Praxton: Book 4
A Vote For Change

N. S. Howard

Published by
Melange Books, LLC
White Bear Lake, MN 55110
www.melange-books.com

Cover Art by Lynsee Lauritsen

Glossary

Some terms and history on the Praxton series, Slaves of the Rogue World

Alliance Worlds: Government offices located on Mars. The Alliance worlds compose over eighty per cent of all habitable worlds.

Charter of Conduct: The Charter of Conduct Office is located on Earth and is responsible for ensuring laws on all Alliance worlds are followed. Praxton was a non-Alliance world, but the Charter of Conduct Office felt Praxton was violating female rights. After the planet refused to change their laws, the Charter of Conduct Office ordered the Alliance Forces to take over the planet. The battle did not go as well as the Alliance Worlds had expected. The end result was Praxton reluctantly joining the Alliance worlds and agreeing to adjust its laws closer to conforming to the Charter of Conduct Office wishes.

Chapter One

Evelyn set up the tripod, making sure the legs were well-supported prior to mounting the camera. She previously programmed the camera to video her news presentation by first focusing on her face and next fading back to zoom in on the building behind her. She stood poised in front of the camera, took a deep breath, put on her camera face and began speaking.

"The Tura Provincial Government is still in heated discussions over the alleged improprieties of cabinet minister Royce Delware. Despite his claims..." Evelyn recited the memorized manuscript she had written earlier, pausing at the appropriate time as the camera changed its view. She studied the politics or topics she spoke about, understanding enough to sound knowledgeable and sincere. She had been told she had great camera appeal with her blue eyes, dark hair and a fair complexion. Tall with a slim figure, she knew her physical appearance had helped to propel her to several promotions within the Pearson News Group.

"...This is Evelyn Montgomery, reporting for Pearson Video News." Evelyn let out a sigh after her smile faded away. *Okay, I'm on schedule. Forty minutes to make it to the office for the interview for that new promotion. I hope I get it. This planet has nothing going on but politics. I need to find something more interesting or my brain will turn to mush.*

She quickly stored the camera equipment in the small personal vehicle and headed to the regional offices of Pearson News. Evelyn had been stationed on a half dozen planets and risen from giving weather reports to complex news assignments, although the dry politics of her latest assignment was trying her patience.

She entered the main doors of the building and after giving a wave to the security guard, entered the elevator. She brushed her short hair back from her ears as she exited the elevator, giving a quick smile to the receptionist. "Hi, I'm here to see Sid Brenner for a two o'clock appointment."

The receptionist invited her to sit while she contacted Sid Brenner. A few minutes later Evelyn was escorted to a large office. The office appeared to be functional for a person who oversaw a large media enterprise with several viewscreens showing various news channels. Sid was a tall, bearded man who appeared to be working on too much caffeine.

"Come in, Evelyn, and have a seat." He shut off the viewscreens by a control on his desk and turned his full attention on her. "I understand you're applying for the news correspondent position on Reggis. It's a minor step up for you, and if you wish to pursue this, I'll give you my endorsement. However, another opportunity has come up for the right correspondent and our head office has asked me to specifically inquire if you'd be interested."

"Head office asked about me?"

"Yes, you're on their radar. This assignment would be a challenging one, and you'd need to be prepared for a quite a change in social behaviour."

"Sir? I don't understand."

"Praxton." He sighed. "Because of the agreement Praxton has signed with the Charter of Conduct Offices, there're a number of changes in their laws. One is that reporters and members of the news media are now allowed to travel outside the tourist zone. Before, they needed permission from the Minister of Defence which was difficult to obtain. Now only a simple permit is needed from the Tourist and Immigration Office. What has also changed on Praxton is that they're going to have elections, and for the first time allow women to not only vote, but also to run for office. Our head office thought that although the conventional wisdom is to send a male reporter, they wanted to send a female reporter to give the viewpoint of women during the change of Praxton society."

Evelyn thought of Praxton with the female population under the control of their male guardians. "Are you asking me if I want this assignment to Praxton?"

"It's yours if you want it. Take time if you need to decide." He gazed at her with his hazel eyes.

Evelyn thought about the reputation of Praxton, of women wearing collars, cuffs and chains. The female population were subject to commands of their male guardians who could administer discipline as they saw fit. Then there were the clothes the women wore, or rather the lack of them, and together with special drugs available on Praxton made them known as the sexiest women in the galaxy. It would be difficult for a woman to be treated as an equal in the chauvinistic society. It would also take a special woman—an independent woman—to open the eyes of the men of Praxton, in order to succeed.

"I'll do it. It sounds like an interesting challenge."

His face broke into a grin. "It'll be a challenge alright, but I've confidence in you. You're going to not only cover the news, but perhaps make some news yourself."

* * * *

Evelyn thought about how quickly she had answered Sid Brenner's offer as she entered the spaceport. She knew her response had surprised him a bit, but remembered what her mentor, Beverly Tobas, once told her at a company social.

"Always take the challenge if it's thrown in front of you—if" and she paused for emphasis, "if you believe you can succeed at it. Unless you reach, you'll never grow taller."

She had kept those words and when Brenner opened the door to a difficult task, she knew she couldn't turn it down. *Besides, I don't have anyone here to keep me. Not that I'm likely to find any guy on Praxton, either. I'll never be any man's slave.*

Evelyn looked up at a blinking sign that indicated her shuttle was ready for boarding. She grabbed her onboard luggage and walked quickly to the departure gate. The green uniformed official checked her identity and passport a final time and she entered the hallway to the shuttle. She relaxed in a seat in the medium sized two hundred and fifty-passenger vehicle and began to read on her tablet about Praxton.

Praxton still has many unique social customs that stand out from the other Alliance Worlds. The first obvious difference is the dress of the women. Typically, their dresses and skirts are shorter than what are usually worn on Alliance Worlds, and slacks or pants are never seen. The second difference is that women wear collars that identify who their male guardians are, plus various restraints to their wrists and ankles.

Another characteristic is the female/male roles. It is not unusual for a male to look after three or more females in the household. The male is responsible for females financially and for their discipline.

Visitors to Praxton will note not only the revealing Praxton fashions, but also the abundant use of decorative chains and cuffs for women. A common form of female discipline can often be witnessed as well. While spanking is usually done at the home of the guardian, it can also be done in public, at the discretion of whoever is in charge of the female at the time. The guardian is head of the household, but there is a hierarchy of the females.

The next highest in charge is the housekeeper. She is not only in charge of keeping the house in good order, but also makes sure the females are behaving during the guardian's absence. Although the housekeeper wears a collar, she is not considered a bed partner for the guardian or for the other females. Rather she is considered an employee of the guardian and is treated as such. The next position is the senior female. The senior female position is not always filled, even with several females under the care of the guardian. Usually the senior female is the guardian's favourite and such a position can be jealously sought after. The senior female is normally given some authority over the other females, including discipline.

A less formal title is the junior female. The newest, and often youngest, female can take on such a title until she has proven she is capable of pleasing her guardian and functions within expected parameters with the other females. Dress, mannerisms and attitude are carefully observed during her initiation into the household. Discipline can be frequent and sometimes harsh during this early period.

Evelyn paused to consider what she read, which didn't conflict with what she already knew about Praxton. She did know the Charter of

Conduct Office was trying to negotiate, or get rid of, several of the Praxton customs around the discipline of females in a guardian's household. Unfortunately for the Charter Office, the females on Praxton were not showing any inclination to support the proposed changes. It seemed to Evelyn if changes were to occur it would have to come from within Praxton society and not from outside pressure. In fact, the insistence for changes the Charter of Conduct Office placed were possibly hindering it, as the population showed a united front against anything to do with the Alliance Worlds and the Charter Office.

Evelyn transferred from the shuttle to the Starship Meridian, going directly to her room. She unpacked her clothes, changed into a fresh outfit and headed to the concourse for something to eat. Food kiosks were scattered along the three levels of shops and entrainment establishments. There were also more fine dining places tucked into the quieter areas of the concourse, but Evelyn wanted a place to eat where she could observe others. Travelling alone on a weeklong journey could be boring and she decided this might have to be a substitute for human contact.

She walked until she saw a restaurant with patio style furniture placed in front of the entrance, giving it a casual appearance. After she sat, a waiter with a white shirt and black pants quickly presented her with a menu and an offer to bring her a drink immediately. A few minutes later she watched groups that appeared to consist of tourists go by. A few more serious, business-type individuals, also went by.

It seems Praxton is still doing a booming business as the entertainment capital of the galaxy. It doesn't look like the new laws on Praxton are having much effect on people wanting to spend their money there. Sin sure sells.

Evelyn noticed that some of the women were wearing collars, and not just the fashionable and simple collars occasionally worn on the Alliance Worlds. Rather, most of the collars were more of the elaborate design Praxton was known for. Occasionally some of women showed a bit of the Praxton fashion by wearing a short skirt or a see-through top. She also saw one male wear a Praxton style shirt with an open front, but it seemed the women were the ones jumping to the Praxton fashions quickly as the Meridian made its way to Praxton.

5

Am I going to have to wear a collar when I'm on Praxton? That's going to feel odd.

Evelyn put her fingers at her neck. She understood while the law didn't require a collar be worn, there was enormous social pressure for women to do so. Even visitors were given stern looks and treated with reserve if they failed to wear Praxton's most acknowledged symbol. "This is going to be an interesting experience."

Chapter Two

Evelyn decided one more pair of shoes would come in handy, and browsed among the shops along the concourse. *Nice shoes but a little overpriced. Those red ones with the high heels look really cute. Maybe I'll try them on.*

She slipped inside the store, looking at the merchandise clustered along a wall.

"Hi, do you need any help?"

Evelyn turned to the green streaked blonde haired girl. She returned a hello to the medium height, slim figured girl that seemed to be bursting with energy.

"Maybe. Those red shoes in the window. Do you have them in size seven?"

"I'll check. Be right back."

Evelyn looked at the purses, belts and collars displayed among the shoes before finding a bench to sit on. The helpful sales clerk presented her with the red shoes and chatted as she assisted Evelyn in sliding them on.

"Are you just visiting Praxton as a tourist, or are you meeting someone? Lots of women have a pre-arranged guardian there."

"I'm going there to work. I'm actually a reporter."

"Wow, you're the second reporter I've met on this flight. I met Max Tremblay a couple of nights ago."

"Really? Max Tremblay? Where?" Evelyn knew Tremblay was at one time one of the veteran reporters who had exposed a fund transfer from the Charter of Conduct Office to Titan parliament representatives, just prior to an important vote on Mars with the Sol government. While his investigation did show some of the inner workings of the politics of the Charter Office, he was also suddenly moved to the outer areas of human space to do reports. It was apparent he had stepped into an area where some powerful people had their ways to deal with problems.

"He was at one of the lounges. He seemed okay but a little tense." She lowered her voice. "I remembered reading he was accused of attacking women in his hotel room. After I talked to him it was hard to believe those stories were true."

Evelyn thought he might have a good reason to be a bit tense. Shortly after his exposure of fund transfer, his personal reputation took a beating with unproven allegations he had attacked a woman in his hotel room. Two other women came forward with similar accusations that occurred over a year ago. While the authorities declined to press charges because of lack of evidence, it became difficult for Tremblay to continue his reporting. He was moved from the mainstream of Charter of Conduct Office politics in Amsterdam to the more outlying areas of human space.

"I think he was set up by those women or by someone who paid them to do so. It's hard to say for certain, but he was never into any trouble until he did his piece on the Charter," Evelyn said.

"Well, to me he wouldn't need to do anything to get women into bed with him. Tall, handsome, and God, those blue eyes. Jeeze, he even had me with that deep voice of his. How do the shoes feel?"

Evelyn stood and walked around. "Really good. I thought with heels this high they would pinch a bit, but these are comfortable. I think I'll take them. So was he a gentleman on your date?"

"Oh no, we weren't on a date. We just talked. I have a guardian and can't date other men. Talking is fine, but as long as I wear my guardian's collar, I'm off limits to other men. As soon as I told him that, he gave me this dreamy smile and just chatted with me. By the way, the shoes are made on Praxton. They make the best shoes for women. Do you want to look at the matching accessories? Purse, collar or belt?"

"Let me see them." Evelyn looked at the small purse that featured several small compartments. She then fingered the collar and found the plastic easy to bend with a soft inside lining. The ends came together to lock in a small catch with a large ring centering the collar. The wide belt the sales clerk held had a large buckle and matched the collar by sporting two rings on the sides.

"Do you have a collar?" the sales clerk asked.

"Not really. I have a fashion collar that I wear occasionally, but it doesn't lock or anything like that." Evelyn studied the collar, curious what a collar locked would feel like around her neck. *It would be an interesting experience.*

"We call them fake collars on Praxton. If a collar doesn't lock, then it's kind of useless. I mean the whole purpose of a collar is to show your guardian controls you. Anyway, you'll need to have a collar or two for when you arrive on Praxton. As the ship gets near Praxton almost every female is going to be wearing a collar, and probably cuffs as well. You don't want to look like a prude by sticking to Alliance Worlds fashions."

Evelyn nodded. "Okay, I'll also take the belt and collar."

"You should pick up a couple of Praxton style dresses or skirts as well. You'll want them for when you arrive on Praxton. Don't buy too much on the ship. Prices and quality are better on Praxton."

"Thanks. Do you like wearing a collar and having a guardian?"

"Oh yeah. I'm one of three females for my guardian. I can't imagine it any other way."

"Is your guardian on the ship?"

"No, I'm with the senior female. She received permission from our guardian to visit her relatives on Tanis and I'm here to keep her company. We both applied for work on the starship, figuring we'd be too bored otherwise. It'll be good to be back home. Three weeks is a long time to be away from our guardian."

Evelyn carried her purchases out of the store, trying to understand how the sales clerk could be so happy sharing a man with two others. *I suppose as a reporter I may have to do a story on that. It's going to be interesting wearing those Praxton fashions, and do I wear a collar when I do a news report?*

Chapter Three

The lounge was noisy with conversing patrons competing with the music played by a holographic band. With two days left before the ship went into orbit around Praxton, Evelyn decided to copy what almost all of the women wore and switched to the Praxton styles. She decided on a black dress with an open back that was short enough to make her conscious of the need not to do anything quickly. She also wore her red shoes and the collar, occasionally touching it with her fingers as she walked through the entertainment section.

She made her way to a tall empty table in one of the crowded lounges, and carefully sat on the bar stool as she watched people. Some women, at least those not from Praxton, fidgeted with the collars and cuffs they wore. A few looked slightly self-conscious of the revealing clothes they wore, but most were having a good time that was partly aided by the alcoholic drinks. Evelyn didn't mind that her dress was long on exposure. She was confident about her body and had worn similar clothes on some of the other worlds she had visited. But the collar was making its presence known and she considered why it felt different from a necklace. *This collar has a presence. The salesgirl was right about it feeling different when it's locked.*

The waitress took her order with a flash of a smile and disappeared between the tables. Evelyn continued to peer around. It was the third lounge she'd visited tonight, and like the night before, she had decided three bars was her limit. Either Max Tremblay would show up or he wouldn't. She had turned down several propositions earlier that night and knew as time went on the men would become more determined to spend time with her.

10

The waitress brought her drink, and as she left, the customers parted in front of her. Evelyn made eye contact with him as he stood by the bar. His lips flinched and finally parted into a grin. Evelyn swallowed hard as Max Tremblay made his way to her table. Tall, broad shouldered, with well-trimmed black hair, he was easy to stare at. His face with chiseled features and steel blue eyes showed why he used to be featured for doing video reports.

"Sorry," he spoke in a quiet but deep voice "you caught me staring at you." He gave a small shrug. "It's not hard to notice you. My name is Max."

"Evelyn." She nodded towards an empty chair. "I know you. Max Tremblay. Why are you going to Praxton?"

"My new assignment. After my run in with the Charter of Conduct Office that sent me practically doing weather reports on Xtedium, I've gradually made my way back up to where I can report for Interworld News again. Not an ideal place to do reports, but with the politics there it should be interesting."

She agreed. "Yes, it'll be that. I'm going to do reports for Pearson News. This is my first assignment where I'll be seen on all Alliance Worlds."

"Congratulations. I'm sure you'll be a success. Of course that means we're officially rivals. We might have to do pistols at forty paces."

Evelyn laughed. "Maybe we can just do microphones instead. You should be happy going to Praxton. There're lots of women that like obeying men."

Max rolled his eyes. "Right. All those women belong to a guardian and leave guys like me alone. The odd single Praxton woman is just looking for a guardian that'll take care of her so she doesn't have to work. That doesn't leave me much. How about you? Are you going to be able to work in a male dominated society?"

"I'll make it work."

He laughed and a deep chuckle resonated across the table. "You sound determined. I wouldn't dare stand in your way." He tipped his glass towards her and took a drink. "To success."

Later Evelyn accepted his offer to walk her to her suite. She was wondering if he was going to try to kiss her, but stood an arm's length away and gave her a friendly good night, promising to contact her again soon.

She closed the door to her suite and sighed. *If you don't contact me, I'll certainly find you again.*

* * * *

The journey from the starship to Praxton in the shuttle was noisy with excited travellers. Evelyn took a quick look around at the seated passengers, but Max was obviously on a different shuttle. She tried to relax until it was her turn to go through the immigration and customs line to enter Praxton, a slower process than the tourist line. The tourist line in the spaceport was longer but quicker for the passengers. They were restricted to a tourist zone that encompassed a large area in the centre of the city of Racon, although that area was big enough to cover any needs the visitor may require.

Evelyn decided she might as well continue to dress in the Praxton style, putting on her collar before she left the ship. The immigration officer, a heavyset man past middle age frowned as he reviewed her application on his monitor. After standing in line, she was finally permitted to enter the small stall where her smile was not returned by the officer.

"You are applying to be a non-permanent resident here to do work as a reporter for Pearson News." He looked back at her. "I see you're wearing a collar, but do you have an actual guardian?"

"No, I don't."

"We encourage females to have a guardian on Praxton. It helps for financial reasons as well as ensuring the safety of the female."

"But it's not a legal requirement, is it?"

"No, but it is advisable." He emphasised each word.

"I'll consider that advice while I'm on Praxton." Evelyn did her best to keep a calm face. *Advisable to look like a man's captured woman? I think not.*

The frown reappeared. "Very well. You've been given conditional approval. Enjoy your stay on Praxton."

Evelyn hurried to exit and entered into an area where returning Praxton citizens were gathering as they were greeted by family and friends. A sign on a wall indicated where waiting ground shuttles were located, and she took one last look behind her before leaving the rest of the passengers behind. *Well, I'm past the point of no return now.*

The shuttle took her to a pre-arranged furnished apartment designed for temporary residents. The lobby was impressive with the high ceiling, black marble floors and decorated stone walls. She registered at the curved front counter made of the same marble material where a young woman examined her identification.

"My name is Shara and welcome to Regis Apartments, Ms. Montgomery. I trust you will find the accommodation satisfactory, but please contact me if you need anything."

"You can call me Evelyn." She took in the red haired woman with a wide blue metal collar and matching wrist cuffs. The green dress was loose fitting but short. Evelyn had noticed all of the women she saw on Praxton so far wore long hair and she wondered if her own short hair was the subject of whispered comments.

"Let me take you up to your suite. I understand you'll be living by yourself." Shara waited for Evelyn to enter the elevator first. "That's a bit unusual here."

"Really?"

"Most females live with at least one other female, and normally all have guardians so they're never alone. I'd find it uncomfortable living and sleeping by myself."

"Well, I've had a few boyfriends, and shared an apartment with women before, but I've slept oftener by myself than with someone. Even rarer was with another woman."

Shara was silent for the trip up the elevator, finally speaking after they reached the forty-fourth floor. "I don't mean to pry, but does that mean you don't like sex?"

Evelyn laughed. "I like sex just fine. I'm just particular which man I share my time with, and I suppose I'm just not into women as partners."

"Oh. On Praxton females are expected to have female partners as well as our guardian."

Evelyn used her thumbprint to open the door to her suite and nodded her approval at the decor. It was a little darker than she thought it should be, and surmised it might be the masculine influence that prevailed on

13

Praxton. Still the furniture had clean lines and the chairs looked comfortable. She entered the bedroom and saw the bed was long, but not as wide as she expected. There was a small indent that ran along the length of the bed in the middle. "The bed looks different."

"Beds for females designed to encourage sleeping physically close together."

"That bed would do it. I noticed there are hooks mounted on the walls. What are those for?"

Shara held up her right hand and pointed at the large ring mounted in her wrist cuff. "They're for restraining females. They're not used much, but it's traditional for most rooms to have them."

Evelyn turned away and rolled her eyes. *Oh, and what a tradition it must be.*

She peered into the bathroom and saw the usual fixtures, plus a large tub and a separate shower stall. One side of the shower stall was a glass wall that adjoined the living room.

"That shower is different. You can see it from the living room."

"Yes. On Praxton when the females shower, and sometimes bathe, they're visible to other parts of the household. Females are encouraged to show off their bodies to others."

"That would certainly show off your body to everyone. Some worlds charge for such entertainment."

Evelyn bid Shara goodbye at the door. "When my stuff arrives, just send it up to my suite."

"Sure." Shara turned to leave but stopped. "Hey, if you want to go for a drink sometime, give me a call. I'd love to hear about Alliance Worlds."

"I need to learn about Praxton. Sounds like a fair exchange." *I've got to understand why a woman would want to live under the control of a man and have to share a bed with another woman and call that normal.*

* * * *

Two days after her arrival on Racon, Evelyn rode the elevator to the ninety-fourth floor of the Praxton Government Administration Building. Her research showed the administration was an all-encompassing bureaucracy that, in theory, followed direction solely from the elected

14

representatives. In practice, the administration also had pressure from the military to adjust how policies were interpreted. Her appointment with the Director of Human Deployment and Immigration was surprisingly easy to make, and at first, she was a bit suspicious if it was only with the director's assistant. However, she was reassured that the director wanted to meet with her and answer her questions.

The elevator opened to a semi-circle foyer with multi-coloured carpet and light green walls. A curved, blue desk sat in the middle of the room with four equally spaced doors behind it. The chestnut coloured doors were wide, tall and imposing, as if protecting something sacred.

She was greeted by a young man in a military uniform, who immediately stopped his work and stood as she approached the desk. Evelyn noted the tall, broad shouldered corporal had close-cropped blond hair and kept his face from showing any expression. He politely asked her to wait in the seating area and offered refreshments before informing Director Simon Bryson of her arrival.

A few minutes later she was ushered into his office and, unlike the corporal, he seemed happy to meet her. "Good afternoon, Ms. Montgomery. I'm pleased to meet you." He stood and walked around his oversized desk to shake her hand.

Evelyn looked up at the middle-aged man. Tall, clean-shaven and surprisingly spry for being slightly overweight, she thought he was rather good looking with his angular facial features. She noticed that like most of the men she had met on Praxton, he appeared confident and in charge.

"Hello, Director Bryson." As she returned his greeting, she looked around the large office. His desk had a glowing top from the monitors built into the flat surface. Behind the desk were the two-corner ceiling to floor glass walls that showed the rest of the city and the reddish landscape beyond.

He smiled and looked at the view. "Ah, I never tire of the sight of the city and the desert beyond. It is such a beautiful planet." He returned to his chair. "Now, I understand you wanted to ask me a few questions."

Evelyn sat on the softly upholstered chair in front of the desk. "Thank you for seeing me so quickly. I was expecting to have to wait a month before meeting you."

He frowned slightly. "We've a mandate to help improve relations and communications with Alliance World representatives. Thus, I make my office available for media requests for interviews as soon as possible."

That sounds like he is quoting from a directive. "Director Bryson, what exactly does your department do? You're the Director of Human Deployment. Is that like being in charge of employment?"

"Partially, yes. You see Praxton has a thriving economy, although it has been negatively affected by the Alliance war." He paused to let the last sentence stand out. "However many of the new jobs are not being filled. Our present work force isn't trained for many of these new industries. So what we need are specialists from other worlds to fill our current needs, and to train our citizens for future requirements."

"If Praxton needs well trained specialists, then why do they restrict the immigration of men but allow almost any woman? It appears as if Praxton is determined to keep the high female to male ratio. Wasn't one of the conditions that Praxton signed with the Alliance Worlds that immigration was to be open to both genders?"

Bryson held a blank expression, and spoke in a clipped tone. "A very good point, and if only it were as simple as that. Praxton did agree to those terms. However, the provision was for the change in the immigration laws, and among other conditions, to be modified over a period of time. Ms. Montgomery, Praxton is proud of its culture and society. The Alliance Worlds, through their illegal military action, have forced us to comply with many aspects of the Charter of Conduct. We will conform to the Charter of Conduct, but at a pace that will not cause undue hardship for the people of Praxton."

Evelyn sat back in her chair, knowing she had struck a sore spot with him. She didn't want their meeting to become confrontational. That would end any special consideration she might receive from him for future news leaks. "Your position is understandable, Director Bryson. But how do you plan to address the need for skilled personnel?"

He pursed his lips. "One method we're deploying is to open immigration to males only with an education and training in the areas we need. That seems to have us run afoul of the Charter of Conduct Office but we are resisting their pressure to accept just any male who applies to live here."

"Are you changing the rules for admitting women? Requiring them to have a skill you need besides having a pretty face?" She gave him a smile, hoping to make him feel she wasn't challenging his position. She saw his face soften slightly and a half smile appeared in return to hers.

"Actually we're looking for better qualified females as well. To that end, there has been a small increase of trained females arriving on Praxton. It's another matter to have them employed in the right areas."

Evelyn recalled her notes she had made earlier. "But isn't part of the problem that most women don't work on Praxton? Couldn't you solve this employment issue by training the women on Praxton for new jobs?"

Simon chuckled and raised his index finger. "I underestimated you. Good line of questioning. I see you're wearing a collar. May I ask how do you feel about it?"

"I'm wearing one because it's impossible for me to do my work on Praxton without one."

"I appreciate that. People on Praxton are very conservative about change and for them a female wearing a collar is a symbol of their society. But I didn't ask you why you're wearing one, but rather how you felt."

Evelyn leaned back her head and looked at the ceiling. "I find the collar has presence. Unlike jewellery, such as a necklace, I can't forget I'm wearing one. It makes me feel a bit vulnerable." She touched the collar with her fingers. "It has a rather powerful effect."

He nodded. "Indeed it does. Females on Praxton feel the same way. When a female wears a collar, it's because she has a guardian. I was curious about how a woman without a guardian feels wearing one. But back to your question of filling jobs with our female population. We can train females on Praxton to help fill the need for skilled jobs. However, there are some problems in trying to accomplish that, in part with the reluctance of females wanting to join the work force."

"You mean women on Praxton don't want to work? I have to say that certainly isn't the case on other worlds."

"I don't disagree with you there, and it's yet another example how the Alliance Worlds believe what works for their society, and by extension the Charter of Conduct, will work for Praxton. The simple fact is Praxton has unique values and culture that cannot be changed by the whim of some Charter Office official."

Evelyn heard his voice rising and quickly tried to calm him down. "Of course, Praxton certainly is known for its unique society. Judging by the number of tourists Praxton receives each year, it'd seem many would like to see Praxton retain that."

"Thank you for that observation." Director Bryson slowly took a deep breath and released it. "Females on Praxton are educated in what we believe is essential to maintain our way of life. This doesn't easily translate into the new job skills we require, so we're looking for a compromise in that area." He touched a lighted segment on his desk. "Corporal Harris, could you bring in some refreshments, please?" He looked back at Evelyn. "We may be a bit longer than I first anticipated."

"Exactly what are the women taught presently?"

"The history of Praxton and social skills."

The corporal brought in a tray of tea and pastries and set it on the desk between them. Evelyn watched the stocky blond soldier walk out, wondering what he looked like under the loose fitting camouflage uniform, but he seemed to be muscular.

Evelyn gave Director Bryson a questioning look. "Armed forces serving tea?"

He shrugged. "The army likes to keep close tabs on the government, and have contracted to provide administration services for the government in many areas. Even though the government is elected, the military has a strong influence on government policy. For example, the Minister of Immigration is an elected member and I was appointed myself to oversee some of the policies. However, the armed forces has the right to veto my appointment."

"So you have, in effect, two bosses?"

"That's one way of putting it. I'm aware of what leeway I have."

She nodded, understanding it must be stressful being watched by the army as he followed the directions of the Minister. "You mentioned social skills. What do those entail?"

"How to dance, walk and act as a Praxton female should. They're also taught, of course, how to please their guardian."

Chapter Four

Evelyn raised her eyebrows. "I assume that means exactly what it sounds like. Can't you train the women new job skills after their ... social skills training?"

"We could, but there's the situation of how Praxton females live today. Most females live very comfortably without having to worry about working and they can do what they want most of the time. So many aren't interested in learning a new job skill, although we're now emphasising during their training that it'd be beneficial that they become employed to help out with the household expense."

"So that leaves Praxton trying to bring in females already trained in the professional skills." She frowned. "It'd seem to me that if a woman had skills Praxton found desirable, then it might be unlikely she would consider Praxton as an ideal place to live. How many would want to accept the Praxton culture of a male guardian who controls them?"

Director Bryson smiled and leaned back slightly in his chair. "Fortunately that question has a favourable answer for us. You mentioned wearing a collar made you feel different and that's understandable. However, you didn't indicate that you disliked wearing it, correct?"

Evelyn shrugged. "It's alright and took a bit to get used to wearing it. But I suppose you're right, I don't mind wearing it."

"It turns out that a large percentage of females in the Alliance Worlds don't mind wearing a collar, much to the annoyance of Charter officials, I might add."

"That may be true, but there is a large difference between not minding wearing a collar sometimes and wearing one all the time.

There's also the matter of obeying a male guardian and the rest of the Praxton culture."

"Agreed. But a common trait many females look for in a male is strength of character, and we certainly have that on Praxton. In fact, you could say on Praxton that the males being dominant is what appeals to many females on Alliance Worlds. Now I'm not saying all females are attracted to the Praxton male and culture, but a fair number are."

"That may be true. However, of the trained and educated women you need, how many of those want to live the Praxton lifestyle?"

He grinned before taking a drink of tea. "We've a question on the immigration forms that asks if the female applicant considers herself a submissive and prefers the male to be in control. As it turns out, well-educated females enjoy being submissive as much as those without formal education. Are you surprised by this?"

Evelyn felt slightly annoyed by the smirk on his face. "I suppose it makes sense." She gave him a forced smile. "Fortunately for Praxton males, women are diverse in their needs."

Director Bryson laughed. "I'm sorry. It wasn't my intention to offend you. I merely wanted to point out that despite the Charter Office efforts, some females, including those who are well-educated, like having a male guardian."

"Well, Director Bryson, it seems you've a plan to address the employment needs for Praxton."

"Thank you for that observation. I trust when you do a news report on Praxton, you'll be able to say that we intend on maintaining our culture within the spirit of the Charter of Conduct."

Evelyn broke into a grin as she stood. "That sounds like a rehearsed line, Director Bryson. I always endeavour to make my reports interesting and without bias. Thank you for your time."

Evelyn returned to her apartment after her interview with Director Bryson. As she entered the lobby, she gave a wave to the front desk. "Hi Shara."

Shara looked up from her work. "Hey, how did the interview go?"

"Interesting. I learned a few things about Praxton, including some of the politics. Have you taken that female education course?"

"Yes, a few years ago."

"What was it like? It sounds really silly to have something he called social training."

Shara smiled. "It was actually alright. On Praxton, females have always been taught that the male is the head of the household and that he must be respected. Most females take a lot of pride in being the best they can be for him and any female that doesn't act that way has few friends. So, I looked forward to taking the training. I wanted to be better for my guardian, Master Philip."

"So you learned how to properly act around him?"

"That and more. Like how to walk correctly, put on make-up, how to exercise properly, even the best way to wear cuffs and chains."

"But the men don't need any training on how to act properly?"

Shara shook her head. "No, I guess it's different for them." She paused as she turned off the console at the desk. "Look, I know this sounds strange to you, and I doubt you approve of how females act towards their guardian, but we're happy this way. Why don't you come over to our home tomorrow for dinner and stay the night? Then you can see firsthand how we live."

Evelyn thought about it for a moment. "I'd be happy to come over, although I don't think I'd be staying the night."

After Evelyn refreshed herself in her room, she ordered a shuttle to take her to do a field report. An hour later, she arrived at the edge of the city where the desert took over.

Evelyn set the camera in front of a military base, well away from the fence that marked the boundary. She called out "Start", and it panned along the road leading to the front gate before coming to a stop where Evelyn stood on the reddish soil.

"Behind me, we can see one of the Praxton military bases. At one time, it was composed entirely of male personnel, but a few years before the conflict with the Alliance forces, female soldiers were finally permitted to enlist. The number of female soldiers is still small, but the implications are large. Praxton is now not only allowing women to take jobs traditionally reserved for men, but is encouraging them to do so. While females on Praxton are still required to take courses on social behaviour that reinforces the male as head of the household, efforts are being made to recruit educated Alliance women to fill the need for skilled workers and professionals. Praxton officials are not pleased that they are bound to comply with the Charter of Conduct, but it is forcing Praxton to look at the roles of men and women when it comes to employment. For the first time, Praxton needs women who do more than just serve a male guardian. Evelyn Montgomery, Pearson Video News."

Evelyn froze her smile for a moment longer. Then she packed up the camera and walked back to the waiting shuttle. The shuttle quietly took her back to her apartment and she began to wonder what her evening with Shara's family would be like. *It might make for an interesting report.*

* * * *

The fine spray of water felt good on her skin as Evelyn washed the sand from her hair, compliments of doing a report in the desert. She twisted around under the overhead showerhead and looked at the living room past the glass wall. She was curious what it would be like to be watched by others as she touched herself with her fingertips. *A little erotic, especially if someone like Max was watching.* She glanced at the hooks on the wall. *I wonder if he would try to make use of those on me. No, I don't need to be thinking those thoughts. I've got to get a man soon.*

She shut off the shower and turned on the warm, dry air fan. Soon her skin was barely damp and she used a soft towel to work her hair a bit more. She picked a soft green dress that showed off her figure but wasn't too transparent, at least compared to the Praxton norm. She put on a black collar with a red stripe running in the middle. The self-locking collar was wide, compared to the one she wore for the news report, but she decided she needed to dress more like the Praxton custom as a visitor to Shara's home. The collar was made out of a leather-like material and had rings inserted at the front and sides. She added the matching wrist and ankle cuffs and, after hesitating, added a pair of chains that went from the centre ring of her collar to the wrist cuffs. Finally, she put on a pair of Praxton made black stilettos. She stood in front of a full-length viewscreen, and with touch of the control, it gave her views from her front, side and back. *I never would have believed I would be wearing this a month ago.* Satisfied, she made her way downstairs to meet with Shara in the lobby.

"You look like you're in a good mood." Evelyn saw Shara smiling as she closed the work station.

Shara agreed. "I had a good day and I'm looking forward to spending the evening with you. You finally added some chains."

"I thought I'd give it a try."

"It looks nice, the silver chains and the black cuffs. Shall we go? The shuttle is waiting."

Evelyn walked with Shara, chatting with her about her earlier report. "I decided to do the report by the military base and didn't realize how far away it was from the city. It turns out it's in the desert. Really pretty, but hot and windy."

"If you live on Praxton you get used to the desert. It covers half the land surface. That's a lot of red sand."

"I ended up with most of it in my hair."

Shara laughed. "Is it customary for females to have short hair on Alliance worlds?"

"No, but not unusual. I notice all the women here have long hair. I feel a bit different with short hair."

"I think it looks good on you. I notice you still call females women and males men. With your accent, short hair and way of speaking you can really tell you're not from Praxton."

"Well, old habits die hard." She entered the shuttle and watched the scenery float by.

The automated shuttle made its way quietly to the suburbs and stopped along a crescent of homes with landscaped yards. On the different worlds Evelyn had been on, few had individual homes. The homes she saw spoke of wealth and an abundance of habitable areas. Most worlds, even wealthy ones, did not have a climate that easily supported having a population spread away from the main cities.

The shuttle stopped and Evelyn jumped out after Shara on the paved street.

Shara happily took her hand and led her to a three storey white home with green trim. The front yard had flowers and small bushes among large boulders, making it inviting to sit on the front porch and relax in the warm evening air.

The front entrance was as large as her apartment living room and she looked around as she removed her shoes, understanding it was a Praxton custom for all females to be barefoot within homes.

Introductions were made, and Evelyn exchanged hellos with Dalina, a tall brunette with a slim figure. Dalina stepped forward and gave her a hug and Evelyn breathed in her perfume. As they broke apart, she took in Dalina's full lips and blue eyes. *She's a real looker.*

Marilyn, a blonde of slightly less than average height but with a curvy figure, was a bit more reserved in her greeting and gave a very light hug.

"I'm so excited to meet you. I've never met a reporter before. You must be famous on Alliance worlds. I hope we can become friends." Dalina spoke enthusiastically.

"It's great to meet you, too." Evelyn smiled at the dark-haired woman.

Evelyn followed the others to the living room, with dark furniture, a pair of large abstract paintings and a large picture window showing the front yard. Light came from lamps built into the vaulted ceiling. A far wall contained a staircase that led to the second floor. Next to the staircase, an elevator with glass doors stood waiting. The couch was comfortable but not too soft, the leather-like material only gently yielding to her body. Overall Evelyn thought the decor was well done, although like her apartment, with a masculine influence. Shara sat next to her and she studied Dalina sitting on a loveseat across from them.

Dalina wore a form fitting red coloured dress that matched her collar and cuffs. The collar and cuffs were made of a shiny red material and were narrow compared to most restraints she had seen. In addition to wrist and ankle cuffs, Dalina also wore cuffs just above her elbows. Black chains went from her collar to wrist and elbow cuffs.

Marilyn appeared to be nervous as she stood next to Dalina, wearing a tight fitting orange skirt that was short even by Praxton standards. Her long sleeved white blouse was loose fitting and open at the front, except from a single button on the bottom. A silver chain could be seen than ran between what Evelyn presumed was nipple jewellery. A thick, wide white belt was tightly fitted around her waist. Silver chains were attached to various rings that were inserted into the belt, leading to her wrist and ankle cuffs. The cuffs and collar were white and made from stiff material. The collar looked uncomfortable to Evelyn as it reached almost to her jaw. A leash was attached to her collar where Dalina held the other end.

Dalina pointed to the floor next to her. "Sit here."

Evelyn watched as Marilyn gracefully dropped to her knees and looked up at Dalina. She saw Marilyn's skirt slide up to her hips as she sat back on her feet. She didn't appear to be concerned about her exposure but rather looked at Dalina for approval. She let out a sigh as Dalina reached over and gently stroked her hair.

Shara whispered, "Dalina is the senior female. Marilyn is our newest female and is still being trained. Unfortunately, she caused a problem yesterday, and there'll be consequences."

"So Dalina is the boss?"

"Yes, next to the housekeeper and Master Philip."

"So what type of punishment will Marilyn get?"

"Restrictions on movement, such as now. She can't pick out her own clothes for a few days and likely will be going to the discipline room later."

Evelyn decided against asking about the discipline room, knowing it was a common feature in Praxton homes, but made a mental note to check it later.

The conversation centered around Evelyn, who told them about her job, Alliance world views of Praxton and the fashion trends on other worlds.

"The fashions are more conservative than on Praxton, although some worlds are still wearing something called skins. They're pants that started on Mars and are made of this thin material that looks about two sizes too small. They fit like a glove and you might as well be naked for all the detail they show. Most women wear a modesty belt that has a front piece that hangs down to give some protection."

Dalina spoke. "They sound interesting."

Evelyn laughed. "Really interesting if you get a snag in them. They can start tearing fast and suddenly you're under arrest for overexposure. The other new fashion style is the phantom sleeves. You can buy dresses and blouses but the sleeves aren't attached. Usually the sleeves go from the elbow to the wrist. You can leave them off but it looks pretty neat with them on and the bare upper arms."

Wine was brought out by a middle-aged woman that was introduced to Evelyn as Ms. Tara, the housekeeper of Master Philip's home. Evelyn thought Tara was pleasant, but looked too busy to stay and chat. The average sized woman quickly left the living room through a side door.

As the wine helped Evelyn relax, she found the sight of Marilyn kneeling in her restraints and leash fascinating. *I'm not sure if I find this disturbing, but she sure does look erotic.*

A short time later, Tara announced dinner and Evelyn followed the others to another room, dominated by a rectangular table that could easily seat ten. Evelyn again sat next to Shara with Dalina sitting across from them. After they were seated, Marilyn was allowed to sit next to Dalina with her leash hooked at the back of her chair.

Tara entered the dining room several times with plates and bowls containing food, but Evelyn understood they were waiting for Master Philip to appear before starting to eat. She saw the women did take small sips of the wine and talk as they waited. Finally, Master Philip entered the room.

The first thing Evelyn noticed was his height. He was slim and easily could challenge the top of a doorframe. She couldn't determine his age easily with his fair features, short blond hair and blue eyes, but she suspected he hadn't reached middle age yet.

Master Philip walked casually to Evelyn, offering her a smile as he extended his hand.

"Welcome to our home, Evelyn. I hope you'll enjoy the evening with us."

Evelyn quickly glanced at the open shirt he wore, showing off a muscular chest and the decorated open fly of the Praxton pants showed his height reflected on other parts of his body.

"Thank you, Master Philip. I'm looking forward to the dinner and the evening."

As soon as Philip returned to sit at the head of the table, Tara presented food dishes to him. Evelyn recalled the Praxton custom was for males to be served first, then the senior female and finally the rest of the females. She was surprised to see Tara pass the food dishes to herself next. She wasn't familiar with all of the food that was placed in front of her but took a small portion of each. She noticed as she filled her plate, each dish was passed to first Dalina and next to the rest of the table.

Master Philip spoke in a deep, but quiet voice. "Dalina, I understand Marilyn is being disciplined for a problem."

"Yes, Master Philip. I'll be continuing her punishment later this evening."

He frowned slightly. "I believe Marilyn's discipline should be considered complete. We've a guest at our home this evening and she may not be comfortable with some aspects of female discipline."

"Yes, Master Philip." Dalina quickly turned to Marilyn and removed her leash.

Evelyn noticed the other women were quiet for a few minutes as they ate. She thought Marilyn looked relieved after her leash was removed, even though she had difficulty eating with her restrictive collar on. She was curious what punishment Marilyn had escaped because of her presence, but decided she could ask Shara later what might have happened. Her thoughts were interrupted by a question from Philip.

"I understand you are doing a report on Praxton for Pearson News and even had an interview with Director Bryson. May I inquire about your impressions of Praxton so far?"

Evelyn finished swallowing her bite of food and answered carefully. She considered one reason he knew she had an interview with Director Bryson was that he had watched her news report. "Praxton is a beautiful world. There aren't many worlds that have a climate where humans can live outside without much protection."

"That's true." Philip took a small drink of his wine and continued in an even tone. "It's certainly part of the reason that Praxton became a prosperous world and never needed any assistance from Sol in the early years. We still don't need any help from the outside worlds, but that argument is now moot. We hope the changes in our society and culture will not be too great."

Evelyn understood the anger many people on Praxton had at the invasion of their world by the Alliance forces, engineered by the Charter of Conduct Office. She knew there was little point in debating that the Alliance worlds only wanted to ensure that the women on Praxton were not being treated as slaves, when even the women on Praxton wanted to keep Praxton the way it was. "I'm sure Praxton will continue as a wealthy world, although there'll be some changes in the coming years. I suppose all worlds go through changes and it may be that the changes on Praxton will be positive ones." She returned to eating, hoping Philip wasn't looking for an argument.

"I hope so, too. What do you see as the coming changes on Praxton, drawing from your knowledge of other worlds, and the intent of the Charter of Conduct?"

Evelyn delayed her answer by taking a drink of her wine. *I'm not going to be able to fool him with some pat reply, and with everyone staring at me, I better come with an honest but non-controversial answer.* "I suppose, in my opinion, the biggest change will be the role of women in Praxton society. They'll be integrated into the work force and will have to be trained in more complex job skills."

Dalina quickly asked a question. "You mean females will need to do more work outside the home, and be educated at the same places males go to?"

"Probably. I don't know too much how the Praxton education system works, but that's how it is on Alliance worlds."

Dalina grinned. "You mean I may have to get up before noon and go to work? What a horrible thought."

Shara laughed. "Don't worry. I'll wake you up the same time I get up to go to work so you'll get used to it."

Dalina stuck her tongue out at her. "I need my beauty sleep."

Philip spoke, causing everyone to turn toward him. "I think you're right, but we may have an issue there. Under Praxton law, a female is not required to work a full shift. A female is given two hours longer than male employees to prepare for her day. We expect our females to look their best at all times and that time is used for exercise, bathing, make-up and dressing."

Evelyn shrugged. "You may have to change the law. Either that or lose two hours of valuable productivity time."

Philip nodded. "More likely the latter. Praxton is slow for any changes and can be stubborn about maintaining the status quo. Believe me, trying to get my females to do extra work would be an uphill battle."

Shara responded, "I work, Master Philip."

"Yes, Shara, you do. However, what Evelyn is proposing means increasing your education and working a full day, about double what you do now."

Shara pouted for a moment and then recovered. "But I'd do it gladly if you wanted me to. I can work hard and I would like to learn more, too."

Evelyn looked at the slightly surprised face of Dalina. *Maybe Shara is the new Praxton woman, ready and able to work.*

* * * *

A sweet liqueur was served in another room on the second floor. Evelyn, like the others, used the stairs. As she entered the room, she was struck by the sight of large floor to ceiling windows along the far wall, and a glass divider for a large shower along an adjoining room. She pointed at the shower as she sat on a couch with Shara. "Do all homes on Praxton have showers where others can see them from another room?"

"Pretty much," Shara answered. "This shower has another glass wall to the outside as well. You can watch the person showering from the backyard. Females on Praxton get used to being seen naked, and I guess there's some enjoyment in watching another female showering. That's one of the things we learn as females is how to shower for the benefit of those watching you. Dalina is really good at it. She makes it look so sensuous."

Evelyn giggled. "So you had to pass a course called showering one-oh-one?"

Shara placed a hand on her knee. "It pleases Master Philip to watch us shower, especially when two or more of us shower together."

"I'll bet he enjoys watching that. Do you get to watch him shower?"

Shara sighed. "No, males are always covered up. They also shower in a private room."

Philip interjected. "Praxton has distinct social rules for males and females. For example, females are required to be barefoot in the home while males must wear shoes." He pointed to his boots. "These are not light shoes, either. Male footwear normally consists of military style boots. Not too comfortable for a full day's wear."

29

Shara's hand moved slightly higher up Evelyn's leg and her fingertips made small, light circular motions. Evelyn wasn't certain if slapping her hand away would be a social faux pas and decided to ignore it. "I can see that might be a bit uncomfortable. So maybe you're in favour of changing some of the social norms here?"

He laughed. "Very clever, Evelyn. While I believe some changes are necessary, we have to move carefully."

"Does that include such things as work for females?"

"Yes, we need to move toward that. Praxton is now a member of the Alliance Worlds and if we're to compete in trade and commerce we need to be competitive in our work force. We simply cannot have the majority of our females sitting at home and expect to maintain our financial position. We have relied on our tourist industry too much to bring in revenue, and while that is a positive source of income for us, we shouldn't depend on that exclusively."

"So the tourist industry still is very profitable for Praxton? Even after the war?"

"Very much so. Despite Alliance worlds condemning our treatment of females, their citizens are still flocking to our tourist zone. Ironically, the female tourists can't seem to get enough collars and restraints, the very thing the Charter of Conduct Office found so appalling."

Evelyn wanted to say there was a big difference between the women tourists playing out a fantasy by pretending to be a slave girl to actually living the lifestyle, but suspected that argument would lead nowhere with Philip. "Regardless, the Charter of Conduct has agreed that women on Praxton could wear collars and restraints as jewellery and accepted it as a long standing cultural custom." She noticed Shara's hand was stroking her inner thigh very slowly. *That actually doesn't feel bad.*

"That was a something we were fortunately able to negotiate. You may want to interview Ambassador Troy LeBlanc. He is the ambassador for the Alliance worlds and his partner is Diane Fulton, who used to work for the Charter of Conduct Office. They're the ones who actually were able to bring about a settlement between Praxton and the Alliance worlds."

Evelyn recalled hearing about the controversy of Diane Fulton actually negotiating for the Praxton side. She had arrived on Praxton as a representative of the Charter of Conduct Office and during her stay at the embassy had fallen in love with LeBlanc. She later resigned her post, accepting completely the Praxton way of life. "Yes, I believe I should do that."

He thought for a moment and raised a finger as he made a point. "Since you're interested in females involved in skilled positions, one of our neighbours, Melvin Taylor, has a female who moved from Earth to Praxton. I understand she's a trained biologist and came here because she couldn't find work on Earth. I can you give you Taylor's contact information, if you want to speak to her about her experience in coming to Praxton."

"That would be great." *I have to ask her guardian if I can speak to her? They've a ways to go for women's rights here.*

Philip stood. "I've some things to take care of. It was good to meet you, Evelyn."

Evelyn watched him walk away. *Good looking guy. I wouldn't mind being his slave for one night.* She turned to Shara. "Can you show me the discipline room? I'm curious what it looks like."

"Sure." Shara took Evelyn's hand. "It's here on this floor."

The discipline room wasn't very big, and was empty except for several hooks along the walls, chains hanging from the ceiling and a rack displaying various whips. Evelyn looked at the restraints attached to the end of the chains. "Wow. This looks scary."

"Usually the female is naked and Master Philip will restrain her as he sees fit. Then he'll whip her a bit. He doesn't hurt a female too much—just to enough to make the skin tingle a bit. This is a small discipline room. Most homes have more equipment and some have a clear wall where the discipline can be seen from another room. Master Philip doesn't believe in a lot of punishment or the use of cages. Many guardians have cages where they'll restrain a female as part of her discipline."

"Nice that he's so enlightened." Evelyn fingered one of the whips. "So you are disciplined in here?"

"Sometimes. Master Philip prefers other types of discipline."

"How? In what way?"

"Different ways. I may have to do some extra housework, no videos

31

or restricted from going out. He also will give us a good spanking. He has big hands and can really make your ass smart."

Evelyn looked at Shara and held back from voicing her first thought. *Really, a spanking, as if it was just one of those things done every day.* "Does he spank you often?"

"I suppose so. I kind of like it sometimes, as long as he doesn't hit too hard. Dalina will spank us as well, but that doesn't usually hurt hardly at all. She has pretty small hands. Do you want to try the restraints and see what they're like?" She pointed at the chains with cuffs hanging from the ceiling.

Evelyn shook her head. "Maybe another time. I should be going home."

"I was hoping you'd be staying the night."

"I guess I'm a bit nervous about that."

Shara nodded. "I understand. It takes a while to get used to the closeness of females on Praxton. But if you want to do a proper report on life on Praxton, you should find out what the discipline room is like and spend the night here. I promise to look after you. Alright?"

Evelyn thought about it a moment and said, "Alright, but another time I'll spend the night, not tonight."

"Good. Maybe we can get Master Philip or Dalina to give you a spanking for the experience."

"Oh, I don't think so." She shook her head and blushed as Shara laughed.

Chapter Five

It took several days to set up an appointment with Ambassador Troy LeBlanc, but on her arrival, he greeted her warmly. She was impressed by his demeanour, his years of diplomacy coming through. His height and dark suit made him slightly intimidating to her and she took a deep breath to relax. He extended his arm to indicate where she should sit in the well-appointed room in the embassy. The furniture reminded her of Earth with the emphasis on pattern fabrics and glass topped tables. Two loveseats and two armchairs surrounded a coffee table where refreshments waited. Evelyn carried in the two small cases that held her equipment, placed them on the floor, and turned her attention back to her hosts.

Standing by one of armchairs was Diane Fulton. She appeared to be average height but had a good posture on a slim frame that made her seem taller. She kept her dark hair long with a bit of curl in it. Evelyn noticed she wore a dark blue collar that picked up the blue colour in her patterned dress. As usual with Praxton fashions, the wrist and ankle cuffs matched her collar, with the chains between her cuffs also of the same colour.

"Thank you, Ambassador LeBlanc, for allowing use of this room to interview you and Ms. Fulton, and also for agreeing to allow me to videotape it."

"The embassy is always willing to help the media present a fair and objective news report. All we ask is to be given the right to approve any edited version of the interview. Unfortunately, there have been concerns in the past about information taken out of context." LeBlanc gave a sincere looking smile and indicated Diane Fulton. "Ms. Fulton, as you know, is my partner. While I'm her guardian, I've always allowed her to express her own views, so please feel free to ask her anything you wish."

Evelyn set up the two tripods and mounted the cameras on them. She knew both cameras contained a microprocessor that analysed voice and used what was called a Viewer Interest Algorithm or VIA. The camera made a decision on whether to zoom in or out on the person speaking. In addition, the cameras could switch from one view to another of the same person. The end result was a video that wasn't static as the person spoke and kept the viewer's interest higher.

Evelyn sat across from Troy LeBlanc and Diane. "Okay, I guess we're ready to go. If something occurs that you feel shouldn't be recorded, just speak the word cut twice and the recording will stop automatically." She waited for them to acknowledge her and started the interview.

"Ambassador LeBlanc, you're regarded as one of the principal architects of the agreement between the Alliance worlds and Praxton that ended the war between the factions. Could you elaborate on those circumstances?"

Leblanc gave the impression of careful thought before answering. "First, thank you for giving me credit for part of the negotiations. I was fortunate to be in a position where I could have some influence. My years of experience have taught me that all worlds, and different societies, have something to offer and we shouldn't all be forced to walk the same walk. There's room in human space for different ways of accomplishing the same tasks. I was able to express the opinion during the negotiations that many aspects of Praxton society were misunderstood. The women on Praxton were not, and are not, treated as slaves. The household roles of men and women are different on Praxton from most Alliance worlds but they're not, as was quoted by one Charter of Conduct Officer, deviant. I've lived on Praxton a number of years as a diplomat and have seen the Praxton people to have strong principles and values, principles other worlds have come to respect." He took a measured pause and continued. "However I would be amiss if I didn't point out the negotiations might have collapsed if it wasn't for a strong performance given by Diane Fulton. She was in a difficult situation at the time, having just resigned her post as a Charter of Conduct Officer, but she turned the tide at the negotiating table with a strongly worded statement."

Evelyn made a mental note not to ask him to elaborate again. She looked at Diane who had a hint of a blush on her cheeks. "Can you inform the viewers what you said at the negotiation?"

Diane nodded. "I actually switched sides to the Praxton delegation, and in a way I suppose I was on the opposite side of Master … Ambassador LeBlanc when I first arrived on Praxton. The sticking point at the time was the wearing of collars and cuffs by the females on Praxton. I simply stated that the collar was a type of jewellery worn on Praxton and it made them no more a slave than a wedding ring. The Alliance worlds accepted that argument and negotiations were able to proceed to less contentious issues."

Evelyn directed her next question to LeBlanc. "Praxton did keep the right to keep collars, restraints and various discipline devices such as whips. However, that came at some concessions. What do you see as some of the possible changes for Praxton?"

"Well, Evelyn, I don't wish to say any one change is more important than another. Some changes will affect some parts of Praxton more than others will. My personal opinion, and not of the Alliance worlds, is the change in the Praxton constitution that allows women to not only vote in the elections, but also to run for office. I believe this has the potential to change Praxton society the most in the long term."

Evelyn turned toward Diane. "Ms. Fulton, you arrived on Praxton as a representative of the Charter of Conduct. What caused you to decide to live on Praxton and accept their lifestyle?"

After a short smile, Diane responded. "Love. I fell in love with Ambassador LeBlanc, and that made my decision easy to live on Praxton."

"Living on Praxton also includes wearing a collar and accepting the man has control over you. How have you adjusted to that?"

"When I arrived on Praxton, I thought of collars with a feeling of apprehension and fascination. When I first tried on a collar there was a moment of trepidation, but it soon passed. It felt comfortable and when the war began it gave me a feeling of security." Diane frowned. "Perhaps a better word to use is feeling protected, because when I looked to

Ambassador LeBlanc, I felt he was in control and would make sure no harm came to me. I do accept his control over me, and while many women on Alliance worlds don't understand this, to me it feels natural. I want my male partner to be strong, to be dominating. If that means I'm under his control, then I accept that."

Evelyn nodded. "I asked Ambassador LeBlanc this question, and now I'd like to get your opinion. What do you see as the most important change coming on Praxton?"

"I agree with Ambassador LeBlanc that allowing women to vote and run for office will be important, but I believe that only gives someone an opportunity to step forward to make a real change. I look forward to seeing the time when a woman will run and win a seat in an election."

"Do you have a woman in mind that someday will claim a seat in an election?"

Diane paused before she answered. "I don't really, except now that you've asked me, a name does come to my mind. Terri Baxter. She has the ability to make things happen."

As Evelyn packed up her cameras and tripods, she tried to remember where she had heard the name Terri Baxter before. She couldn't place it, but had a feeling it was something to do with entertainment. *At least the interview produced some good material. There probably won't be much editing required on it.*

* * * *

Evelyn stepped out of the apartment elevator and headed to the lobby. A few steps later, she saw Shara working at the front desk.

"Good morning."

Shara looked up. "Hey there. Another appointment this morning?"

"More like some fact finding. I'm going to interview some of the retailers in the mall about restraints. I want to get some more information on what's popular and why."

"You've got to wear them to understand that. You should buy a few different styles, or come visit me and try on the ones I have."

"I suppose I could do that. By the way, do you know who Terri Baxter is? I've heard her name mentioned recently, but couldn't place her."

36

"Sure, everyone on Praxton knows who she is. She helped with the war effort against the Alliance Forces. You must've seen her in a famous video called *Strike Her*. Actually it was a group of three songs, *Caught in the Act, Consequences* and *Strike Her*."

"Oh, I do remember that video. I didn't know that was her in it." *Something about females making their master angry. At the end, one of them is stripped naked and lashed with a whip. It was banned on most Alliance Worlds, but that didn't stop it from being seen by nearly everyone.* "I'll have to take another look at that." *Politically incorrect, but that sure was a hot video.*

* * * *

The store manager, a tall middle-aged man, smiled at her request. "Of course, I'd be happy to give you information on the collars and restraints." He indicated the glass counter holding several collars. "The collars are the first item females choose when picking out restraints. Fashion styles change over time, much like clothes do. A few years ago metal was quite popular, especially white. Now brighter colours are more common." He opened the counter for her.

Evelyn picked up a bright yellow collar with several matching rings along the side. Despite the collar being wide, she found it quite light. "Do you think fashion on Praxton has been influenced by the Alliance Worlds? I mean specifically collars and restraints."

"Yes, I suppose they have. The collars have become a bit wider and more vibrant with colours. I believe females here want to show the Alliance World government that they are proud to wear collars, and want to show them off more than they used to. The collar has become the symbol of Praxton."

"I suppose they're showing their defiance that way to the Alliance Worlds. What about the cuffs and other restraints?"

"Well the cuffs usually match the collar, but the chains that link the various collars and cuffs have changed. Females now use fewer of them, which makes them less restrictive in their movements. The collar and cuffs are now more prominent in size and colour. Some now even come with small padlocks, even though they're normally self-locking."

Evelyn visited other shops that specialized in collars and restraints but found their answers similar to the first. She decided to stop at a coffee shop separated from the rest of the mall by a low fence. The server brought her a tea and a pastry as she watched shoppers pass by on the mall concourse.

These women seem very comfortable walking around in their collars and cuffs and skimpy clothes. I can't imagine seeing that on Alliance Worlds, but collars there are getting to be a common fashion accessory. Maybe the ultra-short skirts and going braless will catch on too. She looked down at her top. *I guess one can get used to it.*

As she sat in the coffee shop reviewing her notes, she decided it would be worthwhile to get another perspective on Praxton fashions. Evelyn sent a request to a TV fashion program to arrange an interview with Gina Rosetta, the producer of the program.

This might be an interesting piece. Alliance Worlds fashions are being influenced by Praxton and it'll be interesting to see what influence has occurred on Praxton, though it seems obvious that doesn't include longer skirts.

Her tablet flashed an incoming message. Evelyn opened it and smiled. "Hello Max," she sang out the greeting.

* * * *

"Hi Shara." Evelyn waved as she returned to her apartment building.

"Hi. Did you find out what you wanted?"

"Yeah, and guess what? I was asked to go for a drink with Max Tremblay."

"The reporter you told me about? Good for you. When's the date?"

"Tomorrow evening."

"Do you think he might want to be your guardian?"

Evelyn shook her head and laughed. "No. This may be Praxton, but this girl will never have a guardian."

"Sorry, I forgot." She grinned. "It's just that on Praxton dates are more like interviews for a guardian."

"Really? How do you interview a guardian for yourself?"

"We meet for dinner or drinks and see what the other has to offer. He'll normally show pictures of his home and other females he looks after. Some other details like what he does for a living and if the contract has special conditions in it."

"A contract?"

"Yeah, like how severe the discipline is, how much of an allowance she would get and other details. He has to provide for and discipline the females in his home, and so you would want to know that ahead of time."

"So if you like him and think the contract is okay, then what?"

"Usually we have a few more dates, go to his home to see what the other females are like. If you don't like the other females, or if they don't like you, then the deal is pretty much off."

"Sounds worse than meeting the parents."

"There are a couple of other things, more traditional than anything critical. Usually before the contract is signed, he'll give the female a spanking so she knows what to expect from him in the future. Like if he hits hard or too long she might have to consider that."

"A spanking? That certainly is a Praxton custom."

"I guess so. I kind of like spankings, as long as they're not too hard. Another thing is she has to please him first. The first time they have sex, the female usually gives him a blow job, to show him she can satisfy him."

"Interesting. Although I've got to say I prefer the guy trying to romance me."

"You've got to remember there are two or three times more females than males on Praxton. If you want a guy, you better be willing to give up something to get him. On Praxton it's really tough to survive as a single female. Low paying jobs and legal issues almost force you to get a guardian. Having said that, I'm pretty happy to have Master Philip to look after me. He does care about me and I do love him."

* * * *

Max let out sigh of relief after he put down his mobile. *Thank God she said yes to the drinks. If she had said no I don't know what I would have done next. She's gorgeous and doesn't seem to be aware of it.*

Chapter Six

Terri Baxter carefully pressed the flower shaped nipple jewellery on before slipping on the light cream blouse. She took in a deep breath and checked her appearance once more in the full size viewscreen in her bedroom. She touched a control at the side of the viewscreen and it rotated views of her from the sides and the back. She brushed back her blonde hair with her fingers and examined her clothes, collar and cuffs. Terri wished she could wear shoes that would help accent her legs.

She left the bedroom and headed downstairs, stepping with grace despite the chains between her ankle cuffs. She didn't always use the full complement of chains with her cuffs and collar, but she wanted to look her best for her master when she asked him for a favour.

In the main seating area, she saw Erica and Dezine, and both women were dressed in appropriate Praxton dress of short skirts and light tops with a complement of chains and cuffs. Their collars signified Master Romie was their guardian, a source of Terri's troubles. For a long time she was the sole female under his care but the recent conflict with the Alliance Worlds left a situation of many females seeking a male guardian. Master Romie stressed to Terri he did not want additional females under his care, but felt an obligation to accept at least two from an overcrowded condition at his neighbour's home.

Terri smiled and waved at them. She did like them as women, but viewed them also as competition for Master Romie's affection. She was mollified by the fact Romie had proposed to her to join him in an Affiliation ceremony, which legally bonded them for life. Still, each of the other two women shared his bed on occasion, forcing her to spend the night with the remaining one in a single bed. As with Praxton

40

customs, she was expected to have intimate relations with the other females in the household. While she tried to be as receptive as possible, her heart belonged to Master Romie, and to Allison, a young female in another household.

Master Romie was working at his desk as she entered. He looked up and quickly smiled at her. "Hello, Terri. Is there something you want to talk to me about?"

Terri slowed her walk as she approached him, aware of his preference of the traditional customs of a subservient woman in the presence of her guardian. She made sure she had on an adequate number of chains and cuffs, including a definite restriction imposed on the movement of her limbs by the restraints. She moved around the side of the desk, knelt by Master Romie and looked up at him.

"There's not any problem, Master Romie, although I've come to speak to you about a matter of some importance to me."

"If it's important to you, then it is also important to me."

Terri looked down. "Thank you, Master Romie."

"However before we discuss your problem, can you tell me if your attitude is any different toward Erica and Dezine?"

Terri's face reddened slightly. She quickly recalled the over the knee spanking she'd received from him two days earlier. He told her the two women wanted to remain under his care and didn't want to return to being freelancers. Even though Terri was closest to his heart, he still cared for the other females very much. He had informed Terri she had better start behaving or there would be additional consequences.

"Yes, Master Romie. I'm making an effort to make Erica and Dezine feel welcome and treat them better."

"That's good to hear. I'm glad the spanking helped you see the light. Now what did you want to speak to me about?"

"I wish to speak to you about the recent changes brought about by the agreement between Praxton with Alliance Worlds." She looked back up at his face. "This year there will new elections."

"Yes, for the first time females will be allowed to vote for members of the legislature."

She nodded. "Also, according to the provisions, women will be allowed to run as a member, as well."

Master Romie straightened his back and looked at Terri with curiosity. "That's true. May I ask what your point is?"

"With your permission, Master Romie, I'd like to run for election. I've received much from Praxton and now want to give something back. I believe I can do this by getting involved in the political changes that are occurring."

Master Romie rubbed his chin. "Well, I must say you've caught me by surprise by your request. If any female is capable of standing up for what she believes in, certainly that would be you. If this is what you want to do, then I'll stand absolutely behind you. I'll give you my unconditional support to do whatever you want to do to make your life better."

Terri let out her breath. "Thank you, Master Romie. You're so kind to me."

"Running for office requires a lot of work and support from others. You'll need a campaign manager and others to assist you."

"I understand that, Master Romie, and I was hoping you'd assist me in finding people who are willing to help a female seeking election."

"That I can do. Now, is this going to interfere with our Affiliation ceremony?"

"Our Affiliation ceremony comes first." She rested her hands on his legs. "I'm working with Allison on the details of the ceremony, but there's so much work to do. I have to still pick out the dress and work out the type of ropes and knots to be used. It gets very complicated." She pushed her hands forward to his hips. "I know I'm being selfish, but I'd like to be your only female tonight. Perhaps you'll allow me to please you, Master Romie."

"That sounds fine by me, but now I do have work to do."

Terri stood and reached the doorway of the study, paused and turned to speak to him. "Actually, I rather enjoyed it when you showed me the light, Master Romie. Perhaps you will find a need to do so again soon."

* * * *

Terri walked into the kitchen and saw Anne preparing food. The short, and slightly heavy brunette, didn't turn around as she spoke. "Terri, I presume you didn't come here to learn how to prepare

42

vegetarian stew."

"No, I've a problem. I need some advice."

"Let me guess. It's because Master Romie has allowed those two females to stay here?"

"Yes."

"You cannot change his mind on this, nor should you try. Praxton females must accept their guardian's judgements without argument." She turned to look at Terri. "I have taught you that much, I trust?"

"Yes, I accept their presence here."

"Good. But you do have a window of opportunity to establish yourself as the senior female."

"Master Romie has told me I am the senior female."

Anne frowned. "Just because he names you the senior female, doesn't mean they just accept you as such. Before it's too late you should subdue the other females. Enforce yourself as the senior female."

"Subdue?"

"Dominate them. Make sure they understand you're the senior female. Period. It may not matter that Master Romie said you're the senior female. What really matters is if the other females accept you as such."

* * * *

Terri returned to the sitting room where Erica and Dezine sat drinking tea.

"Hi, can I join you?"

Erica and Dezine exchanged looks and Erica shifted on the couch to make room for Terri to sit between them.

Erica, a tall redhead, spoke. "You seem to be in a friendly mood." She gave her a smile. "Sorry, I'm not complaining."

"Master Romie made me realize I was being less then sociable to you and Dezine. I'm sorry I was being rude. I guess I didn't want to share him."

Dezine touched Terri's thigh with her hand. "We understand. It can't be easy to have us suddenly move into your home, but we'd like to be friends with you."

"And I want to start over and be friends with both of you." Terri put her hand on top of Dezine's. The medium height brunette let out a sigh. "That's good to hear. Anne has given me and Erica some rather severe spankings and even used the discipline room on us. She told us it was our responsibility to make friends with you. We were wondering what to do as you didn't seem to want to spend time with us."

Terri recalled how Anne, the housekeeper, had scared her when she first arrived in the household. Anne was strongly built and had a no nonsense attitude when it came to how she perceived the house should be run. "I'm sorry I made things uncomfortable for you. Actually, Master Romie gave me a spanking for the same thing. He told me neither of you were going to leave and I had better start behaving. I must admit I was being selfish and now want to make amends. I was thinking we could perhaps go shopping and have a drink together for a start."

"That would be nice. But we need Anne's permission first. She has restricted us to the home and property only." Erica shrugged. "She made it rather clear we had best not disobey her."

Terri giggled. "I've been there. I'll ask her for you and explain we're getting along fine now."

* * * *

Terri carried her shopping bags into the house before collapsing on the chair next to Erica. "I need a drink. I think we must have been to a hundred stores today."

Erica laughed. "I was so glad to get out of the house, but now I want to go back and slide into a tub of hot water."

Dezine looked at Terri. "So, how are the Affiliation plans going?"

"Well, I've given it some thought, and did check on the traditional aspects of the ceremony, but decided I want to make it a bit more modern. I'm not much for using heavy chains and collars."

Dezine nodded. "I agree with you there. I like the light, thin metal type. You can barely feel them on. What else are you planning for the ceremony?"

"I want to incorporate some Alliance Worlds customs. I'm going to wear a white dress and have my aides wear black. They'll be still revealing of course, but having black and white is a traditional colour for weddings on Earth. I also want to use rope as a method of restraint rather than cuffs. I know it takes longer to tie them and to undo them but I think they look more elegant and make the female look more sensual. At least I feel that way in them."

Erica smiled. "You look like a thick rope girl to me."

Terri laughed. "I am. I want to ask you two something. I would really like it if you would agree to be my aides. I know it's kind of sudden, but if we're going to share Master Romie, then I want to share the Affiliation ceremony with you as well. I guess what I'm also trying to say is, I want us to be more than just housemates. I want us to be friends, too."

Erica leaned over and gave her a kiss. "I'd love to. It would be a great honour to be an aide for my friend."

Dezine raised her glass. "To friends and Terri's Affiliation ceremony."

Chapter Seven

Evelyn answered her mobile, recognizing the name on the display. She quickly brushed back her hair, still damp from her morning shower.

"Hello, Master Melvin. Thank you for returning my call."

"No problem. I understand you want to interview Jennifer?"

"Yes, if I could."

"Of course. Actually, she has today off, if you want to swing around here. Make it noon and you can have lunch with us."

"That would be great. See you then." Evelyn hurried to put her equipment together and to change her clothes, wanting to dress closer to Praxton customs if she was going to be a guest in a home. Satisfied she was ready, she arranged for a shuttle to pick her up.

Evelyn grabbed the bag containing her equipment and left the shuttle. She took a deep breath and headed up the walk. The home was what she came to expect in Praxton, large with a landscaped yard. She pressed the door chime and waited.

The door opened to a smiling dark haired woman of average height. Evelyn considered that with her full lips, dark eyes and oval face she was quite beautiful. Her curves were visible under her soft yellow dress.

"You must be Evelyn. I'm Jennifer."

Evelyn entered the spacious front hall and into the living room where three other women were waiting.

"This is Helena, our housekeeper, and Celestia and Aatum."

Evelyn received a hug from Celestia, a tall blonde, and Aatum, a brunette with a generous but still fit body. Helena retreated to the kitchen after informing them lunch would be ready in exactly thirty minutes.

Evelyn chose an armchair across from the loveseat where Jennifer and Aatum sat. Celestia took another armchair close to Evelyn.

"I'm surprised you want to interview me. Something about my work?" Jennifer gave a warm smile.

"Yes, I'm doing a news report on the changes on Praxton. One part is the employment for females. It seems you're unique in having a skilled job."

Jennifer blushed. "I don't know if I'm that special. Celestia and Aatum work as well."

Aatum interjected, "But we work just part time. Jennifer works full time and has special training on Earth."

Evelyn asked, "What type of special training?"

"I'm an exobiologist. I went to university, passed with high marks and couldn't find work except in administration on Earth. But Praxton had an opening for me. Good pay too, so I came here."

Evelyn glanced at Celestia who raised an eyebrow at Jennifer's last comment. *There's more to that story.*

Evelyn waited with the others at the dining room table, chatting until Melvin Taylor arrived. She answered questions about Earth and wasn't surprised by Aatum's question.

"How come your hair is so short? Is that something a lot of Alliance females do?"

"No, I just like it this way. I used to have long hair, but decided on a change."

"Oh, on Praxton all females grow their hair long. What does it feel like to wear pants? Don't they feel tight and uncomfortable?"

Evelyn laughed. "Not as tight and uncomfortable as the collar I'm wearing."

Jennifer giggled. "You'll get used to wearing it." She turned to Aatum. "I remember wearing tight pants. You get used to them like the collars."

Melvin entered the room and sat at the head of the table, "Hello, Evelyn. It's good to meet you."

"Hello, Master Melvin." She looked at the barrel chested, dark haired man. *Good looking guy. Definitely has that bad boy look.*

He heaped a portion of food onto his plate. "So Evelyn, how's your reporting on Praxton going so far?"

"Interesting, to say the least."

"As a female, I suspect you're meeting some resistance."

"That's true, but not as bad as I was expecting. I was told Praxton is very chauvinistic, and it is, but so far everyone has been polite and open to me."

"Praxton society can take time to understand, but it does respect the roles of males and females. Even those from Alliance space."

After lunch, Evelyn followed Jennifer to a patio in the backyard. The stone surface held a pair of small tables and several chairs. Beyond the patio, a high fence made of stone separated them from the desert beyond.

Evelyn set up the camera and recording devices and sat across from Jennifer at one of the tables.

"Okay, we're set up. If there's something you wish you hadn't said, just say cut twice and the recording will stop. We'll erase that part and start again."

"Okay, I'm ready."

Evelyn did an introduction and started with a question. "So Jennifer, how do you like living on Praxton and being a slave?"

Jennifer grinned. "It's going well. And I'm not a slave. I've a full time skilled job and am in love with a wonderful man."

"That you share with two other women."

"We've an arrangement. I care very much for everyone in our family."

"Okay. How did you find work in this chauvinistic society? Were there any special problems?"

Jennifer laughed. "Well, that's not too subtle. I applied for my job on Praxton while I was living on Earth. On Earth, I couldn't get a job that I studied for. I did find a job that paid the bills. I was pretty good at it but was passed up for a promotion by a less experienced man. But Praxton was excited about my credentials and offered me a position in my chosen field. I didn't receive any restrictions from immigration, so I moved here."

"Is that the only reason you moved to Praxton?"

Jennifer blushed. "Master Melvin approached me on Earth and made a proposal that I accepted."

"Melvin Taylor lives on Praxton. How did he happen to choose you?"

"When he lived on Earth we dated a few times."

"So he travelled all the way back to Earth just to see you again. He must have special feelings for you. All the same, didn't you hesitate about going to Praxton and sharing a husband with two other women? Also on Praxton, women have to submit to the men and wear a collar and restraints. Didn't that worry you?"

Jennifer took a deep breath before replying. "Well, I'd be lying if I said I didn't want to have Master Melvin all for myself. But I do have a good relationship with the other females and I'm comfortable with sharing him. The last relationship I had with a man on Earth didn't end well. He was a selfish man and didn't care for me like I'm cared for here. I don't mind being submissive to Master Melvin. I like wearing the collar and even the cuffs. The chains are a bit of a nuisance, but are more decorative than functional and we can easily remove them if need be. Overall I feel secure and protected when I wear the collar and cuffs. Being submissive is part of that package."

"How about being with the other women? On Praxton, women are supposed to sleep nude, often with other women on a narrow bed."

"Like I said, I have a relationship with them. There's more cuddling than sex when I sleep with another female. On Earth, I had female partners before, even though I considered myself heterosexual there as I do now. I guess females are more comfortable with same sex partners than males. Most females I knew on Earth had at least one female partner at one time or another. On Alliance worlds there are more females than males, so some sharing is likely to happen."

Evelyn knew the latest statistics showed females made up fifty-four percent of the human population throughout the galaxy. It didn't take much of a calculation to show that meant there were eight extra females in a room of a hundred people. *That sure brings out the nasty side of women when they're competing for too few men.* "How about when you and the other women don't get along? I understand there's discipline involved."

"Yes, if we misbehave, or have a poor attitude, there're consequences. Master Melvin or Ms. Helena will discipline us."

"Such as a spanking? Are there other measures used?"

"Yes, spanking is common. Standing in a corner is another. We also have a discipline room where we can be whipped and put into a cage."

Evelyn gasped. "Don't you consider that barbaric?"

Jennifer shook her head. "No, not at all. I even asked to be whipped once. I was curious what it felt like. It didn't hurt much more than a spanking. I've received a few of those. Females on Praxton consider Alliance females too weak and soft, that they forget what it takes to please a male."

"Interesting viewpoint. What about the special courses females are required to take? I understand to immigrate to Praxton, females are required to learn how to act properly as a female."

"Yes. At first I thought it was a bit silly, but I was glad I took it. I learned a lot. I also met a special female that I have become good friends with, Terri Baxter."

Terri Baxter? Her name sure gets around. "So what do you recommend to women considering moving to Praxton? What should they expect?"

"It's a different lifestyle here. Females give up some of their freedom but gain security. I recommend females considering moving here to choose a potential guardian carefully and ask to live with him for a week before making a commitment. It'll give her a chance to see what Praxton is about first."

Evelyn wrapped up the interview and put away her camera equipment. "So you know Terri Baxter? I keep hearing her name."

"Terri is a wonderful friend and a fantastic female."

"Do you think you could arrange for me to meet her?"

"I can try. I'll ask Master Melvin to contact Master Romie, but I'm sure it won't be a problem."

"Thanks. Do you always refer to him as Master Melvin?"

Jennifer shook her head. "No, I call him Mel when we're in the bedroom. Praxton customs dictate all males are called master in public. It's the Praxton submissive thing I guess."

* * * *

Evelyn changed her dress twice before picking out a matching set of collar and cuffs. She studied her image in a full-length viewscreen, deciding the black dress with a mesh front needed a bit more glitter. She dug into a box containing chains and attached a set that ran from her collar to wrist cuffs.

Better. Maybe one more accessory. Evelyn pulled out a pair of nipple jewellery separated by a chain and put them on. *Okay that makes them stand out but it looks better with them on. If I dressed like this on Earth, I'd be called a slut, but here it's conservative. The danger is I'm getting used to it.*

She took the shuttle to the Red Sand Lounge, named after the view it gave of the desert from the seventy-fifth floor of a downtown building. The viewscreen windows showed the desert in real time but amplified the available evening light so the shifting sand dunes could be seen.

Evelyn saw Max waiting for her at a table. He stood and waved at her, then walked over and escorted her back to the table.

"You're looking even better than the last time I saw you. I like your dress."

"Thanks. I see you've switched over to Praxton attire as well. Looks good on you." *Especially that open shirt. Hard to see anything in this light of that open fly on those Praxton pants. Too bad.*

He held the chair for her, a custom not normally done on Praxton, and sat across from her. A waitress wearing a short black skirt and a sheer sand coloured top took their order. Evelyn noticed he didn't watch her walk away and kept his attention on her.

They discussed the different stories and reports they were doing. She noticed his work entailed more of the economics of Praxton and various trade issues. He listened carefully to her progress on the employment situation of Praxton.

"Interesting. Praxton already is a strong economic power, and if they can attract better educated and trained women they might cause real concern for the other Alliance Worlds. They might regret forcing them to join."

"I think you're right, although that might take a while. There's a bit of misinformation about females on Praxton. The ones I have talked to seem happy and don't feel they're slaves at all. I guess the biggest thing to me is they just accept having to share a male with other females."

"What about the discipline?"

"I haven't really delved into that issue too much. I understand most of its spanking and not too harsh." She giggled. "I think some of them may like it."

He chuckled, "I can see the merits of it."

Evelyn ginned, enjoying the sound of his deep voice. Looking him over, she decided he was handsome, strong and appealing. *I can see the merits of being spanked by you.*

They ordered food and chatted about other personalities in the reporting field. She noticed he didn't run down his rivals, although brought up a few interesting details on how they did work.

"...the bar was where he did half of the interviews, I swear. Now tell me if rum isn't the way to reporting success."

She laughed. "Whatever works." She checked the time, surprised at the hour. "It's getting late."

"I'll walk you to the shuttle." He slipped an arm around her as they made the way to the elevator.

Evelyn was hoping for a bit of privacy, but the elevator car filled up with people as it made its way down. She reached for his hand and gave it a squeeze, hoping he would react as soon as the car doors opened.

He pulled her to a quiet spot in the lobby.

"Thanks. It was great having dinner with a lady again. Can I call you again soon?"

"I'm counting on it." She tilted her head and closed her eyes as he moved closer. As their lips pressed together, she opened her mouth, enjoying the play of his tongue inside her. One of his hands pulled her waist against him while the other gently rested on her ass. Evelyn moaned lightly and carefully twisted her hip, feeling his firmness.

He broke off the kiss and murmured, "Okay, I'll call you tomorrow to see how you're doing."

She gave him another kiss. "I look forward to it."

Evelyn rode the shuttle home, smiling as she leaned back in the seat.

Max relaxed in his apartment with a drink in his hand. *That went well. I've got to make sure I make this work with her. Those Praxton women don't appeal to me. Great looks but no ambition other than sitting at home looking pretty. I wonder if she, and all those other women, know what they do to a man when they walk around half naked and wear restraints.*

Chapter Eight

Terri looked up at Romie as she kneeled by his chair in his office, hoping he would approve of her plans for the Affiliation ceremony.

Romie nodded. "Yes, I concur with your choice of white and ropes for the ceremony. Thank you for including Erica and Dezine as your aides. I'm pleased our talk has led you to being more gracious."

Terri smiled. "Our talk and the paddling you gave me."

He looked at her sternly. "I believe I should inform you that tonight I'll be taking Erica to my chambers tonight. I trust you'll not be acting jealous."

"No, Master Romie. I understand I cannot be with you every night."

After the discussion ended, Terri entered the entertainment room, joining Dezine and Erica already watching a video. She forced a smile and joined Dezine, sitting next to her on the cushions on the floor, trying to find interest in the fashion show they were watching. Not much later Romie entered the room and, after a short conversation, took Erica by the hand.

Terri watched them leave the room and stared at the doorway after they left. Her attention was finally broken when she noticed a glass of an amber liquid held in front of her.

"Look, you've a choice. You can mope that Master Romie has taken Erica for his partner tonight, or you can find a way to enjoy the night with me." Dezine touched her shoulder with her hand. "I say we get a little drunk and find some show to watch."

"You're right." Terri took the drink and made a face as she took a sip. "Let's find a comedy and definitely get a little drunk." She took another drink. "This tastes better after a couple sips."

Dezine refilled their glasses and sat touching Terri. "You're very pretty. I can see why Master Romie loves you so much."

Terri put her arm around Dezine's waist. "Thanks. Master Romie and I had a bit of rough go at one time, but we're very comfortable with each now."

"Comfort is good." Dezine slowly massaged Terri's inner thigh with her fingertips as she looked at her for her reaction.

Terri hesitated for a moment and leaned over to kiss her lightly on the lips, returning for a longer kiss. She opened her mouth and slowly pushed her tongue forward. She heard Dezine moan her approval and slid a hand on her breast over her blouse. She felt the nipple stiffen against the nipple jewellery that imprisoned it, and used her fingers to unbutton the top. Terri pushed Dezine down, with the small of her back resting over the cushion. Terri opened her top. She gently pulled at the chain that ran between the nipple ornaments before lowering her head to kiss the breasts slowly. Terri ran her tongue down Dezine's throat as she undid the clasp on the skirt. With a slow, deliberate movement, Terri joined Dezine's hands together and pushed them above her head.

"Leave them there, no matter what." Terri returned to removing her skirt and the thin panties. "Maybe I should spank you first."

"Maybe you should." Dezine rolled over on the cushion, her ass higher up than her body as she looked back at Terri.

Terri rested her hand on her cheeks first, then started smacking them several times.

Dezine groaned, spreading her legs slightly during the spanking.

"Turn around again," Terri commanded softly. She watched Dezine twist around, keeping her hands above her head with her fingers interlocked. Terri squeezed her breasts and lowered her head to Dezine's stomach, leaving a carpet of kisses as she went down.

Terri lowered her head, licking between her legs, at the apex of her desire. Her hands squeezed Dezine's ass, kneading the flesh. Dezine cried out as her hips rose and fell. Moments later, she collapsed with her knees resting on Terri's shoulders.

Terri disengaged from Dezine but turned her over. She used Dezine's cuffs to lock her wrists behind her back.

"There, naked and helpless. I'm putting you to bed this way."

"Hmm. Sounds good." Dezine twisted around until her head was on Terri's lap. "Thanks. That was great. Maybe I can do you soon."

"Dezine, I've got you naked and cuffed. I want you to submit to me. Obey me. If you don't agree right now, I'll paddle your ass until its red."

She looked up at Terri. "But you're already the senior female."

"Yes. But I want you to be absolutely certain you understand that."

"I do."

Terri grabbed a fistful of hair. "Come with me."

Dezine gasped as she stood.

Terri took the unresisting Dezine out of the room, keeping her head bent down as she was led to the discipline room. Dezine moaned and closed her eyes when Terri released her hair when they reached the discipline room.

Terri briefly freed Dezine's wrist cuffs, and wondered if she would battle her as they stood underneath a set of chains that dangled from the ceiling. Dezine took deep breaths, looking tired. She briefly resisted the chain being attached to her first cuff, but Terri's words caused her to relent.

"Resist me and your punishment will be much, much worse."

Dezine allowed Terri to attach the chains to her cuffs without an argument. Terri went to a wall control and the chains lifted Dezine until only her toes barely reached the floor. She heard the captured woman grunt as she went to another wall to obtain a flogger with knots at the end of the red strands.

"Twenty-five lashes," she announced.

Dezine wiggled at her chains. "Please Terri. I'll obey you."

"This is to make it certain." Terri walked around Dezine, taking her time between each hard strike. Dezine fought now against her restraints, gasping with each strike. She cried out. Dezine was surprised at the strength of Terri's discipline. She had thought of Terri as a bit soft. Intelligent and with a strong personality, but this new side of her scared her. Dezine cried out, trying to escape from the chains uselessly.

Terri saw the marks she made on Dezine, satisfied that, in the future, she would obey her.

"Please, please stop," Dezine gasped. "I'll do what you want. I promise."

Terri struck her again. "Are you sure?" The whip left another red mark.

"Yes. Ow!" She sobbed. "I can't take any more hits."

Terri lowered the flogger. "I'll decide what you can take." Her hands touched the red stripes along her breasts, as Dezine moaned.

"Yes, Terri." Tears rolled down her cheeks.

"You like being punished?"

"A little." She gasped out, "I just can't handle pain very well."

"Well, let's try something a little different then." Terri returned the whip to the wall bracket and returned with a wide belt and a length of cord. She locked the belt around Dezine's waist after making sure it was tight enough to cause her to change her breathing. She attached the cord to the belt at the back and front, pulling it tightly until it pressed deep into her vagina. She was pleased to hear Dezine groan. She smacked her ass again several times. "Okay, I think I'll let you be for a while. I'll be back later to take you to bed."

Later, Dezine looked relieved when Terri returned after she had relaxed with a drink. She released her from the chains and belt, but cuffed her hands behind her back again.

"Come. Time for bed."

"Yes, Ms. Terri."

Terri kept Dezine's wrists cuffed after they climbed into bed, making her struggle to please her. As Dezine worked her tongue on Terri's nipples, Anne entered the room to secure one ankle each to the foot of the bed. She gave Terri a nod of approval as Dezine continued her efforts.

After Anne left, Terri pushed Dezine's head down between her legs. "Don't stop until I tell you," she ordered.

Soon Terri moaned as she came, feeling satisfied physically and mentally.

* * * *

Terri ate her breakfast quietly. She noticed Dezine looked at her occasionally, seeking approval. Terri had given Dezine a hard spanking earlier that morning and told her she was only allowed to wear one garment that day. The light dress made it obvious she had complied and it was equally obvious she had accepted Terri as her superior.

Terri had been fairly confident she could push her will over Dezine. The bigger test would come against Erica. She smiled at Dezine and tried to relax as she waited.

Erica showed up and asked Anne for a large breakfast.

"I'm feeling really hungry."

Terri resisted frowning, smiling instead as she made plans.

* * * *

Shara greeted her as Evelyn stepped out of the elevator. "Good morning. How did your date go last night?"

Evelyn grinned. "Very well."

"Think he'd make a good guardian?"

"No, no, no. I'm not ready for that Praxton custom."

Shara laughed. "Come on. It's how I'd relate to him. Yes or no. If you were a Praxton female, would you take him as a guardian? Don't tell me it's too early to say either."

"Okay. *If* I was a Praxton female, then yes, I'd consider him a good guardian."

"Now that wasn't so hard, was it? What're you up to today?"

"Not much. Some more research. I'm waiting for a call to do an interview with Terri Baxter."

"I'm going shopping after work and was wondering if you'd want to come with me. I want to get a new dress and accessories for a party I'll be attending. Master Philip said I could get whatever I wanted."

"Sure, give me a call when you're ready to go."

Evelyn walked to a teahouse and ordered breakfast. She opened her tablet and searched for the video Terri Baxter was in. The stylized video was a remake of Black Steel and the Steelets original video *Strike Her*, but was changed to make Terri Baxter the featured female dancer. The video was long and involved a lot of dancing and shots of Black Steel interacting with the Steelets. Terri's clothing was revealing and slightly different from the rest of the Steelets. The camera focused on her in close-ups, and while she danced with the rest, Evelyn noticed they avoided comparing her dance steps to the others. *Likely not as good a dancer. But she sure has a nice looking body.*

She watched as Terri had her clothes removed and was tied to a pole where Black Steel whipped her. Evelyn didn't hear the waitress offer to refill her tea as she stared at Black Steel and Terri.

"Sorry, I was distracted."

The waitress smiled. "That's okay. Some of those videos will do that."

Evelyn blushed, knowing the waitress had seen what she was watching. *Not only that, but I feel too warm and my nipples are at full attention. Not obvious at all that I was enjoying that video.*

Her thoughts were interrupted by an incoming message from Pearson Video News head office. She opened the video message and was surprised to see it came from Madison Petry, vice president of Human Interest programming for Sol.

"Evelyn, we are very pleased with your work you're doing on Praxton. We would like you to expand your reports by doing a series on the life in one of the Praxton homes. We thought you could live in a Praxton home over a period of several days, and not just record, but to try to live as they do. We would like you to wear a camera during the time there so you can record continuously. If you send us the raw footage, we will edit here. Please let me know your answer ASAP."

Evelyn sighed. *Oh great. Does she understand what she's asking? And it's not really a request coming from her. Damn.*

Her mobile chirped and she answered after she glanced at the name of the caller.

"Hi Max." She put a smile into her voice.

She listened to what he'd been doing and responded.

"That sounds better than what I've been asked to do." She quoted her new assignment. "I don't think I've a choice but to do it. I can't say I'm thrilled about it."

"You really don't have a choice if the vice president of whatever department asks you. Maybe it won't be as bad as you think."

"Maybe." *Sleeping naked with another woman. Getting a spanking because I forget to do some odd Praxton custom. Yeah, it won't be as bad as I think. It'll be worse.*

"There's a new hologram video of the Screaming Allies group that's being shown at a downtown bar tomorrow night. I was wondering if you want to go."

"I'd love to. They're a crazy group. It helps if you're drunk when you watch them."

He laughed. "That can be arranged. Send me your address and I'll pick you up."

Well that's better than my assignment anyway. Evelyn left the restaurant, calling for a shuttle to take her to a shopping plaza where she planned to do a video report on shopping on Praxton. *This shouldn't be too surprising to most that the stores cater mostly to women. But almost all stores are owned by men, who make decisions on what to carry in the store. No wonder all the women here run around half naked.*

* * * *

She met Shara at a mall and exchanged a hug with her. Shara gave her a quick pat on her ass and led the way to the stores.

"I've a favour to ask of you, Shara. I'm supposed to do a video report on life inside a Praxton home by living there a few days. I was thinking that perhaps I could ask to use Master Philip's home."

Shara grinned. "That's great! I'll check with Master Philip, but I'm sure it won't be a problem."

"Okay, but it was also indicated to me I was to try to live as a Praxton female and use a video recorder at all times. I'll cut out some parts, but there'll be lots of recording."

"You're going to live like a Praxton female? Now that could be interesting."

"That's what I'm scared of."

* * * *

Terri approached Erica and Dezine in the entertainment room.

"Hi Erica, what are you watching?" She motioned with her hand for Dezine to go to sit in the armchair.

"Some sort of comedy. Bit silly actually."

Terri sat next to Erica on the couch, noting she was wearing a skirt and a short top. She was also wearing wrist and ankle cuffs but without chains. "Erica, I do like you but I was thinking I'd love to give you a good paddle."

Erica gave her a smile, "Well, that's nice, but I'm bigger and stronger than you. You'd end up with *your* bare butt spanked."

"Want to see who's stronger?"

"Sure." Erica grinned, grabbing at Terri's wrists and began to push.

Terri let her push at first and began to twist her body. *You may be stronger, but I've had combat training when I was with Charter of Conduct Office.*

Terri quickly had Erica off the loveseat and on her stomach on the floor. She twisted one of Erica's arms behind her back and used her knee to pin it. Terri used her hands to undo the skirt and began to ease it off, pulling the panties with it. When they were down to her knees, she gave Erica several hard smacks on her ass.

Erica moaned, "Ouch, ouch, ouch."

Terri continued to spank her until her cheeks turned a bright pink. "Had enough?"

"Yes. You spank almost as hard as Master Romie."

"Now I want you to strip."

Chapter Nine

Erica slowly stood. After a moment of hesitation, she removed her clothes.

"All right, you win, Terri."

"Good." She sat on the couch. "Over my lap."

Erica rubbed her cheeks. "You really know how to wrestle." She lowered herself across Terri's lap.

Terri stroked the back of her head, and then gave her ass a smack. She repeated the strikes, watching the cheeks turn red.

"Ow!" she complained. "That one really smarts."

"That hurt my hand, too." She gave her a few more smacks. "Are you still going to help me with the Affiliation ceremony?"

"Of course. I have a few ideas about the dinner that I want to...ow...talk to you about."

"Good, I really need your help." She stroked Erica's back. "I've got to admit I do enjoy spanking you."

"Yes, well, I don't mind being on the receiving end, but can I just now agree that you're the senior female and also stronger?"

"You can agree but you will stay over my lap a bit longer, until I'm really certain you get the message."

Romie entered the room, not looking surprised at Erica lying naked over Terri's lap. "Hello, I trust I'm not interrupting anything."

They replied in unison. "No, Master Romie."

"Terri, a female reporter wants to interview you and I gave permission for her to do so. She works for an Alliance news service and left a number for you to contact her."

"Thank you, Master Romie." She kept a hand on Erica's cheek.

"It's good to see you two are getting along."

After Romie left, she gave Erica several more smacks on her ass, satisfied to see the woman's cheeks turning from red to purple. Finally, she said, "Okay, you can get up now."

Erica stood and twisted around to look at her backside. "Now that looks red—purple!"

"It does." Terri stood. "Come on, let's have drink and talk about that dinner."

* * * *

Erica took a sip of her wine. "I know you're trying to incorporate Alliance and Praxton customs together and I've an idea about the dinner. I'm thinking the hors d'oeuvres could be Praxton, you know nude females on a table with appetizers placed on them, and the main course would be Alliance food."

"Hmm, that sounds good. What about dessert?"

"Oh, that should be Alliance wedding cake served by naked slave girls."

Terri laughed. "You *have* thought this out. Okay, that sounds pretty good. At least it's a balance between the Alliance customs and Praxton."

"I think it's going to be great. I like the idea you had about using ropes instead of cuffs to bind you and the other females. Very traditional and I think it's much more artistically pleasing as well. How many females are going to be in your party?"

"I think six females, assuming Dezine and you will be part of it."

"I'd love to. You know I wasn't born on Praxton and I've never been bound with ropes before, just cuffs. So I'm looking forward to the experience."

"It'll be an experience alright. They're not as comfortable as cuffs but can be more sensuous. Now I better contact that reporter and see what she wants."

* * * *

"What type of dress are we looking for?" Evelyn examined a dress hung on a rack.

"Short and glittery. It's for a party," Shara replied and replaced a dress after holding it up against her.

"I thought Praxton dresses were already short."

"I want this to be even shorter. As short as I can get."

Evelyn picked a black dress with sparkles and held it up. "In that case, how about this?"

"Oh, that looks good."

"It's strapless as well. Not much coverage there."

"All the better." Shara smiled. "I want to show off at this party."

Evelyn studied Shara for a moment. "So who's at this party that you're trying to show off for?"

Shara sighed. "Before Master Philip became my guardian, I was hoping this other male would accept me as one of his females. I know I shouldn't have gotten upset, but after meeting me three times, he told me he had chosen another female instead."

"He's going to be at the party?"

"Master Graysen is going to be there along with his females. I want to show him what he's missing."

"You do know that you're a beautiful woman and don't have to prove anything to anyone?"

"I know that, but I still want to make him sorry."

Evelyn grinned. "I can't argue with that."

Shara tried on the dress and came out from the dressing room. She spun around and faced Evelyn. "What do you think?"

"I think if it was any shorter I'd be able to see your cheeks. But, yes, you look very sexy in it. I think you should take it."

The sales clerk packed her dress after taking payment from Shara's mobile.

"So, Shara, you're buying this dress to make some guy jealous?" Evelyn asked.

"I guess, in a way."

"Correct me if I'm wrong, but aren't guardians responsible for all expenses?"

"Yes."

"So your Master Philip has purchased a dress so you can make another male jealous?"

Shara laughed. "Well, if you put it that way. But guardians are also supposed to make sure their females are well cared for and this dress will make me happy. So all is the way it should be."

They stopped at a shop that specialized in restraints where Shara went directly to a display case of collars and cuffs.

"I thought you had enough cuffs."

"I have a few, but I want to get a set where cuffs wrap around your thighs. I think on the short dress it will look really good."

"So what do you do with restraints on your thighs?"

"Well this set here has matching wrist and ankle cuffs as well, and normally you have a chain between the thigh and wrist cuff. I like the look and if you have a long enough chain it doesn't restrict your arm movement too much."

"These are a little pricy." Evelyn looked at the black decorated cuffs with bands of silver in them.

"They'll go with the dress and Master Philip gives me a big allowance. He'll like seeing me in them."

"I'm sure he would. And I'll bet it'll get Master Graysen's attention too."

"I'm counting on that." She bit her lower lip for a moment. "I guess I'm being a little vain."

"That's okay. Sometimes we have to do things like that to feel secure."

"You're seeing Master Max tonight?"

"Yeah, he's coming to my apartment first to have a drink."

"Ohh, maybe a little romance happening?"

Evelyn laughed. "No, just getting to know each other."

"On Praxton after a few dates, the female sometimes lets the male know she wants him as a guardian, even though the male is supposed to ask her first. Something for you to consider."

"I'm almost scared to ask. How does she let him know?"

"There're a few ways. One method is for her to hand him a leash to her collar. Another is to slide over his lap for a spanking, usually with her skirt already lifted. She can also drop to her knees in front of him and take him into her mouth. Usually that's a pretty good hint."

"Pretty obvious hint there. I think I prefer the guy doing the chasing and romancing."

"Yeah, but the competition is pretty severe here. A female

sometimes needs to speed things along." She pointed at an item on the counter display. "Do you know what this is?"

Evelyn looked at the belt that appeared to go around a waist, a strap that went from the front to the back and an egg-shaped item secured in the middle. A small black rectangle rested next to it. "No, but if I was to guess, I'd say that apparatus would hold that round thing between your legs."

"That's right." She placed the egg-shaped item in Evelyn's hand. "Hold this." She used the black controller to activate the device.

Evelyn grinned at the vibrating device. "Oh my, that would be interesting to wear. I didn't think Praxton allowed vibrators for females."

"This is a bit different." She passed the controller to Evelyn. "Try using it now."

She pushed buttons but the vibrator refused to work. "What's wrong with this thing?"

"Nothing. If you're wearing the belt, the controller will not activate the vibrator. Something like a small current is made from the controller to the device. You can't activate the vibrator, but your guardian can."

"That is so wicked. So he can play with you and there's nothing you can do about it."

"Completely at his mercy, wherever you are." Shara looked at the clerk. "Wrap one of these up for my friend."

"Shara! I can't use this, and I'm certainly never going to let Max have the control."

"Maybe not now, but I see a future of you and Max. This will come in handy, I'm sure of it."

Evelyn blushed as she took the package. "We'll see."

* * * *

Evelyn checked her clothes and hair before opening her apartment door to Max. She decided to wear one of her shorter skirts. She also picked a top with an open weave style that meant wearing nipple jewellery. Evelyn decided on a wider collar than the one she normally wore for her broadcasts, adding matching cuffs. As she locked the collar, she realized it made her feel different, the collar thickness slightly restricting her head movement. After a debate with herself, she added a locked chain belt around her waist and attached chains from it to her wrist cuffs. *I hope he doesn't think I've gone completely native with this, but it's an interesting look.*

She swung open the door with a smile. "Come in. We've time for a drink before we need to leave for the concert."

Max scanned the living room before sitting on the loveseat.

Evelyn handed him his drink and sat next to him. They faced the shower and she could see her bedroom through the glass wall, glad she hadn't left any clothes lying around. "Is your apartment like this?"

"A little different. Since I'm a male, they seem to think our needs are different. My apartment is a bit bigger. I have two showers. One is like yours, open to the living room and you can see the female bedroom. I have a second, larger bedroom with a private shower."

"Good grief, because you're a male, you get a larger apartment and a shower where you don't have to shower in front of anyone that happens to be around?"

He chuckled. "I guess there isn't much interest in watching men shower."

"Says who?" Evelyn grinned. "Go ahead and have a shower. I wouldn't mind watching."

He laughed. "Maybe another time. How's the reporting going?"

Evelyn rolled her eyes. "I told you about the assignment that involves spending a few days in a Praxton home. I'm going to have a camera on at all times so we can do a series on what it's like to live on Praxton."

"Sounds like it would be popular with Alliance World viewers."

"Yeah, but I'm not so keen on some of their customs. I'll have to sleep there and females all sleep nude with a female partner. I'm not even comfortable with all the hugging they do between females, let alone being in bed with one."

"I see your point."

"I just hope I'm not going to be disciplined. I find this spanking of females just a little strange. I mean I know it does happen on Alliance Worlds too, but here it happens all the time, even females spank other females."

"So maybe you're going to have to prepare for that, if you're supposed to live like a Praxton female for a few days. Doesn't sound like it's going to be a fun assignment for you." *But it sure is going to be fun to watch. Does she know what this talk of sleeping nude with another woman and being spanked is doing to me? I'm going to need a cold shower if this keeps up.*

"No, but I think it'll help show another side of Praxton to viewers. Anyway I've a theory on why females on Praxton are disciplined."

"What's that?"

"I was talking to a Praxton female and she said its tough competition to attract a guardian. I remember back home in Alliance territory, groups of women competing to attract some guy and I've got to say they can be downright nasty to one another. So if the same thing was happening in a Praxton home where there are three females to one male, there could be some problems. Maybe the guardian has to use discipline to stop the women from fighting all the time."

"Interesting. So the spanking and other disciplines evolved to keep the females acting properly." *Damn, is she hinting she wants a spanking?* He grinned, "So are you acting properly?"

She laughed. "I don't live with anyone so there isn't an opportunity to act improperly. So unfortunately, I'm being a good girl. The bigger problem is we need more men on Praxton, and on Alliance Worlds too."

Max put down his empty glass. "It's a problem I've heard before. Not enough men to go around in Alliance space too. So some women migrate to Praxton where even if they have to share, at least they have a man."

Evelyn stood. "Good odds for guys here. You must be tempted to have a couple of women while living here."

He shook his head. "Not me. I'm more into one woman for one man. To me, two women just means you've doubled your troubles."

She laughed. "You're not suggesting women are trouble are you?"

"Suggesting? No, I'd say that's a fact, ma'am." He thought back briefly to his earlier troubles with the false accusations made against him years ago. *But this one may be worth all that trouble.*

They left her apartment for the lounge. Once they arrived, Evelyn noticed it was large, and able to hold two hundred patrons comfortably. Evelyn noticed that many of tables were made up of only women and

Max was the centre of their attention. She caught herself instinctively slipping a hand inside his arm.

I guess I'm ready to defend my possession. I know he's not going to drop me for any of them, but as soon as one of them stared at him I did the same thing we were talking about earlier on how women behave.

The holographic display at the front stage used several projectors to make the image look real and with high detail. The sound level was high, and Evelyn was certain it exceeded Charter of Conduct Laws that restricted the decibel levels for performances. Still, she enjoyed the concert and the hand holding she did with Max. She was pleased he paid attention to her and the band, and not the women sitting at other tables or the waitress wearing skimpy attire.

After the concert, they returned to her apartment, and she invited him in for a nightcap.

"My ears are still ringing a bit but that was worth seeing." He took the offered drink and stared out of the balcony window. "Nice view of the city." He bent down and kissed her on the lips, lingering a moment after the kiss before looking out to the city again.

"Yeah it is." She leaned against him, looked up and returned his kiss. The kiss was warm, longer and his arms wrapped around her, holding her tight. When the kiss ended, she took him by the hand to the loveseat.

"Max, I'm sure glad I've got you to talk to. I really enjoy your company."

"I like you too." He looked down at her cuffed wrists. "You seem to have adapted to the Praxton fashions rather well."

She had noticed he was wearing male Praxton clothes as well and ran a finger down his bare chest. "I guess we are both forced to blend in if we want to do serious work here."

"True, but I was referring more to how well you can wear chains and cuffs and still use your hands. I would be tangled up in them."

She laughed. "Well, it did take some getting used to. I usually run chains from my collar, to the cuffs but I like this chain belt and decided to wear it tonight. I haven't added chains to the ankle cuffs yet. I'm scared I'll trip when wearing these stilettos."

"So I'm curious, do you feel like you're a slave when you're wearing these cuffs and chains?"

Evelyn frowned as she thought about the question. "No, not really. But the collar makes me feel, well, I guess a bit submissive." She touched the collar with her fingertips. "It constantly reminds me of what it represents."

His hand drifted up and down her thigh and Evelyn noticed a growing carnal look in his eyes. "I like the look on you. The collar seems a bit more prominent on you than some other females. Maybe because your hair is shorter."

"Yeah, I get asked a lot about my hair and why I wear it so short. It must be considered a fashion faux pas here."

"I think it looks great on you." He lowered his head and kissed her.

Evelyn responded by locking her fingers at his shoulders, the chains preventing her from reaching any further. She parted her lips, feeling his hand slide up her leg, over her skirt and under her top. His fingers followed the curve of her back as she pressed against him. She murmured her approval when his other hand went up her rib cage and gently cupped her breast.

When they broke off the kiss, Evelyn sighed and kissed his chest.

"Max, I don't want to lead you too far tonight. I'm not quite ready for the bedroom yet."

"I understand. I think we've lots of time to get to know each other." He slowly withdrew his hands from under her top. *I'm going to have trouble walking out of here.*

"Good, I'm looking forward to getting to know you better."

He stood. "I best get going. Work day tomorrow."

"Yeah, I've the sleep over happening starting tomorrow. I'm not sure of the protocol for going out with you while I'm there."

"I'll call you anyway."

She kissed him at the door again. "Thanks, I may need to hear a friendly voice between the sleeping arrangements and the discipline."

"I doubt there'll much discipline." He shrugged. "At worse maybe a light spanking."

"I hope you're right." *I'd much rather get that spanking from you.*

After she closed the door, she quickly took off her top and removed her nipple jewellery. *I didn't even notice these things until we were on the couch. They didn't exactly adjust to the change in size.*

Evelyn took off the rest of her clothes and cuffs. She started to remove her collar but took one more look in a viewscreen. *It does look good with my short hair. I almost look like a slave girl with it on. Definitely submissive and Max liked the look.*

She turned off the light and crawled into bed, naked except for her collar.

* * * *

Max couldn't sleep. His thoughts kept returning to Evelyn wearing a collar and cuffs. *Maybe I have to buy her a collar and present it to her so she'll accept me.*

He took a shower, dressed and tried to concentrate on his next news report. He felt fortunate to be able to do two interviews via a video link, saving him the time to travel to where they lived. The information he received enabled him to build a series of questions for a face to face interview he had scheduled for the afternoon with the owner of a manufacturing company.

After lunch, he took a shuttle to Gibson Tactical Supply and manufacturing. Stewart Gibson greeted him in his office, consisting of a large desk and work area plus a seating area of armchairs and a couch. Max was expecting to interview Gibson alone, but a female employee joined them.

Gibson explained. "I know you wanted to learn more about the economics of manufacturing, but I thought you may wish to include in your report some of our new employment initiatives. I have listened to some of your reports, and of other reporters, and there seems to be an emphasis on how Praxton is changing regarding the employment of females. Kami is heading up our female training department. Our goal is to have a quarter of our workforce be female by the end of our fiscal year."

Max looked at the raven-haired woman, guessing she was approaching middle age. He also knew, with the abundance of gene therapy available on Praxton, it was difficult to determine the age of most females.

"That sounds like an ambitious plan. What is current percentage of female workers?"

Kami answered. "Approximately six percent. Last month it was just two percent, so we are moving in the right direction."

"Stewart, I understand one of your largest customers is the Praxton military, that you supply spaceship electronics and weapons. With the war concluded, and Praxton under some restrictions in regard to their military, has that had a negative impact on your business?"

"We have had to change what we supply to the military. Less weapons and more devices to enhance the operations of a spaceship. We also make replacement parts for weapons and try to improve on their performance. The Praxton military is hampered in not being allowed to increase their weapon supply but can improve the quality and effectiveness on what they presently have."

Max looked at Kami. "What do your new female employees do?"

"They are trained in the manufacture of various devices and also in the testing of various components."

"How long is the training program?"

"That obviously depends on the aptitude of the new hire and where they will be working. The training can vary from three weeks to two months."

"That must be quite expensive to provide training for a month or more. How does that impact your revenue and profit margins?" He turned back to Stewart.

"The training is subsidized, as well as the first four months of salary when they commence work. It's a good program for us and we are trying to take as much advantage of it as we can."

"So the Praxton government is paying your company to train and employ female employees?"

Stewart shook his head. "The Praxton government is giving us a small allowance to increase our production capability, but it's actually the Alliance government providing us with the funds to increase female participation in the work force."

"Interesting. That is not a well-known fact."

"Only certain firms qualify for this program. Mostly larger concerns that require training that cannot be easily done in technical schools."

Max wasn't surprised. He knew that the Charter of Conduct Office and the Alliance government were able to move large sums of money to areas without official announcements. "How about if I do a video of the manufacturing area? It will be interesting to see how you have incorporated your new employees in the work area."

"Of course." Steward stood and led the way out of his office to a bank of elevators. He stopped from entering. "I'll allow Kami to show you. When you're finished, perhaps you'll have time to join me for refreshments."

Kami pointed out the modern laboratory where men and women worked with test monitoring equipment. "We have up to date equipment here. Being a manufacturer of military grade equipment we need the highest precision possible."

Max looked around the clean environment and at the workers. "I noticed the female employees are wearing collars, cuffs and chains. Doesn't that interfere with their work? The chains seem to restrict their arm movements."

Kami shook her head. "Praxton females are used to the chains and can work around any impedance." She smiled. "Actually, some of the females quite often remove chains while at work. But when they heard an Alliance reporter might be videoing them at work they made sure they were dressed properly. They want all Alliance worlds to know that they are not changing their social norms."

Max grinned. "I understand. A show of defiance." He briefly admired the glittering chains on one blonde that went from her collar to her wide metal cuffs.

"You seem to approve. We don't always get encouragement from Alliance visitors, although those are largely government inspectors."

"I believe in freedom of choice. I'm a bit of an anti-Charter person."

He videoed several workers, men and women, and then asked, "What about discipline? Female discipline seems to be a big part of Praxton culture."

"There were some issues here at first. Praxton females will quickly obey any male if their guardian isn't present. We had to make it clear to the male workers they were not to enforce rules on the females and not subject them to discipline. If problems were perceived the supervisor should be contacted."

"Does the supervisor perform discipline?"

"Max, you have to understand that females on Praxton expect discipline on occasion. It is part of knowing our guardian cares about us. So to answer your question, yes, some of the female workers have been mildly disciplined."

They walked back to the elevators. "So how are you finding living on Praxton? Do you have females living with you?"

"No, I live alone in an apartment."

"There are places where you can search for females looking for a guardian. I'm sure there are a lot of females that would love to have you as a guardian."

"Thanks, but I'm more of a one-woman guy. And I want her to be able to think and live independently. More of the traditional Alliance relation."

"So you have no one to share nights with? That seems like a difficult situation."

"I confess there is one female I'm interested in. Actually an Alliance female. I'm not sure how to approach her. I have thoughts of presenting her with a collar but I'm not sure how she would react to that."

Kami was silent for a moment as the elevator car carried them up. "Whether it's here on Praxton or on an Alliance world, one thing females like in a male is strength. I'm not talking just physical attributes, although tall and a nice body goes a long way. But it is more strength of character and being confident. Be in control when you're with her. She'll let you know when you've gained her trust and be willing to submit to you."

"Okay, thanks for the advice."

The elevator doors slid open. "Is it that female reporter from Pearson news? We like to watch her reports and how an Alliance female reacts to our ways."

"Yeah, that's her."

"Just watching her tells me she would like to wear your collar. She's waiting for you to take charge."

"You really think so?"

"She's living alone, walking around in collar and chains and observing how content Praxton females are. I just know she's thinking how nice it would to have a guardian."

Max enjoyed the coffee and pastries with Kami and Stewart, thinking about the information.

"I didn't realize how the Alliance worlds are trying to influence things on Praxton by subsidizing female training. How does the Praxton government feel about that?"

Stewart smiled. "Officially they remain neutral about it, saying if the Alliance government wants to invest money in Praxton industries they have no objections. Unofficially they are annoyed at this tactic, preferring the Alliance government give them the funds and they would decide on how to use it to increase female employment.

As a company, I cannot afford to refuse this injection of capital. I'm also a believer in allowing females to join the workforce. Praxton cannot sustain having the majority of our females staying at home or doing menial work. Having said that, I do hate the Alliance inspectors hinting broadly that the chains and cuffs are a work hazard and they should wear appropriate clothing."

Max chuckled. "That's hardly a surprise. Government money always comes with baggage. I have to say I enjoy how females dress here."

Max concluded the interview and went to a waiting shuttle. *Okay, now just how should I show Evelyn I'm in charge?*

Chapter Ten

Evelyn faced the camera mounted on a tripod and began to speak.

"For this series we're going to spend a few days in a Praxton home. I'll have a camera attached to my ear and hair and you'll see what I see. I promise it will be a very interesting video, but once again we warn you this is for adult viewing, as there'll be some nudity and perhaps a glimpse of the famous Praxton discipline methods."

She stepped slightly to the side. "This is a view of my apartment's living room. As you can see, the furniture is similar to that on Alliance Worlds. However, the two pictures are a little unusual. One is of the deserts that covers much of Praxton. The other is that of a woman wearing a full complement of a collar with matching cuffs and attached chains. She is wearing only a short skirt and no blouse so breast jewellery can be seen. Note she looks relaxed and pleased in her pose. This is considered on Praxton an image of ideal feminine beauty and you will see other examples of this in our series."

Evelyn directed the camera to focus on the glass shower wall. "The other unique feature on Praxton is the belief all women should be seen nude occasionally. Thus, the showers usually have glass walls so women can be observed washing. In my apartment, you can see my bedroom through the shower in the living room. If you're shy or modest you may find living on Praxton difficult if you're a woman.

"Finally, in this series women are referred to as females and men as males. Females normally only use their first names, although the title of Ms. is used by a female addressing one of much higher status. The males, when addressed by a female, always begin by the title Master. This is Evelyn Montgomery with the Pearson News Group reporting."

She held her smile for a few seconds longer and let out her breath. *Now the adventure begins.*

* * * *

Shara greeted her warmly when she arrived at Master Philip's home. Dalina took her suitcase after giving her a hug. Marilyn stood away from the rest and gave a hesitant smile to Evelyn.

Evelyn returned the smile. "Hi Marilyn. How are you?"

"I'm good." She quickly looked at Dalina and seemed to retreat further into the wall.

A few minutes later, Evelyn was led upstairs to a bedroom by Dalina.

Dalina pointed to the bed. "Normally one female sleeps with Master Philip and the other two females sleep together. Usually when we have a female guest she gets to sleep with one of us, but Shara said you would prefer to sleep alone. So this is your own room." She placed the suitcase by the bed. "You packed a lot of stuff for only a few days. You do know you're going to be half naked around the house, don't you?" She grinned. "You won't need a lot of stuff."

"I brought along some Alliance clothes to show you. I thought you might be interested in seeing what they looked like."

Dalina nodded. "That would be great."

Evelyn unpacked and attached the waterproof camera to her ear with the lens on a thin tube poking through her hair. The pea size camera was almost unnoticeable and sent a signal to a small device attached to her belt. She slowly spun around in her room, showing off the bed, closet, dressing table and the shower, adding voice commentary. She walked into the shower stall and looked down at the living room below.

"As we can see, the shower is visible from the living room below, which means I'll try to be the first one up and showered before anyone else can see me."

She went downstairs and saw Master Philip entering the living room.

"Hello, Master Philip."

"Hello, Evelyn. Are you prepared for your stay with us?"

"I hope so."

He chuckled. "I suppose we'll find out soon enough. I just want you to be comfortable staying here. I want to discuss the matter of discipline with you. If a situation arises where you would normally be disciplined, I'll permit you to decline without incident."

"Thank you."

"Of course, I hope that you'll go through with the discipline anyway." He gave a smile. "It would make your report more authentic."

"I'll keep that in mind."

Evelyn watched him walk away. *No pressure there at all*, she thought sarcastically.

Lunch was served by the housekeeper, Tara. Evelyn sat next to Shara and whispered to her. "Marilyn still looks withdrawn. Is she doing okay?"

"She's adjusting. I think it'll take a while for her to feel comfortable."

After lunch, Evelyn joined the other women on the backyard patio. She watched Marilyn pour wine for everyone. Before she could sit down, Dalina took Marilyn's hand and pulled her to sit down on her lap. Evelyn joined in the conversation about the upcoming elections and how females were going to vote.

Shara was of the opinion most females would vote as they saw best, but Dalina thought they might vote as their guardians wanted.

"I mean we're so used to obeying them, it might be most females will ask who they should vote for." Dalina frowned. "I hope not but I guess we'll see." As she spoke, she began to undo Marilyn's blouse.

Evelyn watched as the blouse was removed and tossed on the brick patio surface. Dalina took a sip of her wine and began to touch Marilyn's breasts.

This is interesting for the camera. Dalina obviously controls Marilyn. The girl didn't even protest being undressed. Mind you, being topless in a Praxton home isn't exactly news, nor two females enjoying each other.

Shara gave out a sigh. "Dalina, this is being recorded. Why don't you take Marilyn inside and have some privacy?"

Dalina shrugged. "Alright." She stood and took Marilyn by the hand and went inside.

Evelyn mouthed, "Thanks" to Shara.

Shara watched them leave. "No problem. Dalina is a bit of an exhibitionist and Marilyn wouldn't dare protest what she wants—or doesn't."

"Tell me, Shara, is it common for females to have relationships with each other like Dalina and Marilyn?"

"It depends on the household. We do get turns with Master Philip. In some households, the guardian only sleeps with one or two females, so the other females have to search for companionship. Dalina just seems to like to dominate Marilyn. I don't believe she's mean to her, but I wish she would give her some space. Dalina likes both male and females, but I think Marilyn definitely prefers males."

"But she goes along with Dalina anyway?"

"If you're a female on Praxton, you end up having sex with another female occasionally." She shrugged. "Sometimes it's more like just cuddling and kissing, but we also have sex. Evelyn, have you ever had sex with a female?"

"No. I kissed a girl once out of curiosity."

Shara laughed out loud and covered her mouth. "I don't think that counts. Really? Never?"

"No. Just men." She giggled. "And it's been too long."

"If you lived on Praxton it might have been a different story when it comes to females. Either that or it'd be even longer between getting laid."

After a dinner of too many courses, Evelyn brought out her suitcase containing Alliance clothes to the entertainment room. She began to take out the clothes.

"These are the pants females wear."

Shara held up the pair of pants. "These are a lot different than male pants. They don't have a fly and are really thin."

Dalina touched the material. "Feels soft. Put them on so we can see how they look."

Shara slipped off her skirt and pulled on the pants. "They feel really strange."

Dalina touched her leg. "Hmm, I can see some appeal in them. They shape your behind really nice."

Marilyn joined in trying on the clothes, putting on a bra.

"It feels like your boobs are being squeezed and pushed. I don't like it very much."

Philip walked into the room. "What are you females doing?"

Dalina stood and held up an Alliance blouse. "We're trying on some Alliance clothes, Master Philip."

He shook his head. "Odd looking stuff. Pants for females? I don't see that catching on here."

Shara commented, "The pants show off the figure nicely from the back."

"I suppose so. Anyway I wanted to tell Marilyn to come to my bedroom tonight."

"Yes, Master Philip," Marilyn replied quickly.

After Philip left Marilyn clapped her hands. "I was hoping he was going to pick me soon."

Evelyn saw Shara sigh. She looked at Dalina, who didn't look happy.

That evening, Shara escorted Evelyn to the spare bedroom.

"Sorry you have to sleep alone."

"That's okay. I usually sleep alone."

"You know females sleep only in the nude, don't you?"

"I heard."

"Also Tara will come in soon and cuff your ankle to the bed. In theory, you have to remain in bed until morning when Tara will come by to unlock it. If you have a need to get out of bed, you're supposed to ring a bell asking to be released." She pointed to the headboard. "At the side is a spare key for the ankle cuff. If you need to go to the toilet, you can unlock the cuff. Just make sure to lock it again or there'll be severe punishment."

"Okay, I heard about the cuff thing before."

"Remember, you can't leave the bedroom without your collar on. You can be dressed or naked, but the collar must be on."

"Got it. Collar is essential."

"I'll come by in the morning and help you get ready with the make-up. I noticed you don't use all the stuff Praxton females do."

"Thanks. I was wondering about all those containers on the dressing table."

"Good night." She patted Evelyn on her ass and kissed her on the cheek.

Evelyn watched her leave the room, feeling slightly surprised. *I guess I better get used to all the affection between females.*

She removed the camera, undressed and slid under the blanket. Shortly later Tara came in and attached the ankle cuff. After a brief reminder that she wasn't to remove the cuff, Tara left the room.

The chained ankle felt odd at first but a few minutes later, she fell into a deep sleep.

* * * *

Evelyn woke up to the morning sun beaming through the window. The reddish light of the Praxton sun wasn't hard on the eyes as she slowly sat up. She waited for Tara, hoping it wouldn't be too long as she eyed the bathroom.

Shortly, Tara greeted her and quickly unlocked her ankle cuff.

"Breakfast will be served in two hours, so you'll have plenty of time to get ready."

Two hours to get ready? I'll be starving by then.

She looked into the shower stall and didn't see anyone in the room below. She quickly turned on the water and stepped into the fine spray. *Well, if someone does see me I guess that's normal here, and I better get used to all their customs if I want to survive here as a reporter.* She was pleased she managed to finish her shower before anyone appeared in the room below.

Evelyn sat at the make-up table wearing only her panties. She examined containers of creams she hadn't seen before. Ignoring those, she applied facial cream and make-up when Shara entered the room.

"Did you sleep well?"

"Like a log. I was either tired or the wine got to me." She looked at Shara wearing only her collar.

"I thought I'd come and help you first thing this morning." She picked up a small jar. "This cream is for your neck. After using that, apply this..."

Evelyn listened to which cream to apply where and the use of make-up in places she never considered before. "Really, on my nipples?"

"Yes, it deepens the colour and contains a substance that helps keep them slightly swollen."

"Oh great. I don't want more attention drawn there."

"Don't be silly. Our breasts are in the middle of our chest and are meant to be noticed."

Shara gave her a kiss on the cheek. "I better get ready now. See you at breakfast."

Evelyn put on a dress and added cuffs to complement the collar. She added chains from her collar to her wrists and finally a chain between her ankle cuffs. *I hope I don't trip.*

She took a video of herself using a viewscreen as a mirror.

"This is a typical set of collar, cuffs and chains used by Praxton females. In the homes, females are usually barefoot." The camera focused on her feet and ankles. "Here you can see the ankle cuffs match my collar, and like the collar, they are locked. The chains between the cuffs are meant to lightly restrict movement of arms and legs. I can still walk with these chains but certainly not manage any running. The chains are just clipped on, so I can easily remove them. Sometimes the chains are locked as well, depending on the situation. In that case, which is also true for the collar and cuffs, a key is kept close by so they can quickly be removed if needed." Evelyn shut off the camera, frowning. *I likely looked like a proper sex slave. That should do wonders for my professional career.*

Breakfast consisted of sweet pastries, hot cereal and fruit. She tried to eat slowly as was the custom on Praxton, but did take a second helping. As she was eating, Shara and Dalina joined her.

Shara commented on what Evelyn was wearing. "I like your dress and collar and chains. Looks good."

"Thanks, I wasn't sure about the chains."

"No, the chains are fine. You're following our customs really well."

As they left the table, Marilyn came into the room, smiling.

Evelyn turned to Shara. "She sure seems to be in a good mood."

Shara giggled. "I think we can guess the reason for that." Shara continued. "I think it's great you put chains on between your ankle cuffs. Not many Alliance females try that."

"Since I'm a guest in your home, I thought I'd try adding more of the Praxton custom of chains."

"Let's go outside and sit on the patio."

Evelyn followed Shara outside.

"I thought it was a bit more private here. I want to make sure you're comfortable being in our home and if you have any concerns."

"I'm fine so far. I'm trying to get used to the touching and kissing between females. I guess I've always been a bit of a loner and not used to a lot of human contact. I am surprised I've adapted so easily to the collar, cuffs and chains. I hardly notice them most of the time, although when I was with Max, I felt like a sex slave with them on." She smiled. "Something about wearing that collar made me feel a bit submissive toward him."

"That's the point of the Praxton collar. You're supposed to feel obedient towards your guardian."

"He's not my guardian. Just a guy I'm dating."

"Right, just try and convince a million years of biology that a female doesn't want the male to be dominant. When we put on a collar, it just reminds us the males are in charge, and it's something we find alluring. At least it does for me."

"You may be right. I guess there's part of me that likes the fantasy of being in collar and cuffs in front of a big strong man. But like my other fantasies, such as being a princess that's rescued by a handsome knight, maybe they should remain fantasies. If Praxton females are going to be part of the future by being in the work force, maybe the submissive female in chains has to go."

Shara frowned. "You might be right, but I hope that there'll be room for wearing cuffs and chains and being in the workforce. So far I've been able to do both."

"True. But wouldn't wearing cuffs and chains be a problem for a shuttle pilot? There're probably a host of jobs that'd require free use of arms and legs."

"In that case, the female could remove the chains until it's time to go home. I can see what you mean, that the work environment will cause changes on how females dress, but maybe we just have to be more flexible on what is appropriate during work time."

"Good point. Do you believe most Praxton females would prefer to continue to wear the traditional attire of short skirts, collar and cuffs with chains?"

"Oh yes, females fought for the right to wear a collar and restraints when the Alliance Forces invaded our planet. We think Alliance females are prudes and don't really appreciate strong males. This collar represents to me security and love." She tugged at the ring in the centre of her wide, red collar.

Evelyn nodded, believing she had some interesting material for the report. One thing she had noticed several times was the reference that Praxton was invaded by Alliance Forces. The Alliance government, and the Charter of Conduct Office, insist they came to Praxton to rescue the oppressed female population. However, the female population on Praxton, typified by Shara's view, didn't agree any rescuing was required. "You made a good point. You certainly have managed to do your work while wearing restraints."

"Thanks. I wanted to ask you if Master Philip talked to you about discipline yet."

"He did. He said I could bow out if there was discipline."

"Okay, I just wanted you to know that likely tomorrow all the females will be disciplined. It has been a while since we were punished and I sense he'll do something soon."

"Why are you being punished?"

"Nothing specific. He, like most guardians, believes occasional discipline is necessary to prevent bigger issues from happening."

"What will be the punishment?"

"It varies. I'd guess a small whipping for each of us. Maybe just a spanking. I'm just letting you know in case you want to go through with it. It doesn't hurt much. All the same, remember Praxton females resist crying out or struggling when they're being disciplined."

"I'll try to remember that. Would it be bad form if I chickened out?"

"Well, I guess word would get around that the Alliance females aren't very tough. My opinion of you wouldn't change, but maybe some of the other females would think of you as a wimp."

Oh great. It looks like I don't have much choice here.

* * * *

Evelyn joined the other women to watch TV in a large squared room. One wall featured the holographic screen, while the adjacent wall had a glass surface that showed a large shower stall. She wondered how often it was used and directed the question to Shara.

"Not too often, as there are showers and baths attached to the bedrooms. But the shower is next to the exercise and sauna area. So after a workout, or using the sauna, we would shower there."

Evelyn smiled. "It would be in competition with what's on the screen for sure."

"Well, I've taken a long shower in there a couple of times while watching part of a program on TV. If you shower right, as taught in our female classes, you can be a real distraction to some of the shows."

"So how do you shower the Praxton way?"

"A lot of tilting your head back, soaping and rubbing body parts, especially the breasts and thighs. Then you stand on your toes on one foot as you wash. That angles your hips, which is enhanced if you do a slow circle under the shower of water."

"That would do it for attention. Maybe I should video one of these times as you shower." Evelyn grinned.

"Sure. Next time I do a workout, you can video me."

Evelyn accepted a glass of wine from Dalina and soon was trying to get up to speed on a Praxton crime mystery series. *The Charter of Conduct Office would be having a fit if they saw this on Alliance Worlds. Half-naked women wearing restraints trying to please their male guardians, and earning a spanking for almost anything. The trouble is, after being here only a short time, I don't see that much wrong with it.* She fingered her collar. *I'm used to wearing this already. It feels odd when I take it off at night. Maybe I'm submerging myself too much into the Praxton culture.*

Dalina sat on the floor, resting her back on the couch where Evelyn and Shara were sitting. She looked over at Marilyn sitting on an armchair, and waved her hand for her to join her on the floor.

Evelyn saw Marilyn responded, not quickly, but she didn't show any sign she would refuse Dalina. Marilyn sat next to her, and trembled slightly, as Dalina undid her top and removed it. Evelyn watched as Dalina took Marilyn's hair in her hand and pulled her over her lap. She lifted up her skirt and quickly smacked the exposed cheeks several times. Then she stroked her fingernails over her back and ass.

"Did you enjoy that?"

"Yes, Ms. Dalina."

"I thought so. Come, rest your head on my lap."

Marilyn slid across the floor and rested her head on Dalina's thighs.

Evelyn was glad that was as far as it went. She would have been hesitant to video Marilyn being stripped completely, regardless how well such a scene would be received by the network. The spanking was acceptable as well. Praxton customs were well enough known by Alliance Worlds that it would not have been a shock. She looked at Marilyn as her hair was being stroked by Dalina. Her ass, now pink in colour, was still exposed, as Marilyn made no effort to pull down her skirt. Only her thong gave a hint of modesty.

The wine glasses were refilled, once by Evelyn, who checked the bottle. The percentage of alcohol was much higher than what was allowed under the Charter of Conduct Laws, but she had to admit it did make the wine taste better. The body was fuller and not as sweet. *It may be hard getting used to the watered version we have on Alliance Worlds again.*

She was happy to receive a call from Max. She excused herself from the room and stepped outside to chat with him on the patio. She switched on the camera mode and showed him the patio and the surrounding area.

"You can't see much since its dark, but it's really beautiful here. Next time I'll show the other girls. One is pretty much naked, so you'll have to wait until next time."

"I only have eyes for you anyway."

"Right." Evelyn laughed. "But I shall not lead you into temptation."

After a talk on some of his doings, she said goodbye and went back to the TV room.

Dalina looked up at her. "A forty-five minute call? You must really like him."

"Just a good friend. He's also a reporter from the Alliance Worlds."

"And you talked about the news? I'll bet someone will be on her knees in front of him before long."

"That's not how I plan for things to happen. I'm an Alliance female."

"Yeah, one wearing a collar. I say that's another Praxton custom you're going to want to do."

Evelyn blushed as she sat.

Shara gave her a hug. "Don't mind Dalina. She's just teasing you because we all like you, and want you to have a man. Notice I said a man and not a guardian? You see I'm really trying to respect your Alliance views."

"Thanks." She noticed Shara still had her arm around her waist. She put her arm around Shara's shoulder and gave her a kiss on her cheek.

They resumed watching the show on TV and gradually Evelyn relaxed with her arm around Shara. *This isn't so bad. At least Shara doesn't push past my comfort zone with women.*

* * * *

Evelyn woke with a slight headache. She relaxed in bed, waiting for Tara to undo her ankle cuff. She didn't check the time, but it seemed to her it was later than the previous morning when she was allowed to get up.

When Tara did arrive and unlock the ankle cuff, Evelyn didn't hurry to shower. *If someone wants to watch me shower, so be it. That wine did a number on me.*

The fine water spray felt good and she reflected on how Shara described how to do a sensuous shower. She tried to tilt her head back and wash and found it wasn't hard to do, except that she was used to watching where her hands went. When she stood on her toes on one foot, she found that fairly easy to do. *Maybe those moves will come in handy for when Max gets to watch me shower. Correction, if I let him watch me shower.*

Evelyn applied the make-up and creams that she learned from Shara. She put on nipple clips attached by a gold chain, and slipped on a blouse. Like all tops on Praxton, it had extra closures along the sleeves so it could be removed even if her wrists were cuffed together. She put on a pleated skirt, a pair of panties and a few chains to go with her cuffs. She decided to try on a wide collar, wondering how it felt to try to eat and carry out normal functions.

She entered the dining room and saw everyone but Dalina had arrived. She went to sit next to Shara and greeted her.

Shara leaned over to whisper to her.

"When you wear a loose fitting skirt, lift the back so you're sitting directly on the chair."

Evelyn nodded, stood, and lifted the skirt behind her.

"What if the skirt is tight?"

"You sit down normally, but you don't tug the skirt down. You let it ride up as high as it wants to go."

No such thing as modesty on Praxton. "I'll have to remember that."

* * * *

After breakfast the women were gathered into the living room by Philip. They sat as Philip stood and gave a lecture. Tara stood behind him with her arms crossed.

"I cannot say I'm pleased with some of the actions going on. Tara has told me that clothes, on occasion, are left lying on the floor or the bed. Towels in the washrooms are simply left on the floor after a shower or bath. In particular, I'm concerned how Marilyn is being treated. Dalina was given responsibility to show her how to behave properly in our home. However, she seems to believe that gives her permission to abuse her with various punishments. While this is something Dalina is doing, I'm left wondering why Marilyn accepts this and hasn't approached me for help. Shara, I'm disappointed you allowed this to go on without some sort of intervention."

Dalina spoke up. "I'm sorry, Master Philip. I shall be mindful how I treat Marilyn in the future."

Philip nodded. "Good. However, after lunch there'll be discipline to reinforce proper behaviour. All of you must learn that this attitude is not acceptable."

Evelyn watched Philip, but also saw Tara nod her head in approval. *I suspect she's the one that approached Philip about the problems. I'm not sure what I'm going to do here. Getting punished with the others might be something I'll have to endure.*

Later, Evelyn lightly tapped on the doorframe of Philip's study where he looked up behind his desk.

"Master Philip, may I have moment of your time?"

"Of course." He gestured at the armchair situated to the side and front of his desk.

She sat, remembering to flare out her skirt first. "I have an appointment at lunchtime with Terri Baxter, and I hope you won't mind if I leave the house for that. Actually I mean to say, may I have your permission to go out at lunch time?"

He nodded. "I see. When do you expect to be back?"

She swallowed. "I expect the interview to last only an hour. I can be back right after that. I understand you would want me present for when the discipline is to be done. I know you told me I could bow out of any punishment, but I decided I should accept whatever a Praxton female would normally receive."

Philip smiled. "I'm pleased to hear that. I also appreciate that you're asking for consent first to go out, and I do grant you permission. I have to say you're showing a great deal of willingness to accept and try Praxton customs. You're wearing the proper clothes and a sufficient amount of restraints, not just a token amount as most Alliance females do. Your behaviour is also in line of a Praxton female, and if it wasn't for your accent and your short hair, you wouldn't draw attention here as an outsider."

"Thank you for saying that. If I don't try to follow Praxton customs, then the accuracy of my reporting may suffer. I would be only like many other reporters that view things only as an outsider."

"Excellent. I shall wait until your return to do the discipline."

She stood. "Thank you, Master Philip, for your time and permission."

Evelyn left the office, not sure if she really was ready for the discipline. *Reporters have gone into war zones to get the news. I shouldn't be afraid of a little punishment.*

Later, Evelyn finished her conversation with Gina Rosetta on her mobile. Gina agreed to an interview, providing Evelyn appeared as a guest on her show. Evelyn accepted her proposal, wondering what it'd be like to be interviewed for a change.

Chapter Eleven

Terri Baxter worked through the evening on various emails and messages. She didn't stop, other than a sip of her tea, until Romie entered the study. "You're still at it?"

She turned and smiled at him. "There's so much to do. I have a hundred things for the Affiliation ceremony. That by itself is a lot of work. But I also have to prepare for the election."

"Perhaps you have too much on your plate. Are you sure running for election is a good idea?"

"I do. If I was to get elected, I will have to be able to handle multiple problems. This is good training for me."

"That's a good point. But if you were to get elected and faced these multiple tasks, then you would have to learn how to delegate. I suggest you do that now. Establish your priorities, pick the ones that you believe only you should do, and hand off the rest. Trust those around you and you will be rewarded."

Terri swallowed and thought over what he said. "When I worked for the Charter of Conduct Office and trained as a spy, it was drilled into me to only rely on myself. Don't trust others. Do it yourself." She smiled. "But those days should be behind me now. I'll take your advice and get help with this work."

"Good. Now make a list of what you want to do tomorrow and come to bed. My bed, that is."

Terri quickly finished her work and went upstairs.

* * * *

Terri found Erica and Dezine at the table eating breakfast and soon joined them eating and talking.

"Hey, I know we talked about the Affiliation ceremony before, but I was wondering if you two would handle more of the plans. You know what I like and maybe you could do the leg work of finding the hall, caterers, music and dress designs for the bridal party. I'm finding I've more work than I can handle lately."

"Terri, we'd be happy to help out. Dezi and I will do our best."

Terri felt relief. *This is turning out really well.* "Thanks. I have to run. I have an early lunch meeting with a reporter. I think it might be a good opportunity to announce my candidacy."

* * * *

The El Tiempo restaurant attempted to provide an old Earth style of Mexican cuisine. Terri, originally from Earth, smiled at the menu items. *As far as I can remember, pizza wasn't a Mexican dish.*

She didn't have to wait long at the casual eating cafe before spotting a dark haired woman standing at the entrance looking around at the tables. Terri stood and waved at her. *Only an Alliance female would be wearing short hair. Good looking though, and she is adhering to Praxton fashions.*

They exchanged greetings and Evelyn quickly moved to the interview after the waitress, wearing only a poncho and high heels, took their orders.

"How difficult was it to make that video *Strike Me?*"

"In what way do you mean? The dancing?"

"Well, the dancing is one part. But you were naked, tied up, whipped and made love to on video. Millions, maybe billions, saw it. When you made the video, you must have known a lot of people were going to see everything of you. How did that make you feel?"

Terri smiled. "A little excited, actually. I mean, first I get to be part of a video with the famous Black Steel and the Steelets. What female wouldn't jump at a chance at that? But I believe you're referring to the nudity part of it. As a Praxton female, I'm used to nudity. The female form is expected to be shown off here, I don't have a problem with someone seeing me naked. On Alliance worlds, clothes are used to cover up the body. Here on Praxton, they're used to decorate and enhance the body form. On females, that is. Males have an entirely different set of fashion guidelines." She grinned.

"On the video you were tied up and whipped. Don't you feel that presents the wrong image to Alliance worlds and to women in general?"

"In the video Black Steel was my lover and my guardian. On Praxton he has the right to do what he wants to me. I'll put a caveat on that. Praxton guardians are not allowed to use excessive force. They cannot leave permanent marks, or cause mental anguish. The laws are strictly enforced and a guardian who abuses his females soon finds he has none. So I, when I was on the video, felt sexy and alive. I hoped everyone would see it."

"I believe almost every adult did." Evelyn smiled. "Okay, you're one of the most well-known women, or to use the Praxton term, female, in the world. What are you going to do with that? What are your future plans?"

"My future plans?" Terri repeated. She took a drink and leaned back in her chair. She laughed. "Well, I do have plans."

Evelyn looked at Terri as she laughed. *Whatever it is, she's got it. She's gorgeous and exudes that girl next door image at the same time. She's smart and turns every question I have into a statement.*

"Can you elaborate?"

"The most important one is my upcoming Affiliation ceremony with Master Romie. Believe me, that takes a lot of planning."

"Can you explain what an Affiliation ceremony is?"

"It's like a marriage ceremony but more legally binding. Once the ceremony is performed, it's almost impossible to break it. Most guardians shy away from that commitment because of that."

"So is the Affiliation ceremony like a marriage? I mean do they have a dinner, dance and gifts? Do the men wear tuxes and the ladies white dresses and horrible bridesmaid dresses?"

Terri giggled. "We do have dinner, dance and gifts. The men, as in Alliance customs, don't wear clothes much different from normal formal wear. The females get to wear special dresses, and I do mean special, that would scare Alliance viewers."

"I'd like to hear more about that."

"The dresses for the bridesmaids are flimsy, fairly thin fabrics. They are meant to be torn off during the ceremony by the groomsmen who then secure them. In my ceremony, we are going to use rope. The females are treated like captured slave girls, and while I haven't worked out the details, could involve a whipping and perhaps being placed in cages. My dress is different. It's going to be white in following Alliance customs, and won't be torn off as is often the case in Praxton ceremonies. But it will be removed at some point and I'll be tied up as well."

"Wow. That is an unusual ceremony to say the least."

"The ceremony comes from when Praxton was first colonized. There were two warring factions and they fought for land and females. Even after a truce was called, there were still raiders that captured females and sold them in auctions. If a guardian wanted to have a female, he would have her captured or buy her at an auction. To make her his, he would throw away her old garments that may have come from her previous owner. That's the ripping of the dresses part in the ceremony. He then needed to secure her so she wouldn't try to run away, and we see that in the ceremony by the use of rope. The whipping was often done to new females so she knew to respect her new guardian and obey without question."

"So there a historical reason for the Affiliation ceremony. Naked women tied up." Evelyn smiled. "I'll bet a lot of people will accept invitations to that. Now you have naked females but the men get to wear tuxes. That seems hardly fair."

Terri gave a small shrug. "I don't write the rules. However, Praxton men do wear open flies on their pants, usually with a string or open weave covering. For this ceremony, I'm going to ask the men to go commando and let the females see what they have."

"Yea, one for the females. You said the most important upcoming event was the Affiliation ceremony, but you implied there are other things."

Terri bit her lower lip for moment. "Well, I'm not sure how to announce this. I was thinking of holding a press conference, but maybe I'll give you a scoop. I've decided to run for the election. I don't know what my chances are, and I'm still looking for help to run the campaign, but I believe I can make a positive change for Praxton as a member of the government."

"That's really big news. Are there many females running for election?"

Terri shook her head. "I doubt there will be. However, I've heard that there may be two other female candidates in my riding."

"Congratulations on your upcoming Affiliation ceremony and your decision to run for election." *This woman really has something. She is a doer and makes things happen.* "I'd love to follow your campaign. Could you keep me informed of what you're doing? I think a female running for office on Praxton will be big news for Alliance viewers."

"I'd be happy to. I'll send you details later when I get things up and running. And if you like, I can include you as a guest for my Affiliation ceremony. You can bring a guest as well."

"I'd love to see that. It sounds more risqué than the Dutch adult-only theatres."

"I don't know about that, but I guarantee it won't be dull."

* * * *

Terri was pleased with her meeting with Evelyn. *For an Alliance female, she doesn't act shocked at what we do on Praxton. At least with her I think some positive news about the Praxton way of life will be reported.*

She stopped in at the home of Master Alex Greggory, a neighbour who was the guardian of her closest girlfriend, Allison. Terri wasn't sure how she fell for the slim brunette, who was also several years younger. But Allison was able to do something that surprised Terri, and that was to dominate her. Terri gave in to the aggressive female, including being spanked in front of the other females in Master Alex's household.

Terri rang the chime at the front door. Moments later it was opened by Allison.

"I saw you on the monitor walking up here." She gave Terri a hug and a kiss. "I missed you so much." Allison led Terri by the hand inside. "Pretty quiet in here today. Almost everyone is out."

Terri followed Allison to the patio in the back and accepted a glass of wine.

"I'm sorry I haven't seen much of you lately." She sat on a three-person couch on the brick patio and curled a leg underneath her.

"That's alright. I know the Affiliation ceremony is keeping you busy."

"Well, that's one of the things I want to talk to you about. I need your help on my dress. It has to be a bit like the Alliance world wedding dresses, but with a Praxton influence."

"You know I'd be happy to help out in any way." Allison sat next to Terri. "I'll scout out some designs and take you around to try them on."

"Thanks. I know I can count on you. There's also something else I want to talk to you about. I've decided to run in the election."

"You are? Wow, that's really something. What does Master Romie say?"

"He's given me permission and has offered to help me get a campaign manager. I'm really excited about this. I also just got interviewed by an Alliance reporter who is stationed here on Praxton. She works for Pearson News, so I may get some far reaching publicity."

"Terri, I'm so happy for you." She gave her a kiss. "But I'm a bit unhappy about your lack of visits to me."

"Sorry, but you know how hectic things got with Master Romie accepting two females into the household. I wanted to stay around as much as possible because…well I was jealous and wanted him to see only me."

"How did that work?"

"Master Romie gave me a hard spanking and told me I better learn to get along with them. Erica and Dezine are nice, but I was being mean to them. So after learning my lesson I made up with them and they're going to help me with the Affiliation ceremony. They're also going to be two of the selected females."

"That's good that you worked it out with them." She hooked a finger through the ring in Terri's collar. "I believe you're overdue for a spanking from me."

"Yes, Ms. Allison." Terri looked down.

Allison pulled on the ring and Terri complied, sliding over her lap. Moments later, she felt her dress being lifted to her hips. She relaxed and soon felt Allison's fingers trace circles on her cheeks. The sensation was enjoyable and she sighed. The first few slaps were light, but soon increased in strength. Allison soon stopped and lightly stroked the pink flesh.

"Did you like that?"

"Yes, Ms. Allison." Terri knew Allison only gave her a spanking to establish her dominance over her, and not to inflect any pain. She enjoyed the light spanking and made her aroused for more contact, but felt the pressure of returning home soon. "I'm sorry I can't stay long."

"That's too bad. I'd like to strip you naked and take you to my bedroom."

"Hmm. I'd like that too, but maybe I better take a rain check." She felt another smack on her ass. Terri hadn't received permission to get up and relaxed until she was allowed to. She kept her cheek muscles relaxed, knowing bruising could result if she tightened them. She heard padded footsteps on the brick patio and turned her head to see Cassandra. The long legged strawberry blonde female walked over to the loveseat opposite of where Terri lay.

"Hi Terri. Long time no see."

"Yeah. I've been busy."

"Allison told me." She looked at Terri's prone position on Allison's lap. "Am I interrupting anything?"

"No." Allison sighed. "I want to strip and spank her good, but she has to return home." She gave Terri another smack and pulled down her thong panties to her knees.

Terri sighed, knowing Allison had decided the spanking was going to continue a while longer. When Cassandra showed up, she knew Allison wanted to show that she belonged to her. That reminded Terri that she needed to make sure she reasserted her authority over Erica and Dezine occasionally as well. *I think maybe I'll take them to the discipline room together. Strip and whip, as the saying goes.*

Terri felt her panties pulled down past her knees and bent her legs so Allison could remove them. Terri placed her hands behind her back without prompting from Allison. The cuffs were joined together.

Cassandra stood. "That looks too tempting." She walked over and gave Terri a couple of small smacks. "I'll let you two talk. I'm going to do some sunbathing."

Terri understood that Cassandra's smacks were a sign of friendship, but also didn't cross the line of joining in what Allison was doing. Terri knew that as the junior female in the household, Allison often had to give in to the wishes of the others. The one person she had control over was Terri, and Cassandra made sure she didn't threaten that ownership in any way. Terri allowed Allison to control her in public, but in the bedroom was much more forceful and sometimes took the dominant role. She looked as Cassandra walked naked, except for her collar, to a lounge chair and turned it toward the sun. She felt another smack and flinched.

"Don't stare at her too much."

Terri smiled. "Sorry. She has such a nice body, it's hard not to. Don't be jealous. You're the reason I come to visit."

"I guess I better let you go now," Allison said as she undid Terri's cuffs.

Terri lifted herself slowly from Allison's lap and stood. She found her panties and pulled them on. "I'll ask Master Romie if I can spend the night here soon."

Allison walked her back to the front door. "Don't make me wait too long before I see you again." She gave Terri a kiss.

"I promise." She gave Allison a pat on her behind. "Maybe one of these days I'll get to give you a good spanking."

"Maybe. I'd rather spank you though."

Terri waved goodbye and headed home.

* * * *

Romi was sitting in the living room when she arrived home. She quickly saw he wasn't alone, and was introduced to Thomas McGrath. She smiled at the bearded man. He looked well-groomed, was medium height and slightly on the heavy side.

"Thomas wants to talk to you about your need for a campaign manager. He's has a lot of experience in politics and is intrigued about your desire to run for election."

"I hope you'll be able to assist me, Master Thomas."

"I'm sure I can. I'm intrigued by a female running for election, and it does present some challenges."

"Anything in particular?"

"Yes. You will have public debates with other candidates. You will have to navigate to presenting a strong image of yourself while also appearing to be respectful to the male candidate. He will press the advantage of being a male and try to make you appear weak and subservient to him."

"I understand. That's something I'll have to work on."

"No worries. I'll help you on the problem. For now, let's go over what message you want to deliver to the voters."

* * * *

Evelyn felt nervous as she returned to Philip's home. Her luncheon with Terri went well, and she received more information on Praxton customs. She was looking forward to the Affiliation ceremony and suspected she might be the first Alliance reporter to get an invitation to one. *I wonder if they ever allow kids to attend the ceremony. It doesn't seem likely, but I've heard of stranger things.*

A few minutes after her return Philip called everyone into the living room. Evelyn copied the other women and kneeled on the floor, getting a look of surprise from Shara. She tried to slow down her breathing and relax as she saw Philip holding a wide strap in his hand. The black strap had a loop on one end and he twisted it on his wrist.

Chapter Twelve

"I cannot accept the lack of respect you females have for each other. I do hold all of you responsible for this problem. That includes Marilyn, whom most of the actions are directed against." He looked at her. "You have to learn to defend yourself. You are not a slave to Dalina's desires. When I put Dalina in charge of teaching you proper behaviour in this house, I didn't say to you that you had to obey her every whim. I wish you had come to me about this." He looked at each woman in turn. "Therefore, all of you shall receive punishment, and it will be sufficient to remind you that poor behaviour will not be tolerated." He paused, letting his words have effect. "Stand and strip off your clothes."

Evelyn took off her clothes, folding and placing them on a chair like the others. She suddenly realized her nudity didn't bother her, but the sight of the leather-like strap certainly did. She knew better than to show it and she managed to maintain a passive expression.

"Shara, you shall go first." Philip pointed at the arm of the couch.

Shara bent over the arm, stretching her arms in front of her and spread her legs to shoulder width. Philip's long arm swung the strap against her ass, striking it with a sharp slap. Her body jerked in response.

The arm swung down again and again. Evelyn saw Shara open her mouth in a silent scream. Her legs twitched as she tried to remain in position. Evelyn counted ten slaps and Philip stopped. Shara was allowed to get up. Her ass was red, looking painful. She didn't make any effort to touch or examine herself, but a fine sheen of perspiration was on her forehead.

Philip pointed to a wall and growled, "Stand there."

Shara walked to the wall. She stood on her toes with her hands behind her head.

Marilyn took her place and assumed the same position. Evelyn studied her, expecting the younger woman to show more emotion due to her punishment. She was surprised that Marilyn, even though she shook from the pain of her spanking didn't utter a sound other than small gasps from each strike. She managed to keep her composure until she made her way to the wall when tears broke free and rolled down her cheeks. *Damn, she's tough. I hope I don't cry like a baby.*

Evelyn watched as Philip struck Dalina next, punishing her with the same even strokes. Dalina's cheeks vibrated with each hit. It seemed to Evelyn that Philip was putting more effort into punishing Delina than the first two women. The pain was too much for her and she let out several cries from the blistering attack. After the ten hits, Dalina slowly went to the wall with her hands on her head. Her cheeks looked red and bruised.

Okay, that looks really painful. It's too late to chicken out now. I've got to remember not to scream out. For Evelyn, Dalina's punishment was over too soon. She took small steps to the couch and placed herself over the couch's arm. She was surprised when Philip whispered in her ear.

"If it gets too much, make a fist and I'll stop. Do not tighten your ass, or you'll end up with bruising."

She nodded and placed her hips on the arm. She spread her legs and slid her shaking arms forward. *I can do this. I can do this. I can do...Ow!* Instant tears flooded her eyes at the pain. Evelyn concentrated on not closing her hands into fists. *How many is that now? This isn't so bad. It hurts, but not as bad as I thought.* The straps alternated from one cheek to another. Evelyn thought he wasn't likely hitting her as hard as he did the others. Still the burn spread over her exposed skin and suddenly she felt warmth expand at her groin. *Oh, don't tell me there's a part of me that likes this. Let's see. Naked, check. Big male spanking the hell out of me, check. Other naked women aware I'm being punished, check. Yeah, that would do it.*

"You may get up now."

Evelyn stood, wiping away the tears that wet her face, and went to the wall to join the others. Standing on toes wasn't hard, although after a few minutes her calves began to ache. She spread her legs slightly to help to keep her posture, as she wavered slightly with her hands behind her head. Occasionally her erect nipples touched the cool wall, making her realize how sensitive her skin everywhere had suddenly become. She heard the slow, deep breaths of the other women, listened to Philip walk behind them and the sound of a cushion sighing as he sat. The stinging on her ass had changed to a pleasant warmth, a feeling that had moved to her groin. Evelyn wondered how long she would have to pose with the others, sure that he was looking at her naked form.

"You may now carry your clothes into your rooms. You will all make use of the entertainment room until it's time for dinner."

Evelyn turned to where her clothes were piled. She made brief eye contact with Philip, knowing he had taken in her body, scooped up her clothes and carried them to her room. She was aware they had not been given permission to get dressed and inspected how red her ass was in the viewer.

"How're you doing?"

Evelyn looked at Shara. "I'm all right. That was quite the strapping, at least for me."

"You did really well. I think Dalina and Marilyn were surprised that you took the punishment and didn't scream out."

"I wanted to, believe me."

Shara took a jar from the dressing room table and placed some of the cream on her fingers. "Here, this will help." She smoothed the cream on Evelyn's red buttocks.

"Thanks, I can do that." Evelyn attempted to reach for the jar.

"Don't be silly." Shara pushed Evelyn's shoulder back. "Let me do this. I can see what I'm doing."

Evelyn blushed. *Great. I'm getting my ass cheeks rubbed by another woman.*

"That should help. Now let's join the others." She took Evelyn's hand and pulled her along.

When she entered the room, she noticed Dalina and Marilyn staring at her.

She smiled. "Yeah, it hurt like hell. But I'm glad I went through it. It gave me a new view on the life of a Praxton female."

Dalina laughed. "You sure did that. I didn't think you'd last after one strike." She poured some white wine into a glass. "Here. This will help ease the pain."

"Thanks." Evelyn sat on a loveseat next to Shara, acutely aware of her nudity and of Shara's. She tried to focus on the screen showing a weekly drama, but felt Shara move closer to her.

"I think you need to drink your wine and relax a little." She placed a hand on Evelyn's thigh. "We're all naked, we have wine, we have a show to watch and soon that burn we have on our asses will disappear."

Evelyn thought the drinking of the wine was good advice and soon had a second glass, and then a third. The show made little sense to her, but by the comments of the others, decided she should hate one of the main female characters. The hand that occasionally was placed on her leg began to feel less invasive. She slowly reached across and placed a hand on Shara's thigh, squeezed it for a moment and withdrew her hand.

Marilyn refilled her glass again and smiled at her.

She is rather pretty. In fact, almost every female on Praxton is. I wonder what they put in their water. She looked at her half empty glass. *Maybe it's not the water.* Evelyn realized she was having a good time and the touches she exchanged with Shara were friendly and not necessarily sexual. She also knew the wine was getting to her head. *And it's not even dinner time yet.*

Dalina looked over at Evelyn. "Shara tells me you're a virgin when it comes to females. Is that true?"

Evelyn laughed. "Yup. Just men for me."

Dalina replied. "You're missing half the fun."

"Yeah, well, it was the way I grew up. One guy. Get married. Have a family. Happily ever after."

Shara grabbed her hand and raised it. "Yeah, happily ever after with one guy. And I know who the guy is."

Evelyn blushed as Shara revealed Max's name. She tried to refute their opinions on her romance but in the end agreed he may be the one. "But I'm going slow with him."

Marilyn, in a rare moment of vocalizing her thoughts, spoke. "How do you survive that long without sex? I like males too, but out of sheer necessity alone I have sex with females."

How do I survive that long without sex? Not very well. "The truth is my comfort zone. I'm not comfortable with sexual touching with women. Therefore, I don't have sex with females. I want men, but I'm willing to wait for the right time." She grinned. "I also have a vibrator, an essential item denied to females on Praxton."

Dalina exclaimed, "A vibrator! Oh, I've heard stories about those. Battery power to heaven. I'm so jealous. I mean, I love sex with females and males but there are times you want your own private journey. It's hard to do that just yourself with fingers, if you know what I mean."

Evelyn waited for the laughter to die. "Maybe I can start an import business."

Shara kissed her cheek. "You're just too funny. Jokes with an accent."

Evelyn laughed and saw that they had been called to dinner. "What accent? You guys have the accent."

The dinner was good, but Evelyn hardly noticed the various foods. She drank wine, talked and laughed. She was still naked but didn't feel it was unusual. She noticed Philip occasionally looking at her and adding bits to the conversation. It was the only time she felt naked.

Evelyn relaxed after dinner in the living room with Shara on the couch and Marilyn and Dalina on a loveseat. Philip sat alone in an armchair, contributing little to the conversation. *He's damn good looking, but despite having three women under his control he's still nervous around me. He wants me and is that tempting right now.*

Her thoughts were broken by the chirping of her mobile. She hurried to a table where it rested and after glancing at the display, sang out a hello. She walked out of the room to the kitchen.

"It's good to hear your voice, Max."

"Good to talk to you. How's your adventure?"

"It has been interesting. I've just been disciplined with the other females. It was an experience."

"Do you want me to come over? Maybe take you out for a coffee?"

"I can't. Master Philip hasn't released us from detention yet. Besides, I'm naked along with the rest of the females."

"Now I really want to come over."

Evelyn laughed. "Shame on you. I'll tell you what, I'll ask Master Philip if you can come over for dinner sometime soon."

The conversation drifted to other topics and finally Evelyn said goodbye.

When she returned, Shara looked up from where she sat on the couch. "No, it's not serious at all. Not sure about him at all. Just decided to talk to him for an hour. No biggie."

Evelyn laughed. "Okay, so maybe I'm liking him a bit more now." Evelyn sat on the couch again. She found it difficult not to press her legs together or put her hands between her legs.

Philip looked over at Evelyn. "Is this male someone you're involved with?"

"Yes, Master Philip. He's also an Alliance reporter."

"On Praxton we believe all females should have a male to protect them. If this male is someone you're going out with, then perhaps we should invite him over."

Evelyn was surprised. She didn't like the statement that females needed a male protector, but the surprise offer to invite Max over precluded any resentment. "Thank you, Master Philip."

"You're welcome." He stood. "Everyone may get dressed now. I trust I won't be hearing of any more problems." He left the room. He looked at every woman in the room with his eyes lingering on Evelyn a fraction longer.

Evelyn wanted to hurry upstairs to get dressed, but the others seemed content to sit around as they were.

Marilyn looked at her with a smile on her face. "Tell me, what's he like? Does he treat you like a Praxton female?"

"He's tall, good looking and has a voice that makes my heart flutter. And he treats me as a lady on Alliance worlds."

Shara giggled. "And you think that's a good thing. I really want to meet this guy someday and see how Alliance men act toward females."

Marilyn persisted. "So how does he treat you that's different?"

He respects me. I guess that wouldn't go over so well saying that. "Little things, like holding a door open for me or pulling out a chair for me to sit. He told me he's a one-woman man, and is taking our romance slow."

Marilyn sighed. "I think I can see the attraction in that. Like those old fashioned movies we watch from the Alliance Worlds."

Evelyn saw Dalina give Marilyn a curious stare. *Marilyn doesn't like being a Praxton female. She may be submissive, but she longs for a life on an Alliance world. I wonder how many other females on Praxton see Alliance videos and long for that type of lifestyle.*

Dalina retorted, "The problem is that's just a fantasy world. Real life females on Alliance worlds aren't living happily necessarily. Remember there're more females than males, and a lot of females are alone."

Marilyn shrugged. "Still, can you imagine going to bed every night with the same guy? That would be heaven."

Shara jumped in. "Things are what they are. We do have a partner every night, just not always our guardian. What seems to be perfect on the Alliance Worlds may not be reality. Remember there's still a lot of female immigration to Praxton."

Marilyn nodded. "I know, but a girl can dream, can't she?"

Evelyn saw the faraway look in Marilyn's eyes. *She's not entirely happy here.*

* * * *

Max leaned back in his chair, closing his eyes. *Does she understand what thoughts are going through my head when she talks about being naked and disciplined by Philip? She claimed the Praxton customs of the female role on Praxton were not for her and yet her lack of protest indicate otherwise. Maybe she's hinting that I should be more dominate. If so, I better act if I want her.*

* * * *

Evelyn faced the camera. "As you saw in the previous segment, the Praxton discipline can be made up of different parts. In this case, Master Philip first gave a lecture on what he perceived to be behaviour problems. Next, in my view, came the humiliation part. We were all ordered to strip off our clothes. While females on Praxton are used to showing off their bodies, being naked before the discipline made me, at least, feel very vulnerable. The strapping was not as painful as it looked, although it did sting.

You may draw your own conclusions from what transpired, but this is considered normal in a Praxton household and it does have an effect on behaviour."

Evelyn signed off. *Boy, it's hard to say anything like that in a neutral voice.*

* * * *

The next morning Evelyn started the day by taking her time in the shower, deciding after the discipline yesterday, she had nothing to hide from anyone. After breakfast, she found Marilyn sitting in the living room on a loveseat. Dalina was in an armchair absorbed in her tablet.

"Hi." Evelyn sat by Marilyn. "I was thinking of going for a walk and was wondering if you would join me."

Marilyn thought for a moment, her eyes flickering toward Dalina. "Sure. I'll ask Master Philip if I can."

Evelyn followed Marilyn to his study. *I guess I better ask for permission as well.* She noticed Dalina frowning as they went by.

Philip was in an agreeable mood and quickly said yes to their request. "No problem, but why didn't you ask Dalina?"

Marilyn licked her lips. "I was worried she'd say no."

"I thought we had that problem resolved." His eyes squinted at her.

"I hope so too, Master Philip, but I don't want to make an issue of it now. Dalina feels she needs to exert her authority over me as she is still supposed to be training me."

Philip smiled. "Well put, Marilyn. You show a talent for diplomacy there. You're quite right. I should remove her from her duties as your trainer. She still is, however, the senior female and you must respect her decisions."

"Yes, Master Philip. I will."

He looked at Evelyn. "I'm going to take this opportunity now to say I was most impressed with you during the discipline. In fact, surprised might be a better term. You didn't flinch and held the proper position of a Praxton female."

"Thank you, Master Philip."

He continued. "Perhaps you may be interested in a small session in the discipline room. One of the females, or myself, could help you experience that aspect of Praxton life."

"Thank you. I'll consider it." *Naked and in chains with Philip holding a whip. I don't know if I'm excited or scared.*

After they left the house, Marilyn spoke up. "I've a feeling you asked me to go on this walk to ask me some questions."

"I do have a few. Some as a reporter, some as one woman to another. I have to admit I don't understand Praxton customs fully, but to me Dalina is not just training you, but bullying you too. Why do you take it?"

"When I arrived in Master Philip's household, Dalina was given the job of training me. I know now she went too far, but at the time, I was too scared to say anything. Then it became too late."

"Master Philip found out from Tara, I assume."

"Yeah, she told him and he was upset I didn't approach him earlier."

"He also disciplined you."

"He had to. If he didn't, the other females would've resented me. It wasn't too hard this time."

"So what're you going to do if she's still aggressive with you?"

"I don't know. She's stronger than I am."

"I think you have to draw a line in the sand. Push back if you feel she's gone too far. I'll stand up for you. You're not alone."

"Thanks." Marilyn looked at her and briefly squeezed her hand.

"I'm under the impression you'd prefer not to have female company at night."

"Well, yes and no. I like to sleep with Shara. She's content to just cuddle and doesn't push me if I'm not in the mood. I don't like sleeping alone, so it's good when she's my partner. Dalina is hungry every night, and doesn't take no for an answer easily."

"You've got to tell her no and mean it. If that causes a commotion, then she may be the one in trouble."

"I suppose you're right. What's it like on Alliance worlds? Is it really hard to get a male?"

Evelyn laughed. "Depends on what you mean. To get one for one night, no problem. To get one to stay and make a commitment...well, let's just say that's why a lot of females decide to go to Praxton."

"But it does happen?"

"It does. A lot of my girlfriends have settled down with a guy. Are you thinking of travelling to an Alliance world and trying your luck?"

"No. I don't have the money, or the courage, to do that. I don't really know how to do things and so it'd be tough to get a job."

"If you ever decide to try, contact me and I'll help you any way I can."

"Thanks. You're really nice. I'm glad you're staying at the house with us."

"How did you end up being one of Master Philip's females?"

"When I came of age, I advertised myself. I had three guardians interested in me and after I was interviewed by them, I decided he was the best choice. I was only the third female, so I knew I'd get some bedroom time. He also was the best looking of the males. The thing was, I got along with Shara right away but knew there'd be problems with Dalina. During the interview, I could tell she was more interested in me as a bed partner than as a friend. I went with Master Philip anyway. Maybe it was a mistake, but you've given me some courage to fight back."

Advertising yourself? I'll have to look into that later. "Master Philip seems pretty nice, and was concerned about how Dalina was treating you."

"He's a good guardian. I just wish I could sleep with him more often." Marilyn took Evelyn's hand. "Come on. I want to show you the desert."

Evelyn walked with her on the brick pathway. They passed a few other walkers along the path, most of them females enjoying the warmth from the red sun. Marilyn led the way to an intersection and turned down the path to go between a pair of homes. She pointed to a place where two walls overlapped but left an opening between them.

"The walls prevent the desert sand from blowing in too much."

Evelyn stepped through the opening and marveled at the vastness of the red sand desert. "So Master Philip is your first guardian. How about Dalina and Shara? Did they have previous guardians?"

"Master Philip is Shara's first, but Dalina had another one before. Most females don't like to change guardians. To change guardians is hard. I mean it has to be a serious situation to want to leave. It's also a legal hassle, but a female can leave if she really wants to. The problem is finding not only the right guardian, but also if she and the other females can get along."

Evelyn followed Marilyn's example and removed her shoes before they began to walk on the sand. "So before you chose a guardian, where did you live?"

"A boarding school. All females live in boarding school before they become adults. Males too, but the schools are separated."

"You don't get to live at home?"

"No, from the age of three on Praxton, children are in school most of the time. By the age of seven most are sleeping at a boarding school. Up until age twelve, they get to go home on a schedule. It depends on the school, but usually they have a few weeks each year they can stay at home. I liked boarding school. It was where all my friends were."

"I lived with my parents until I could afford to move out. Don't you miss your parents?"

Marilyn shrugged. "Well, I don't really know them. They helped me make decisions, such as school subjects and finding a guardian, but we never got really close."

Boarding school from a young age? That explains seeing so few kids around here. "So do you want to have children?"

"I do. It's something I've got to discuss with Master Philip. I hope he will agree to let me have at least one, but boarding schools are expensive, at least the good ones are. And he does have two other females who want to have children too."

Evelyn found the stroll along the desert relaxing, and the sand warm to her feet. "I thought the sand would be hotter."

"It will be later this afternoon. But the sun doesn't get too hot and you get used to the sand. I like taking walks in the desert. There are some interesting creatures that live in the desert, all of them small. If you're willing to go for a long walk, there's a couple of sand dunes that-a-way." She pointed opposite of the way they were travelling. "You take a plastic mat with you and slide down a dune. It's lots of fun but you end up with sand everywhere. And I mean everywhere." She laughed.

"I'll bet."

"There's also a lake, maybe a two-hour journey, you can go swimming in."

"A lake? It doesn't evaporate?"

"I guess some, but there's a lot of water, like a sea, trapped underground. The lake is in a low part of the desert, so I guess this sea keeps it filled." Marilyn stopped. "Here we are at the back entrance." She opened the solid metal gate set between the stone walls, revealing the backyard.

"Thanks for the walk. The desert was really interesting."

"I like going out first thing in the morning. That's when small creatures, insects and birds are most active. Also a few plants will open up their flowers."

"I'll have to check that out sometime. Right now, I need a drink."

Evelyn went to the kitchen, poured a glass of water, and saw Shara enter.

"That was a long walk you took with Marilyn." She smiled. "It seems she must have taken a liking to you."

"She was really nice, and told me a fair bit about the desert and information about boarding schools."

"Oh yeah, the infamous boarding schools."

Evelyn asked, "I assume it wasn't all pleasant."

"The schools are supposed to prepare you for life as a Praxton female. There's instruction on everything, including social graces and how to treat a male."

"That sounds reasonable, considering how Praxton social modes work."

"The thing is, we learned all about how to act in front of a male, but we never got to meet any. There were the male instructors at the college, but not any young males. It was pretty frustrating to be taught how to please a male without any around."

"I can imagine." Evelyn laughed. "So what did you do?"

"We had to sneak out at night and visit some of the males. I was a virgin far longer than I want to admit."

"And here I thought Praxton females had sex all the time."

"I wish. There's little action when we're young and when we finally have a guardian, we have to wait our turn with him. Sleeping with females is fine, but not a substitute for the real thing."

Evelyn put her arm around Shara as they walked out of the kitchen. "Let me take you away from all this. On Alliance worlds you can meet boys at any age."

Shara laughed. "Oh so tempting. But I'm here and I'll have to make the best out of it."

"Okay, but I offered." Evelyn joined her in laughter as they entered the living room and sat on a loveseat together.

"You did. I don't want to leave you with a bad impression of the schooling. We learned a lot and it prepared us for being adults. It's just the lack of males that was frustrating. One thing you have to understand is how close we became to other females, as friends."

"Like you're friends with Dalina and Marilyn?"

She nodded. "We may have our differences, but we do love each other. We're family."

"A family of three females and one male. Doesn't that cause more than just a few problems?"

"We make it work." She smiled. "I see you don't believe me. Tonight I'll show you how we get along so well. We socialize and party together."

"So does this involve drinking?"

"It does."

"Then I'm in."

* * * *

Evelyn changed her clothes after dinner, deciding to put on a skirt with a slit that nearly reached her hip. Her sleeveless top, which she borrowed from Shara, had buttons along the top of the shoulder and along one side. She looked forward to spending an evening drinking with the other women, deciding to dress more as if she was going out to a nightclub. She put on one of her more expensive collars and cuffs, made of green and white striped metal. She saw the cuffs had a hinged clip that could be used to be attached to chains, or directly to another cuff. She debated on adding chains, but wanted the freedom of her limbs. *Those Praxton drinks are potent. I'm still pretty clumsy with chains even when I'm sober.*

She went downstairs to the entertainment room. She was pleased Marilyn and Shara complimented her on how she looked, with Shara offering the opinion the top looked better on Evelyn than on herself.

The drinks made the average video show appear funny. Evelyn sat on the floor next to Shara, their backs against the couch. She looked up where Marilyn sat on a loveseat next to Dalina, noticing Marilyn had allowed Dalina to touch her and give one kiss, but firmly pushed her hand away at her attempt to undo her top. Dalina looked upset for a moment, but soon resumed drinking and joining into the conversation.

Shara poked Evelyn's ribs with her finger. "So was that the first time you were disciplined when Master Philip used the strap on us?"

"It was. We don't do that sort of thing where I come from."

"That doesn't sound much like fun. How about just a spanking? Do you get some of those at least?"

Evelyn shook her head. "No, I've never been spanked."

Shara giggled. "Wow, thus far, you've lived a boring life. Never been spanked? I mean I've talked to other Alliance females before and it seems being spanked is not uncommon."

"I guess it isn't. But a guy has never tried to spank me." She thought a moment. "Maybe a couple of smacks on the rear the odd time. Nothing I'd call a spanking."

"You really don't know what you're missing."

"I think it's something I can live without." Evelyn grinned as Shara poked her again. "Stop that." She reached to block her hand.

"I think you need to find out what a spanking is." Shara grabbed Evelyn's arm and began to pull.

Chapter Thirteen

Evelyn laughed. "What're you doing?" She began to lean over Shara's lap.

"You're in my home and have to follow our customs now. Don't resist or the situation will get a lot worse."

"Worse than what?" Evelyn looked back at Shara as she was pushed over her knees.

"There are spankings, and then there are spankings." Shara positioned the nervous, laughing Evelyn down over her lap. She rested her hand on Evelyn's skirt. "This is something you need to experience, as a reporter, of course. Also as a female. Also because it's just fun." Shara lifted up Evelyn's skirt, exposing her ass.

"Shara, you can't do this." Evelyn giggled, reaching a hand behind her to cover her exposed cheeks.

"Want to bet?" She smacked Evelyn's ass, alternating between sides.

Evelyn waved her hand behind her back in a fruitless attempt to block Shara's hand. Shara grabbed her wrist though and pinned it to the centre of her back.

"Give me your other hand." Shara gave a sharp hit on her ass for emphasis.

"Shara, this isn't fair." Evelyn reached back with her other hand, where the wrist cuffs were joined together. She decided to try to relax, realizing she wasn't going to stop Shara. *I'm not sure how, or if, I give a report on this. I know females on Praxton do like to give each other spankings as a form of friendship, so I guess I should feel flattered Shara considers me that. Oh lord, she's taking off my panties.*

Shara tugged the panties down her legs and tossed them to the side. She gave another series of quick, light slaps. "Don't worry, we'll get those cheeks nice and red."

Evelyn groaned as Shara's hands fumbled with her skirt closure. After a moment of hesitation, she lifted her hips to allow it to slide down easier. A few more smacks were placed on her ass, and then fingers gently massaged the skin, running up briefly under her top. She saw Marilyn slide off the loveseat and kneel next to her. A moment later, she received several more slaps.

"I wanted to get in the fun too." Marilyn spoke.

"Some fun," Evelyn retorted. She had to admit the hands rubbing her skin felt nice, and the spanking was more stimulating than painful. She tried pulling her hands against the cuffs in a symbolic gesture of escape. There was a sound at the doorway and she saw Philip enter. Evelyn joined the others in greeting him. "Hello, Master Philip."

He looked at Evelyn lying over Shara's legs. "You're letting her experience another Praxton custom, I assume."

Shara responded, "Yes, it turns out she had never been spanked before. I thought she might enjoy it and learn more about how we do things here."

"Good. I'm sure she'll like it." He turned his attention to Dalina. "I want you to report to the discipline room in one hour. I'll be taking you to my bedroom after that."

Evelyn watched him leave, aware he had taken a long look at her exposed ass. There was little she could do but remain where she was, feeling erotic and aroused under his gaze. Her thoughts were interrupted by another smack on her ass.

Marilyn commented on Dalina's being chosen by Philip. "Lucky you. I wonder what type of discipline he has in mind."

"I don't know, but I commented to him last week he hadn't used the flogger for a long time. I hope he uses that. I'm looking forward to whatever he has planned."

Marilyn teased one of Evelyn's buttons on her top open. "Maybe we should take this off too."

Evelyn knew this was her opportunity for her to say no and preserve her dignity. *If I was to say no, then what? The end of this rather personal attention? This spanking is rather humbling, or is that humiliating? But it's also strangely enjoyable. I think I've waited too long to say anything now anyway.* A slight coolness arrived on her skin as her top was opened and removed.

"Now we've got you naked." Shara announced. She stroked Evelyn's back slowly, and then dragged her fingernails along the skin.

Evelyn gave out a soft moan. Suddenly she received multiple hits on her ass from both Marilyn and Shara. "Oh, oh, oh. My poor ass." *Why does that feel good? I like men, not women.*

"Do you like that?"

"Yes." *There, I've admitted it. That doesn't make me a lesbian, just someone who isn't confined to one set of standards.*

"I want a turn. Bring her here," Dalina announced.

Marilyn helped her stand up, taking her to the loveseat and over Dalina's lap.

Evelyn guessed Dalina would be more severe than Shara and Marilyn. Her toes touched the floor and her face pressed into a pillow. Her legs were pushed apart as Dalina inserted one of her legs between them, pinning an outside leg down. She gasped as successive hard hits made her skin burn. Dalina also smacked her upper thighs, returned back to her ass at the end.

"There. That's how spanking should be done."

Marilyn escorted Evelyn back to Shara, helping her to sit again on the floor. "Your cheeks are nice and red now. How does it feel?"

"It hurts a bit." *And it felt good.* Evelyn was glad Marilyn placed her on her side with her head on Shara's lap. *Looks like the spanking is over. I wouldn't want to take another hit after what Dalina did.*

Shara stroked her face. "So did you like the experience? If you don't say yes, we may need to do it again until you do enjoy it."

Evelyn laughed. "Alright then, I did enjoy it."

"Now are you just saying that to avoid another spanking?" She slowly rubbed her shoulder and arm.

"No, I did like it. It just felt strange being spanked naked by another woman."

"Perhaps, but females on Praxton have to do things with each other." She reached over and gently squeezed Evelyn's breast, releasing and squeezing again.

Evelyn nodded. "How long are you going to keep my wrists cuffed together?" She felt Shara circle a finger over her engorged nipple.

"A little while longer."

Marilyn spoke from the couch upon which she'd stretched out. "I think Shara just wants you to relax and get comfortable being naked with us. We don't want to push you past your comfort level, but we want you to experience a bit what it's like to be a Praxton female."

Evelyn considered Marilyn had a point. If she was going to report on Praxton, it was good to try a bit of their culture. *Actually, this doesn't feel too bad. It's a little strange to be naked with my hands cuffed behind my back, but I do trust Shara not to push too far.* "Thanks, although I may have to draw the line at some of the experiences." She took a deep breath as Shara continued to fondle her breast.

Shara laughed. "Don't be a coward. Roll on your back."

"Hey, I think I've done pretty good so far." She twisted on her back with her head on Shara's lap.

Shara stroked both her breasts, occasionally lightly pinching the erect nipples. "You have. For an Alliance female, you sure are willing to try being a Praxton female."

Evelyn was surprised by how Shara's soft touches were making her feel. After a period of conversation, Shara helped Evelyn sit up and unclipped the wrist cuffs. "Now that is how females sometimes act in bed. Just light touches, some kisses, but not all out sex," Shara warned her. "Now don't get dressed. You're with friends, and we like you as you are."

Evelyn nodded. *It didn't occur to me get dressed. I guess I'm over my inhibitions of nudity.*

She watched Dalina leave the room after saying good night, briefly wondering what Philip was like in bed.

Shara laughed. "Well, she's going to have a fun night. Discipline room and then sex."

"Why would she want to go to the discipline room?"

"Did you like the spanking?"

"Yes."

"Well, the discipline room is like that, only more intense. The

116

discipline room is used as a form of punishment, and Master Philip can be quite harsh. But it's also used on occasion as a prelude to sex. Praxton females love our guardians to be in full control, and a light whipping while you're naked in restraints can be quite stimulating."

Evelyn nodded, picturing her being placed in the discipline room. *Naked, and with Max holding a whip. I can go with that.*

"I'll show you the discipline room tomorrow, and give you a better idea what I'm talking about."

"Okay, but no whipping."

"Relax, I wouldn't hurt you. Well, no more than the spanking."

Evelyn took another drink when she heard her mobile chirp. She quickly reached for it, noting it was Max calling.

She exchanged greetings with him and found out he had flown to another city to do a report on mineral mining.

"Pretty lucrative business potentially. If Praxton can get enough skilled operators for the mining equipment, they'll do really well with exports. But that's the big issue with them with a lot of things. Not enough skilled labour."

"That's a problem alright. They're pretty slow to change. They believe they can get skilled labour by doing minor changes to their immigration policy."

"What did you do today?"

"Not too much. More of the series of living in a Praxton household."

Shara called out, "Tell him you're naked and received a spanking."

Evelyn waved a hand at her to be quiet.

"What's this about? You got a spanking from Philip?"

"No. Well, he gave all us females a strapping yesterday. Apparently we weren't behaving properly." Evelyn walked to the far side of the room, wagging a finger at Shara. "So you're able to come over for dinner tomorrow?"

"Yup. I was planning to bring a bottle of wine over, but are there any other social graces I should know about first?"

"No, just be yourself. Dress as a Praxton male, of course. You can go commando, a lot of males do." *And be prepared to be stared at by these females.*

He laughed. "I think I'll keep some coverage on there for the time being."

"Okay, but if us females have to show off our bodies, I think it's only fair you guys do too."

She chatted a few more minutes with Max and then sat on the couch. "Shara, I could kill you. He doesn't need to know I'm naked and that you spanked me."

Shara laughed. "You should have seen your face. He's going to find out eventually, you know."

"He will if you keep blabbing." Evelyn failed to look stern and ended up smiling.

"You should tell him. Maybe that'll inspire him to spank you. I told you before, a Praxton female will lie across a perspective guardian's lap to let him know she interested in him."

"Oh no. He can let me know he likes me and do a little romancing."

"Okay, but don't string him along too long. There's a lot of hungry females out there."

Unfortunately, she does have a point. How long can he resist all these half-naked females looking for a man to take care of them?

* * * *

Evelyn opened the door to Max, who held a bottle of wine in one hand and bouquet of flowers in the other. She gave him a quick hug and kiss before showing him inside.

"These are for you." He gave the brightly coloured green and red flowers to Evelyn.

"Thank you. They're beautiful." She slipped a hand under his arm, hampered slightly by the chain going from her collar to her wrist cuffs. Her dress was light pink, sheer at the top and reached mid-thigh and was snug at the waist but loose elsewhere. Evelyn introduced Max to Philip first, who shook hands, and next the women where they were in the living room.

Philip initiated the conversation. "Evelyn tells me that you're a rival Alliance news reporter. I assume that's a friendly competition."

"It is. I work for Interworld News. They prefer the dryer side of news, such as politics, economics and business ventures. Evelyn's employer, Pearson Video News, is more social and people orientated.

They like showing the news versus Interworld's style of reading the news with a bit of video background. However, regardless of the network, most reporters get along fairly well. Evelyn and I met on the starship coming here. It was a chance encounter, but it sure was nice to know someone when I first arrived here."

"Has it been tough adjusting to the different culture and social customs here?"

"For me it hasn't been too bad. I do find the behaviour of females takes a bit to get used to, however, the males act much the same. I've had to adjust a bit for the social norms here." He smiled. "Evelyn has helped me understand how to act appropriately and she seems to have adjusted faster than myself."

Shara interjected, "But, Master Max, you date her as if you were still on an Alliance world."

"Well, yes. It works on our comfort level. I'm not sure about dating her as if she was a Praxton female. At least not yet."

Evelyn looked at him. *What does he mean, at least not yet? Does that mean he will later on?* She briefly touched her collar.

Philip commented. "You're right that Evelyn has adjusted to life on Praxton. I mentioned to her the other day that she has fit in very well. She does have an accent, and short hair, but has managed to blend in. I expected problems with her trying to adapt to staying here, but haven't noticed any. She's intelligent and observant about what is happening around her. She certainly has changed my opinion of Alliance females."

Evelyn felt her cheeks grow warm. "Shara has been very kind in helping me learn the household rules."

Tara announced dinner was ready, and they entered the dining room. Philip sat at his customary spot at the head of the table and Max was seated across from him. Evelyn wanted to sit next to him, but knew Praxton customs were rigid on where guests sat and how food was presented. Max was served first, followed by Philip, Evelyn and finally Marilyn.

Philip waited until the meal was underway and a toast was made with the wine before asking a harder question to Max about Praxton.

"Praxton is going through some changes as the Charter of Conduct laws are introduced. Many of us are worried about the economic impact of such change. What is your perspective on this?"

"That's a difficult question to answer because there are so many variables." He took a drink of wine and continued. "I think the concern about the adaptation of the Charter of Conduct laws is a red herring. It's easy for the political leaders to blame that that's the source of problems, but Praxton has a long term serious problem. On the short term, it's going to be fine, but eventually a lack of action is going to cause difficulties. At least, as I see it."

"Please elaborate."

"The Charter of Conduct laws might change social norms, but won't negatively affect economics. It may actually help a bit. As I view it, Praxton has a huge female population that isn't providing any support to the economic engine. Praxton is going to have to compete against the rest of the Alliance worlds with only twenty-five percent of the adult population working. That won't make it easy to maintain your current lifestyle. You have a huge tourist industry that works because you provide something other worlds can't—cheap drugs, potent drinks, wild entertainment and a fantasy theme of females as slaves. However, going forward, now that Praxton has joined the Alliance worlds, your drugs and booze will be the same as most worlds thanks to the special taxes charged on entertainment products. Other worlds are already setting up special tourist and entertainment facilities to compete with Praxton, with some gearing towards the whole family and not just adults. I know that a lot of people want to visit Praxton just because of the female in collar and chains concept, but overall your tourist industry will shrink."

Philip nodded slowly. "That's true. We do depend on our tourist industry to bring in revenue. We have a lot of natural resources, such as mineral deposits, and they are providing an increasing share of income."

"They are, and at first I was impressed with the increase of production of the mineral exports. But as I looked into the matter, it turns out many of the resources are being controlled by non-Praxton industries. They buy the right to dig out the minerals, give a royalty to the Praxton and Alliance governments, and spend the profits outside of Praxton. Praxton doesn't have enough skilled labour to harvest its own deposits. Eventually that will cost Praxton dearly. It will be exploited by Alliance companies that have no interest in Praxton, other than as a place to carry out mining."

"That's a serious problem then. Our politicians are telling us it's all under control, and that they're resisting the influence of the Charter of Conduct and Alliance worlds as much as possible. Perhaps they're blind to what's actually happening."

Evelyn added her thoughts. "My interview with Director Bryston was interesting, but one thing came out was his resistance to follow Charter of Conduct laws. It seemed to me he felt Praxton could carry on with the status quo. He did say they wanted to bring in better educated females, but at the same time believed females came here so they didn't have to work. If he's typical of the attitude of Praxton government officials, change will be a long time coming."

Philip frowned. "I don't know what the answer is. We want our females to look pretty and wear collars, cuffs and chains. How do we also ask them to work and add to the economy?"

Shara spoke quickly. "Perhaps like Evelyn, Master Philip. She dresses and acts as we do, but she also works full time."

Philip looked at Shara. "That's a very good point. Perhaps what we really need is a leader to take us to the next step. I think it will have to be someone new. The present officials are all from the old guard."

After dinner, Evelyn showed Max the house. She took him upstairs to her bedroom, pointing out how her shower overlooked the living room.

"I try to be quick in the shower before anyone is in the living room."

He laughed. "Do you set the alarm early?"

She shook her head. "Wouldn't work. Praxton has this custom for females. I have to sleep nude and they cuff my ankle to the foot of the bed. I have to wait for Ms. Tara to release me."

"Now that's an image. You chained naked to a bed."

She punched him on the shoulder. "It could be worse. At least I don't have to sleep with another female. That's a custom here and you can see how narrow the bed is."

Evelyn moved next to the discipline room. "Fortunately I haven't been ordered to report here yet."

"Interesting devices." He touched the various whips and handled one flogger.

"Shara told me they don't hurt that much. I'm not keen to find out, but I guess that may happen if I stay on this assignment too long." She looked at his hand as he absently moved the flogger back and forth. "All females in the household end up spending time in here, and apparently some even enjoy it." Evelyn walked to a wall and reached up to a pair of wall hooks. She faced him with her arms extended up and to her sides. She grinned at him. "What do you think? Do I look like a Praxton female in trouble?"

"I don't know about being in trouble, but you sure as hell look sexy."

"I better show you the downstairs before you get any ideas with that flogger." *Because I sure do. What is with me? I'm teasing him about whipping me and I think he seems quite willing to do so.* She led the way out of the discipline room, not noticing he was slowly blowing air out of his mouth.

Max was surprised that showers for the females all had at least one glass wall so they could be seen showering. "Even to the outside? That would make it easier for Peeping Toms."

"I guess if you're a female here, you better get used to showing off your body. The clothes don't hide very much anyway."

He put his arm around her as they went downstairs and to the patio. "I didn't write the social rules, but I like how you're responding to them. You look beautiful."

"Thanks. It took a bit getting used to the feeling I'm half naked all the time. These collar and cuffs are a bit harder to adapt to." She lifted a hand, showing the chain attached to the cuff. "I know the chain can be removed and it's more decorative than functional, but I'm aware of what they represent."

"I like the look actually, especially on you. Maybe the short hair accents the collar more, but there's part of me that finds it a bit exotic."

"I'll bet it does." She gave him a smile. "I'm glad you like it. It's something I've finally gotten accustomed to wearing." She grinned as they sat on the patio. "Well, almost." She tugged at the ring in her collar. "Every so often it seems to call out to me that it's there."

"I can understand that. I want to call out to you too."

Evelyn laughed as Marilyn and Shara came outside, carrying wine and glasses.

Shara spoke. "I hope we aren't interrupting, but we'd like to have a drink with you and Master Max."

Max smiled. "Two pretty women bringing me wine? How could I refuse that?"

Marilyn giggled nervously. "May I ask you a question about Alliance men, Master Max?"

"Of course. Anything."

Marilyn licked her lips as she next to Shara on a loveseat. "I heard the Alliance males have their choice of females. Like maybe they can have only one, but they can choose any female they want. Would I be considered pretty enough to attract an Alliance male?"

Max took a deep breath. "Marilyn, you're pretty enough to attract men on every planet in the galaxy. As far as having a choice of any female in the galaxy, it hasn't exactly worked out for me. I don't wish to pry, but aren't you committed to Master Philip? Why the interest in Alliance males?"

Marilyn lowered her head. "I'm happy here, but I wonder what it'd be like to have a male just for myself. I know that sounds bizarre."

Max shrugged. "It sounds reasonable to me. But, Marilyn, you may find that there're advantages and disadvantages no matter where you live. For example, Praxton has a wonderful climate, a healthy environment, wealth and you do have a family. Some Alliance worlds require their citizens to live inside protective domes. In others, almost everyone lives in apartments. No lawns, small rooms and people everywhere. Living on another planet may not bring you happiness."

Marilyn slowly nodded. "I know. I was just curious about living elsewhere. I love Master Philip, and I don't want to leave his household, yet I can't help but be curious about other places."

"You're young. You've plenty of time to learn more about life. Make sure you do talk to Master Philip about your wants. I only just met him, but he seems to be the type of man who would listen and try to help you."

"Okay, I will."

Shara refilled the wine glasses. "I've a question for you, Master Max. How come you're still single?" She smiled. "I'd thought you'd have several females now that you're on Praxton."

"It's a long story. Suffice to say that I prefer to take my time in getting to know a female. I'm also more of a one-woman man and not inclined to have a harem."

"So is Evelyn your one woman?" She grinned at Evelyn, who was turning red.

Max chuckled. "She is right now, but we're still getting to know each other." He pointed a finger at Shara. "You really are a bit of brat, trying to put Evelyn and myself on the spot."

Shara laughed. "I guess I am. Maybe I deserve a spanking. From you."

Max held up his hands. "I think that's Master Philip's department."

Shara gave a fake pout. "He's given me a lot of those. I thought getting one from you would be interesting."

Max shook his head. "Praxton females can be rather troublesome."

"Well, if you won't spank me, how about Evelyn?"

Chapter Fourteen

"Shara!" Evelyn raised a finger to her.

"Just saying she may need one." She stood. "I best leave you two alone, but take it from me that Evelyn has a very spankable bottom." She left, grinning, with Marilyn following her.

Evelyn turned to Max. "Don't ask." Evelyn hoped her face wasn't as red as it felt.

"I won't ask right now, but your friend Shara likes to stir things up."

"She does. She really does deserve a spanking."

"I suppose so. Maybe Philip will give her one."

"You do know that as a male, you've the right to spank her? If Master Philip was in the room, then he has the final say. But since he wasn't present, you could've spanked her."

"Really? Any female?" *Does she want me to spank her right now? I sure would like to.*

Evelyn decided to change the subject. *Good grief, I practically told him he can spank me anytime he wants.* "What's your next report going to be about?"

"I want to show more how Alliance industries are taking advantage of the lack of skilled labour here. They're buying up land rights and if they find something worthwhile to dig up, they bring in their own skilled labour. Those workers don't get to mingle with the rest of the population, other than visits to the tourist zone, so most of Praxton aren't aware of the number of Alliance workers living on their planet."

"That sounds better than my next interview. It's with the hostess of a fashion show."

"No one can say Praxton fashions are dull. I guess I should be going,

125

but thanks for getting me the invite to come over."

Evelyn walked him back inside where he said his goodbyes to Philip and the rest of the household.

"By the way, can you recommend a good restaurant? I want to take Evelyn to dinner and I'd like to find a place with a bit of a wow factor."

Philip thought for a moment. "Try Normand's. They have a very traditional way of presenting a meal. It will be a unique experience, especially for those not used to Praxton customs."

"Alright. I'll give them try."

Evelyn kissed him at the door and he responded.

She whispered, "I hope I can see you again soon."

"You will if I've any say in it. Besides, I have the incentive of knowing I can spank you if I should choose." He gave her a light pat on her ass. "Good night."

Evelyn watched him leave. *Well, I sure opened the door to that possibility.*

Evelyn slumped in a chair in the living room with a glass of water. She smiled at Marilyn and Shara sitting on the couch. She pointed a finger at Shara. "You have caused me a major problem. Thanks to you, I mentioned to Max he has the right as a male to spank a female whenever he feels there's a need to."

Shara laughed. "I think that's a good thing. He's going to give you a spanking and there's not a thing you can do about it."

Evelyn sighed. "I know. He was also rather intrigued by the discipline room. Praxton does strange things to men."

* * * *

Evelyn woke up to the sound of Tara entering her bedroom. She looked at the housekeeper who stood at the side of her bed with her hands on her hips and a stern expression on her face.

"I've noticed you haven't put away your clothing and left your underwear on the floor. This is not acceptable behaviour." She jerked off the blanket. "Put your pillow in the middle of the bed and roll on top of it."

Evelyn felt surprised at the lecture and sudden removal of her cover. "I'm sorry. I'll pick them up right now."

"No. First you better do as I say and lie on that pillow." The words were sharp, without room for argument.

Evelyn reluctantly complied, placing her stomach over the pillow.

"Legs apart and hands above your head."

"Please, Ms. Tara, I didn't know I was breaking any house rules."

"Did you hear me?"

"Yes, Ms. Tara." Evelyn parted her legs and put her hands on her head.

Several hard slaps landed on her ass, stinging her buttocks.

Evelyn bit her lower lip, trying hard not to cry out.

Then the hits were repeated in an even harder fashion.

This time she cried out, making hands into fists.

Several more hits caused Evelyn to kick her feet. She tried to muffle her scream, weeping out her pleas for Tara to stop.

By the time the discipline ended, Evelyn was gasping out sobs.

"Now you will remain in that position until I return. Understood?"

"Yes, Ms. Tara."

Evelyn heard the housekeeper leave the room. *All that because I left my panties on the floor and my clothes on the chair? This is humiliating!*

Long minutes passed before Tara returned.

"I've decided that you need to understand the rules of the house better. Since you like leaving your panties lying around, you won't be allowed to wear any for the next two days." She unlocked Evelyn's ankle cuff. "You may get up now."

"Yes, Ms. Tara."

Evelyn rolled out of bed and quickly picked up her panties off the floor under the watchful eye of Tara. When the housekeeper left, Evelyn sighed. *Not a great way to start the day.* She looked at her ass in the viewscreen, seeing her cheeks covered in red and blue marks. *Oh God, no wonder it hurts so much. How am I going to even sit down?*

By the time she was in the shower, she saw Dalina was already downstairs, observing her as she washed.

Feeling annoyed, Evelyn put on a loose fitting skirt and tight fitting top. She made sure she put on a full complement of cuffs and chains besides her collar, not wanting to endure Tara's wrath from a lack of adherence of Praxton customs.

At breakfast, it seemed everyone was aware of her morning punishment. Shara whispered to her to not to worry about it as Tara was looking for something and someone to lay down the law about.

"She feels Marilyn's problem came about because she wasn't being strict enough. I guess you became her target this time. It could have been any of us. I once got into trouble for leaving a wash cloth in the sink instead of putting it on the counter."

"Thanks. But I have an interview to do today and I'm not allowed to wear any panties."

Shara giggled. "Not a big deal. Dalina rarely wears any. Praxton panties are pretty low in coverage anyway."

After breakfast, Evelyn carried her recording equipment to the waiting shuttle. She sat down on the seat, remembering to flare out the skirt first. Evelyn was planning to do a report to send to Pearson News, but decided to do it later when she was in a better frame of mind, although she felt she was falling a bit behind schedule on her reports. *They'll have to wait until this evening. I'll do a couple of reports then.*

Her mobile chirped and she was pleased to see it was Max. He told her he was heading to do a report in a remote area and decided to call her in case time was short later.

"How's your morning going?"

Evelyn hesitated, then decided to tell him of her ordeal. "I received a spanking this morning from the housekeeper for leaving my panties on the floor. Tara smacked my ass but good. She also ordered me to go without panties for the next two days."

He laughed. "Wow, and I thought my job was tough because I had to get up early. At least you're getting used to spankings."

"Too much so."

"As long as I get a chance to get in on the act and give you a paddling."

She laughed. "I'm a good girl now and won't need a spanking for a long time."

"We'll see about that next time I see you."

"And when might that be?"

"How about I take you out for dinner tomorrow?"

"I'd like that."

She closed off the conversation, aware that the dinner could end in a spanking for her and she would still be without her panties.

* * * *

Max watched the scenery drop by as the shuttle gained altitude. *Okay, Evelyn has practically told me she expects me to spank her. If I don't, there's a chance she'll drop me for a man who will. She's acting like a Praxton female and wants me to assume the role of a Praxton male. Well, I can do that.*

* * * *

Gina Rosetta stood as Evelyn entered the studio. "Hello, it's so nice to meet you. I'm thrilled an Alliance news reporter is interested in my show."

"I'm excited to meet you too." Evelyn shook her hand and sat in one of the black swivel chairs.

"As I discussed with you, I'll be happy to answer your questions, then perhaps we can do a short interview with me asking the questions for my viewers."

"Sure, I've never been on the receiving side of an interview before. It'll be an interesting experience."

Evelyn accepted coffee and began her interview. "We have seen the influence of Praxton fashions on Alliance Worlds. What influence have Alliance Worlds made on Praxton?"

"A few things. First, there are the reactionary fashions. Since the war, collars and cuffs are much more noticeable. They're wider with more vibrant colours. The chains are more subdued, although that's partly due to more females going into the work force. The more noticeable Alliance fashion influences are the tighter skirts and dresses with a slit on the side. Praxton skirts are normally short enough that slits are not needed, but that detail is showing up more often now. We have also seen the introduction of the uneven hemlines, and that's a little more difficult with the Praxton short skirts. On Praxton that means part of the hip is exposed, and if you look where the other part of the hemline is, that's a little dangerous." She laughed as she finished speaking.

"What about male fashions?"

"Males are slower to change than females, and the changes that have come about are more conservative. For example, the famous pant fly is now more likely to be a weave and a bit harder to see through. The shirts are still open, and here we see more colours than in the past, in particular in patterns."

"So would you say the fashion change has been more positive from Alliance influence?"

Gina laughed. "I would say change can usually win the day in fashion. I love seeing the new colour and patterns, as well as the different cuts that Alliance fashion brings."

"I'm curious how you manage to have a show on fashions under Praxton customs. Were you required to have permission from your guardian?"

"Yes." She paused in her answer. "On Praxton it's almost impossible for a female to work without a guardian's permission. Now there are some females that work as freelancers, but they are in the, shall we say, the adult entertainment industry. Even so, they often have a guardian that acts like an administrator. They don't necessarily live with him, but use him to operate their financial affairs."

"That's one of the changes that the Charter of Conduct Office wants to introduce, that females be allowed to live independently if they want to. How do you feel about that?"

"It probably wouldn't change my life at all. I'm content, and most females are, to allow our guardian to handle all finances. However, I do believe that it should be possible for a female to handle her own affairs, have her own apartment and work where she wants without having a guardian's permission."

"So when you wanted to work as fashion show host, did your guardian resist giving you permission? How difficult was it to get the permission?"

"My guardian never had an objection to my working. He paid and supported my desire to go to college to learn broadcasting. I started as a reader of news, and gradually worked my way up the ladder."

"Was that difficult to do? To move to where you're the hostess of your own show?"

"It was. Tough competition, and being a female you have special obstacles to work around."

"What were they?"

"A female has to respect the males around her. Males can, if her guardian isn't present, decide if she requires discipline. It seems some of the males resented my success, and on some occasions I had to be very careful to avoid conflicts. My guardian at one time went to the station manager and asked him to use his authority to protect me from abuse."

"And now you feel safe from abuse?"

Gina laughed. "More or less. I get along with everyone here on the show. Most of the males have given me a spanking, as well as one of the females. On Praxton, there are two different types of spankings. One is for discipline, and normally it's done with a paddle or a cane. That can really hurt. The other type is with a bare hand. Now that can sting a bit, but on Praxton it means you actually like the person. It's a bit sexual as well, but most importantly it's a sign of friendship."

"Oh. I didn't know that."

"Have you been spanked here?"

"Uh, yes. I'm staying in a household for a few days to do a report on Praxton lifestyle. I received a spanking, as all the females did, with a strap from the guardian. I also got a spanking from the females, and that seemed to be part of having had too many drinks. Finally, this morning I was spanked by the housekeeper for leaving my clothes lying around."

Gina smiled. "Okay. The strap was a punishment. But the females and the housekeeper are telling you they like you. The housekeeper views things differently than most members of the household. Her job is to help maintain traditional aspects of female behaviour. She was obviously pleased with your attitude. If she wasn't she would've ignored you or spoke to the guardian and have him speak to you."

"Oh, so it wasn't really a punishment?"

"No, but if you really want to endear yourself to the household, you may want to have the guardian spank you. The other females will see this as a sign you are a member of the household."

"Well, he hasn't shown any sign he wants to spank me, other than the strap that he told me I could've refused."

"It's good you didn't. But often the female has to take the initiative by bending over in front of him, or lying over his lap. Sometimes she just has to ask him to spank her."

Evelyn shook her head and laughed. "Well, that's a lot different than asking a guy to go out for a cup of coffee."

"You're on Praxton now. Try living as we do. I think you'll find we have something to offer."

"Okay. I've been trying to do that. I just have trouble being submissive to a man."

"You just need to meet the right one. Now, I've got to get ready for today's show. When you come back, could you wear some Alliance clothes? It'll make the show much more interesting and we'll get you to model them."

Evelyn agreed and went to a shuttle to take her back to Philip's home. *So am I supposed to try to get him to spank me so I'm more accepted? It's an interesting thought.* She smiled. *What a girl has to do as a reporter.*

Chapter Fifteen

The camera was carefully positioned to show off the entertainment room, programmed to a sweep as Evelyn did her report.

She did a final check of her clothing and hair, and began to speak.

"This is part of my series of reports of living in a Praxton household. I'm trying to experience life as a woman, or female to use the custom here, on Praxton. One of the misunderstood areas is the use of discipline of females. Many people on Alliance worlds have images of females being taken to a discipline room and being whipped. During my week here, I have yet to observe that. However, I personally have received spankings here."

She paused to smile. "I assure you that while it was embarrassing and somewhat painful, it left no lasting feelings of discomfort. On Praxton it's considered a sign of friendship to give someone a light spanking. My female housemates gave me one the other day as a way of showing they accept me as friend. The housekeeper also spanked me for leaving my clothes lying around. My mother will appreciate that. However, I'm told that the spanking was really to show she appreciates my effort to follow Praxton customs. With that in mind, this is the entertainment room used to watch videos, drink and socialize. Next room over is the exercise room, and like all good exercise rooms, it has shower facilities."

She paused as the camera focused on the glass wall of the shower with Dalina showering behind it. She knew the steam and water made it difficult to see her completely, but still the image of a naked woman would take some of the viewer's thoughts off her confession of being spanked. *Come on people, focus on Dalina.* She stopped recording and went back to her room to send her report to Pearson News, knowing they would appreciate the adult content.

Evelyn checked the time. *I've got an hour to get ready and get back to the studio. I better get moving.* She quickly packed up her camera and headed to her room. She saw Tara, and stopped to talk to her. "Ms. Tara, thank you for correcting me this morning about not leaving my clothes lying around."

"I believe you're making a real effort to follow our customs and wanted to help you learn." She smiled. "I trust you understand I wouldn't have spanked you if I didn't care about you. All of us do like you."

"I was told that I should consider asking Master Philip to spank me."

"You should. I believe he would like to, but doesn't want to cross a boundary you have as an Alliance citizen."

"I want to experience life as a Praxton female during my stay here, even if it is uncomfortable."

"I'll mention our conversation with him. I'm sure he'll understand."

Evelyn continued her journey to her room. *Okay, I guess that'll just about assure another spanking in my future.*

* * * *

Evelyn changed her clothes at the studio, finding it odd to put on tights after having bare legs since she arrived at Praxton. She examined her image in the viewscreen; black stilettos, dark grey tights that sat low on her hips and a short sleeved orange top that left her midriff bare. She left off her cuffs, but wore a thick black collar. She considered she would have normally worn a bra under the snug fitting top back home. *I'm used to be being without one now.*

A knock on the door indicated it was time for her turn to be interviewed. She followed the female escort to the curtains at the side of the stage and received a few simple instructions. She heard Gina give a short introduction and Evelyn began walking to the centre of the stage to the applause from the audience.

"Welcome to Fashions and More, Evelyn." Gina gave her a hug and Evelyn sat on a swivel chair. To her left, Gina sat on a slightly larger armchair, and to her right two of the show's previous guests sat on identical swivel chairs.

Evelyn smiled. She didn't feel nervous with the cameras pointing at her, although the audience was making her aware how she was being studied. She exchanged greetings with the other female guests and then focused her attention on Gina.

"So, Evelyn, how does it feel to be living on Praxton after being on so many other worlds doing news reports there?"

"Every world is different and unique, and Praxton is certainly no exception to that. You have a beautiful world and your weather seems to be a series of one perfect day after another."

"Now how about fashions? What do you see as different? Let's start with the male fashions."

"There are some very obvious differences. Praxton shirts are loose, open at the chest and usually with long sleeves. Alliance males wear tighter fitting shirts, often with short sleeves and lots more colour and patterns. Pants usually don't have the famous decorative fly, and certainly aren't open. The pants are not as loose, and again we see more colours with different cuts. For example, the legs aren't always the same width and the waistband can vary quite a bit. Finally, the shoes on Alliance worlds have a lot more style to them for males. Praxton males wear boots, and there isn't much difference between every day wear and formal dress."

"So would you say the Alliance male fashions are more interesting?"

"There are more choices for Alliance males. I do like the open shirt for Praxton males. I'd like to see that incorporated into Alliance fashions."

"Alright, now how about female fashions? I see you wearing Alliance fashions and could you do a walk for us and describe it?"

Evelyn laughed. "Now I'm nervous. I've never done a catwalk before." She stood and looked at the raised platform that extended from the stage to halfway into the audience.

With the encouragement of the audience, she made her way across the stage and to the walkway. She was conscious of her walk, trying to slow down as she shifted her hips. "This is a common casual wear on most Alliance worlds. The shoes have a higher heel than normally worn, but I like height. These pants, or tights, vary a bit. They're usually dark colours and come in different weights and how snug they fit. I have a belt with mine, but that's for show only. This is a mid-height for pants and some can be quite a bit lower, to the point of showing cleavage of the cheeks." She reached the end of the runway and turned around. "Alliance tops are usually tighter fitting than Praxton ones. And usually worn with a bra that I neglected to bring. Bare midriffs are common, by the way. As far as skirts are concerned, they are longer than Praxton's. We don't always have bare legs either, stockings with colours and patterns are common." She reached the stage and did a final turn-around before sitting.

"That was very interesting. I noticed you are wearing a collar. Are they becoming more common on Alliance worlds?"

"They are indeed. Most collars don't lock, but they are becoming closer to Praxton's in style. Cuffs are rare and chains are very rare. Instead, most females wear jewellery in place of the collar and cuffs, such as necklaces and bracelets. I like this collar. It's become my favourite."

"It looks really good on you with your dark hair. Is short hair common on Alliance worlds?"

"Not especially. No one hairstyle predominates. Long, short, curly, straight, coloured, streaked or even partially shaved. It all can be seen."

"Now I want to put you on the spot." Gina grinned.

"I thought you did already." Evelyn laughed.

"What do you think of our quaint Praxton custom of females being spanked?"

Evelyn looked up at the ceiling. "Oh, my lord. That's a special custom. I was never spanked until I arrived on Praxton. Now I can say I have been."

"By your housemates?"

"Yes. Apparently, the females decided they liked me after all. I'm staying at their home for a few days to do a report. I also got a strapping from the guardian. Not so much fun that time." Evelyn laughed.

"Are you seeing anyone special right now? Have you picked out a possible guardian?"

"I'm seeing someone. He's also a reporter from Alliance worlds."

"Is he aware of the spanking customs here?"

"I'm afraid so." Evelyn grinned.

"And..."

"And I think I'm going to get one from him." She laughed and covered up her lower face. "I hope he's not going to see this show."

Evelyn was glad the next and final guest came on. She chatted with Gina after the show and concluded Gina and her were very similar in their attitudes.

"You know, Evelyn, maybe someday you could host a show as well. You have a great personality for the viewers. Now I hope you'll return to my show someday."

"I'd love to."

* * * *

Evelyn returned to Philip's home, pleased how the studio interview went. She hurried to her room, wanting to change before dinner. Shara followed her into her room.

"So how did it go?"

Evelyn gave her a short version. "I can't believe how fast days are going by. Soon my stay here will be over."

"You have a couple more of Praxton customs to go through first. One is a turn in the discipline room."

"Well, maybe I should look into that."

"And I want you to sleep with me. I don't mean for you to have sex, but this is Praxton, and you should see what sleeping with a female is like."

"I'll have to think about that."

"Okay. Better hurry dressing. Dinner is soon."

Evelyn sighed as she added cuffs that matched her collar. *Just when I got used to collars, cuffs and spankings, another Praxton custom pops up.*

Dinner was filled with questions about appearing on the Fashion and More show, with Evelyn feeling like she was a celebrity. Philip didn't say much, but listened to the chatter while occasionally raising his eyebrows.

The normally reserved Marilyn was especially intrigued with her appearing on the show, asking a series of questions that surprised the others at the table.

"Marilyn," Evelyn laughed, "I was only on there for a few minutes. I wasn't a big star, just a different guest."

"Yeah, but it's something I really think is interesting. I'd love to do something like that."

Philip leaned forward and stopped eating. "Are you interested in broadcast or fashion or both?"

"Both. It's something I really like. Fashions in any form."

"Have you looked into any courses?"

"Yes."

Philip took a deep breath. "Marilyn, if this, or anything, is something you wish to pursue, then please come to talk to me about it. We can send you on any course you want to take. In fact, I want to encourage you to do so."

"Thank you, Master Philip."

He looked at Evelyn. "You seemed to have inspired Marilyn. Thank you for that. When Max and yourself spoke about the need for more training of females, I never expected for that issue to come up so close to home and so soon. And that, I can say without any reservations, is a good thing."

* * * *

Evelyn entered the living room carrying a glass of Praxton beer. She normally wasn't a fan of the beverage, but this particular one had more of a fruit favour to it. She sipped it faster than she normally would have, but was nervous about the upcoming event. She noticed all the females and the housekeeper were present in the room. Tara stood in her normal position just inside the doorway from the kitchen, with the other females sitting in various chairs. She stopped and took another drink of her beer and looked at Philip. He gave a slight nod of his head.

How in the world did I end up following this strange custom? I have to ask him to spank me so the others will respect me? It's almost like a hazing ritual. "Master Philip, I believe I'm in need of discipline." She licked her lips and placed her glass on a table. Evelyn slowly approached Philip, standing by his side.

Philip watched her keenly, his hands fidgeted at her approach. He gently put his hand at her waist and pressed her forward. Evelyn leaned forward, bent her knees, and rested over his lap. She felt his hand rest on her buttocks briefly and her skirt being lifted over her hips. She wished the spanking wasn't being done on a day when she wasn't wearing panties, but was almost getting used to being exposed in front of others.

His large hand came down with force, enough to make her gasp after the first hit. It wasn't as painful as the strap, but she noticed a big difference from what Shara and the others were able to inflict. Once again, a rush of warmth covered her cheeks and penetrated to her groin. She rested her hands on the floor, counting out each hit. She gasped after four strikes. Her hip felt his hardness press against her and she let out a small groan. After eight strikes, he stopped and helped her stand up.

"Well done, Evelyn. It seems that you're truly accepted as a member of our family."

"Thank you, Master Philip. I never would've thought that this would happen when I first came to Praxton." She took a quick look at his fly, seeing the definite bulge.

Shara was the first to give her a hug. "Maybe it's time for a drink to celebrate."

Evelyn nodded as Dalina, Marilyn and Tara all gave her a hug. *I really do feel part of this family. They make me feel welcome, strange customs and all.*

* * * *

Evelyn readily accepted refills of her drink. She had a strong suspicion that Shara was going to take her to the discipline room, and after that ordeal was over, was going to bed her.

"I want to call Max before I drink too much."

"Call him on your tablet. We can all say hello to him." Shara suggested.

"Okay, let's sit together on the couch."

She placed her tablet on a table, using its built in stand for support.

After a delay Max answered on his own tablet, his head and shoulders filling the screen.

After few hellos from Evelyn, Marilyn, Shara and Dalina, Max responded after his initial surprise at seeing the group. "It's wonderful to see all of you again."

Evelyn explained, "I wanted to include the other girls, I mean females, in our nightly talk because, well, I survived another Praxton custom. I requested and received a spanking from Master Philip tonight. It was rather humiliating and exciting at the same time."

"Really? Another discipline? Did you at least enjoy that experience?"

Evelyn didn't hesitate. "I did." She laughed.

"Well that's something I'll have to keep in mind." He raised his eyebrows.

"How come we can only see your face?" Evelyn knew tablets gave users a choice of just head and shoulders or full image.

"I did a field report on mining and came back with a lot of dust and dirt. So I was about to take a shower when I heard your call."

"So are you naked?"

"No, I have underwear on.

"Then put on the full view."

He shook his head and laughed. "I don't know about that."

Evelyn raised her voice. "Us women have to walk around half naked, wearing collar, cuffs and chains. I got spanked bare ass in front of everyone and you don't even want us to see a video image of you? Do you want me to start covering up every time you see me? Full view or this call is over."

"Alright."

He frowned and she saw him reach to the tablet. Suddenly the view changed.

Evelyn heard the women giggle and give whispered comments. She saw he had more muscle on his chest than she expected, with just enough chest hair to not be distracting. A flat stomach descended to a pair of black briefs. He looked embarrassed as he sat on an armchair.

"Thanks. You have a nice body. You have to admit it's only fair that males show off what they have as well."

"Maybe. I wouldn't mind one on one but I'm facing a group of ladies here."

"I had to do a video report with myself partially undressed. Millions of people saw me. Get over it."

He chuckled. "Okay, you have a point there. Tell me what you did to deserve a spanking."

"Nothing really. I guess it's more of a custom. I'm staying in Master Philip's household and to be accepted better by the family I asked for a spanking. It wasn't painful, although a bit embarrassing." She saw his eyes widen as she talked. "I also agreed Shara can take me to the discipline room tonight. I thought I should see what the fuss was all about."

"Are you going to video that as well?"

"I hadn't planned on it."

"I think you should. You may be able use part of it in your news report. Besides, I'd love to see it."

"I'm sure you would." Evelyn laughed. "But no camera. I don't want those images accidently being released."

"Okay. Remember we have dinner tomorrow."

"I won't forget. Before we say goodnight, will you please stand up?"

"Why?"

"You know why. So far we have seen only your chest."

He hesitated and finally stood. Evelyn saw the strain on his underwear. *I guess my talk of the spanking and going to the discipline room did have an effect on him.*

They ended the call and the women burst out laughing.

Dalina spoke, "I would say he was excited at your conversation. You can tell he's an Alliance male. A Praxton male never would have shown off his body on video. Good looking male I have to say. He could get a lot of females if he wanted to."

"Yes, but he wants me and he knows I don't share my men."

Shara took her hand.

"Come with me. It's time."

Evelyn nodded, putting down her empty glass on a table. She went upstairs to the discipline room, wishing she had more wine to drink. Evelyn stood still as Shara undressed her, gave her a kiss, and attached her cuffs to a set of chains hanging from the ceiling slightly wider than her shoulders. She looked up at the chains, tugged at them, and looked back at Shara who had stepped toward the wall.

"Don't worry. It'll be just a little tug." She touched a pad on the wall.

A rattle of the chains and a tug of the cuffs initiated Evelyn being lifted just off the floor. She received a smile from Shara as she retrieved a pole from the wall that held an assortment of devices. The spreader bar was attached to her ankle cuffs, spreading her legs further apart than she felt entirely comfortable with. "Oh Lord. Can I change my mind on this?"

Shara laughed. "Do you feel sufficiently helpless? I can add a gag or a blindfold if you want."

Evelyn gave a nervous giggle. "No, no. I'm fine the way I am."

"You sure? You may want to scream out." She laughed as she flicked the flogger. "I won't really hurt you. Well, not much."

Evelyn looked at her and the doorway where Dalina and Marilyn stood watching. *Great. An audience.*

Shara grinned as she used the flogger. "This is fun. I'm going to enjoy this."

Evelyn felt the light whipping on her skin, moving from her legs, to her ass, back, breasts and between her legs. She found it didn't hurt as much as she feared, but she still jerked against her restraints.

"How does that feel?"

"It hurts a bit." Evelyn gasped.

"Good. I'm going to strike you a bit harder now. Since this is a discipline room even Praxton females will cry out during the punishment. You don't have to be brave." Shara selected another whip from the rack and struck Evelyn again.

"Ow!" Her legs stung from the harsh straps. She jerked on the chains as the whip lashed at her ass. Evelyn gave up trying to remain quiet. She cried out as the whip struck her back several times.

Shara placed her hand between her legs, slowly rubbing the lips. "Normally the session is longer and more intense, but I don't want to push you on your first time. Did you want me to continue?

"No, please, I really had enough."

"Okay. I think you did really well for your first time."

Marilyn spoke as Shara undid Evelyn's restraints. "I'm a bit of a chicken when it comes to the discipline room, but I've found that Master Philip knows how to make it enjoyable. He has a way of knowing which area to strike. Now Dalina likes it rougher than I do, and I can say from experience she is also tougher on the other side of the whip."

Dalina laughed. "The rest of you females are too soft."

Evelyn shook her head. "I have to say that's as far as I want to go in here."

Shara handed Evelyn her clothes. "How about if Master Max was here?"

"Oh, that might change things a bit." Evelyn giggled. "I think he might be rather handy with a whip too."

Shara led Evelyn out of the discipline room. "I believe we're seeing a bit of the submissive side of you. Master Max will no doubt want to exploit that."

"No doubt he will." *And I'll let him.* Evelyn allowed Shara take her to her bedroom. She removed her collar and cuffs before slowly sliding under the blanket. Shara undressed and quietly joined her.

"How's your back?"

"A bit sore but I'm okay. It feels like a bit of a sunburn."

"We will be doing some touching—the bed design encourages it. But I won't be pressing myself on you." She smiled. "Well, maybe I'll do a little bit of extra touching, but nothing serious." She leaned over and gave her a kiss on the lips, lowered her head and lightly kissed a breast.

"There, that's as far as I'll go."

"Thanks."

"But if you're ever curious and want to stop being a female virgin, I'm here for you."

Evelyn laughed. "Thanks, but my main focus is on a man right now." She took Shara's hand and gave it a squeeze. "But you'd be my first choice if I ever did get tempted." She saw Tara enter the room.

The housekeeper gave them a tight smile as she locked the cuffs on their ankles and bid them goodnight.

Evelyn wondered how easy it would be fall asleep next to another naked woman in close contact with her. *It doesn't help I'm as horny as hell. She's awfully good with those light finger touches and I wouldn't have much resistance if she did push. Am I ever going to fall asleep?*

Later, Evelyn drifted awake. The room was dark, she heard the deep breathing of Shara, and realized their arms were wrapped around each other. Shara's leg was between hers, her thigh pressing her groin. *This feels comfortable.* She returned to her dreams, not waking until the red sun began to peer through the window.

"Good morning."

Evelyn looked up at Shara, felt her body weight on top of her. "Morning."

"My hands are kind of caught underneath you, so I decided just to lay here while you slept. I didn't want to wake you, and besides its nice having a warm body under you." She kissed Evelyn's forehead.

"I don't mind. I slept better than I thought I would. And you're not heavy. It is kind of nice."

Tara entered the room, unlocking the cuffs. She looked at Evelyn. "I assume you slept well." She gave a smile as she left the bedroom.

Shara laughed. "I think she thinks we did more than sleep."

"My reputation is ruined." Evelyn laughed with her.

Evelyn found they had to share the shower, and took turns with Shara in washing each other. Shara's touches were soft and bordered on being more than needed for washing, but while she did give her another kiss, she stayed in Evelyn's comfort level.

Evelyn went to her room to dress, putting on clothes suitable for doing business interviews. In particular, she wanted to catch up with Terri Baxter and see where she was in her campaign. She went downstairs for breakfast, realizing she'd adjusted to the later time of eating in the household.

* * * *

"So what is so special about Normand's restaurant?" Evelyn asked Shara as they sat in the living room. The afternoon sun had made sitting outside uncomfortable as the temperature rose.

Shara curled a leg under her as she leaned back in the large armchair. "Very traditional on how they treat males and females. You should have a leash on as well. The maître d' may let you enter if you don't, but he'll likely let you know he's not impressed with uncivilized behaviour. Also, the dinner choices lean more towards meat. I know you do eat some meat, but I understand on a lot of Alliance worlds, meat isn't eaten at all. Just warning you it might be more than you're used to."

"Thanks, I'll keep that in mind. A leash? That will be a new experience." Evelyn rolled her eyes as she sat alone on the couch.

Shara continued. "Master Max will enter first into the restaurant holding the end of your leash. He will pass it to one of the restaurant staff who will lead you to the table. Max will sit first, by the way. He will also be given the menu and will order for you."

"Really? So am I even allowed to talk?"

Shara laughed. "I'm sure you'll find plenty to talk about with Master Max."

That evening Evelyn examined her image in the viewscreen. She sighed and decided she had better stop second guessing herself. Her dress fit her well, the navy blue satin-like material showed off her body in more detail than she liked. She was also aware she wore nothing underneath the dress, save for a pair of flower shaped nipple jewellery that made an imprint against the dress fabric.

Shara and Marilyn helped her with her make-up and hair, trying to help her achieve a Praxton female look. Marilyn mentioned that the short hair did help bring awareness to the extra wide, red collar that she borrowed from Shara. She also added matching wrist, elbow and ankle cuffs. Evelyn elected to keep the chains to a minimum, joining the wrist and elbow cuffs to one of the collar's four rings.

Evelyn stood in front of a camera on a tripod, smiling before speaking.

"I'm about to go out for a formal dinner at one of the better restaurants on Praxton. This particular restaurant, Normand's, is known for its traditional settings and guests are expected to conform to those expectations. One of those traditional Praxton customs is for the females to be on a leash as they follow their male guardian into the restaurant." She paused and held up the end of the leash with the other end attached to her collar. "The guardian is seated first and he is given the only menu. He makes the decision on what they will eat and drink.

"The food itself is different from what most Alliance worlds serve. Meat is considered the main item and unlike on most Alliance worlds, it comes from living animals. Not soymeat flavoured imitation or vat culture grown selected meat, but from ranch raised or wild animals. This is certainly something I will have to work around mentally as I eat my dinner.

"Evelyn Montgomery, Pearson Video News."

* * * *

Evelyn waited, sipping on a glass of wine before Max's arrival. She felt nervous, wondering why this date was having this effect on her. Then it dawned on her. *I'm acting the part of a Praxton female and Max the dominant male. I think I'm falling under his control. He can do what he wants with me and do I have enough strength and will to refuse him?*

The front door was answered by Shara and Evelyn cautiously stepped into the entrance hall.

Max greeted Shara and Evelyn. "So are you ready for a Praxton dinner and all its tradition?"

Evelyn forced a smile. "Let's not go for all of Praxton's traditions tonight, shall we?" She passed him the leash handle for her collar. "Apparently you'll be needing this."

Max looked at the leash and gave a small shrug. "Shall we go? I'm getting hungry."

Evelyn took his arm and headed to the shuttle, trying to ignore the leash in his hand.

Max was content to let the silence continue as the shuttle made its way to the restaurant. Normand's was located in the middle of a one hundred and thirty-six story circular building. The elegant restaurant slowly revolved, giving alternate views of the city and the desert.

Max finally spoke about the meal. "I assume you do eat some meat, having moved around different worlds."

"Yes, although I prefer poultry and fish to red meat."

"I'll keep that in mind, although I've been in some restaurants on Praxton where red meats seem to be the main thing on the menu. Perhaps Normand's will have a wider selection."

The shuttle stopped and Max led Evelyn to the bank of elevators. One quickly opened its doors and they joined several other passengers.

As the elevator rose, she took a deep breath and dropped her hands down to her sides. "I hope this dinner doesn't hold too many more surprises."

He held up the leash in his hand. "It's just for show. Don't be worried."

She nodded and followed him out of the elevator after it came to a stop.

The maître d' greeted them warmly, giving them both a hello and a welcome. A woman, dressed in a black dress, took the leash from Max and they proceeded to follow the maître d to a table at the perimeter of the restaurant. The woman gave Evelyn a warm smile and whispered to her. "I like your hair. You must be from somewhere besides Praxton."

"Thanks. I am. It is a bit hard to get used to wearing collars, cuffs and chains, not to mention the Praxton style of clothing."

"It seems you have adapted well."

The two chair table had one chair facing out toward the glass exterior and the other toward the inside the restaurant. The maître d' indicated the chair facing the outside for Max to sit in.

Max stood and pointed at the view. "It is a lovely view, but I believe my companion should share in it. Can we rearrange the seating?"

"Of course, sir."

The table and chair were quickly changed so both Evelyn and Max had the window seating to their side. Evelyn sat after Max and had her leash handle attached to the top of the chair. She saw how Max had his water poured first and all questions were directed at him by the waiter, who took over after the maître d' seated them.

The woman bent down and whispered to Evelyn again. "Remember to wait for your guardian to drink and take a bite first. If you wish to use the washroom, place your napkin on the arm of the chair. I'll come by and escort you to the washroom."

Evelyn nodded, deciding it wasn't the place to correct her about Max being her guardian. *After all, he is acting as my guardian tonight.* She watched as Max studied the menu, had a quiet discussion with the waiter and then focused his attention on her. "Lovely view, isn't it?"

Evelyn glanced back at the window, seeing the desert stretch out past the city. "It is. Can I ask what you ordered for us?"

"Raw..." He paused as he watched her face lose its expression, "salad." He smiled at her as she let out an exasperated sigh.

"Not funny, Max." She grinned back at him.

"I also ordered soup that has a meat in it, and then for the main course I decided against choosing meat where one had to pick how well done it was to be. I ordered froler, which is a type of domesticated bird. I thought that was the safest bet."

They tore open a small bread roll each, nibbling between sips of wine. The discussion went to the upcoming election in the city.

"The incumbent, James McKinney, has a good lead coming in. Something like a third of the votes according to a poll. All the rest have about the same percentage and are way behind him. Of course, that will likely change after the first all candidate speeches rally. That will quickly determine who will challenge McKinney."

"I believe there are some female candidates for the first time in Praxton history?"

"Yes, I interviewed Terri Baxter. Interesting woman. She wasn't born on Praxton but certainly has adopted their customs. Smart, pretty and very composed. It will be interesting to see if she can pull votes. It's hard to say how male and female voters will react to a female candidate. There is bound to be some backlash that the Charter of Conduct laws forced Praxton to adopt the right of women to vote and run for election."

"I think Praxton needs fresh ideas if they are going to continue to keep their high economic status."

The food arrived, one dish at a time. Evelyn commented they certainly did know how to present the food and everything tasted better than she expected. Before dessert arrived, she placed her napkin on the arm of her chair and shortly later, the same woman came to escort her to the washroom.

"Are you enjoying dinner so far?"

"Yes, everything is delicious. Were you born on Praxton?"

"I was. Actually, on a farm, which was a bit different than most Praxton females. Our parents, rather than send us to boarding school, kept us at home so we could help with the chores. I have two sisters and three brothers, and believe me brothers can be awfully bossy." She laughed.

They stopped at the washroom door.

"When you are finished, just wait here and I'll be back to escort you to your table."

Evelyn considered it wouldn't be easy for a girl to grow up in a household where brothers, and possibly sisters, could order you around. *On the other hand, growing up on a farm was likely more fun than a boarding school.*

Evelyn finished and waited outside the washroom doors. She looked around at the other tables and saw what Praxton women wore for formal dining, and was surprised to see several topless outfits. The women with their front exposed wore more jewellery, including some elaborate metal spirals that encircled their breasts. Nipple ornaments were also more apparent and more intricate in design. One close by table featured two men at opposite ends of a rectangular table with the women sitting between them. The women wore much more revealing dresses than her own simple dress and she now understood why Shara had tried to convince her to wear something with less coverage. *Maybe next time.*

She was escorted back to her table and she asked quietly, "Am I dressed okay?"

"It's fine what you have on. Most women use formal occasions to expose more of their body and wear the real fancy breast and nipple jewellery. But wear what you're comfortable showing, otherwise your body language betrays you."

Evelyn nodded and sat down. She looked at the dark blue sauce covering a steaming pudding.

"I was told it is the speciality of the restaurant. I can't tell you exactly what it is, other than the pudding is infused with the special fruit and berries that are native to Praxton."

"It looks interesting." She waited until Max took a bite. "Well?"

"Rather sweet with what I would call a rhubarb finish to it. Quite tasty actually."

Evelyn tried her dessert. "It is rather good. I like the sauce. A hint of spice in it."

"So how much longer are you staying at your friend Shara's house?"

"Just another day. I should have more than enough for the report on living in a Praxton home."

"How was the time in the discipline room?"

"Very interesting. I was suspended and spread apart. Shara whipped me with two different whips. The first didn't hurt but the second really stung me."

"Sorry you had to go through that."

"Praxton females expect to be occasionally punished. I was glad I tried it."

They finished dinner with a liqueur and went back to the shuttle. The pilotless two-passenger shuttle gave them privacy and kisses were exchanged. Max pulled her close and she felt his hand slip under her dress, his hand squeezing her ass cheek.

Evelyn moaned and kissed his neck and stroked his bare chest with her fingertips. Her short dress was pushed up around her hips and he had easy access to massage her skin.

The ride was too short as Evelyn reached down and pressed at his pants, pleased at the firmness of his member. "Oh, I wish we could go somewhere private."

"Me too. When you move back to your place we can spend more time together."

"Yeah, that will be nice."

"I noticed you're still without panties."

"Yes, Tara ordered to go without them yesterday and today."

"So you can wear them tomorrow?"

"Yes."

He tugged on her leash. "Well I'm ordering you leave them off for another two days."

Evelyn opened her mouth in surprise, then recovered. "You can't order me to do that."

"Just how hard a spanking do you want later?"

"I can see you're adopting to this male guardian role very quickly." She gave him a final, deep kiss and headed to the house with him. Then she gave him one more kiss and quietly entered the home.

Shara was waiting up for her in the entertainment room and wanted to hear about her date. Evelyn filled her in with the details, including the end.

"He ordered me not to wear any panties for two days. He's acting like he's my guardian."

"You were on a leash already. I think he's just taking the natural next step. He's giving you an order and seeing if you'll obey. If you do, he'll continue to assume control. If you don't, you'll be saying you don't

respect him. It's a test."
    "Oh great. Some choice."

Chapter Sixteen

Evelyn slept in slightly and joined others at the breakfast table. She apologized to Philip for being late and sat.

Shara asked quietly, "Did you or didn't you?"

Evelyn sighed. "I decided to obey him this one time. I'm not happy about this."

"You did the right thing. All you're telling him is that you like him enough to obey him."

"Yeah, well he also implied I'd get a hard spanking if I didn't."

"Good for him. You need to be put over his lap." Shara grinned at her.

"I don't think so."

"Doesn't matter what you think. It's going to happen."

Evelyn smiled. "Maybe I'll let him."

"You'll let him? Oh you are the defiant one. I'm sure Master Max will take care of that attitude in a hurry."

Evelyn was glad when breakfast was over and she could escape the teasing at the table. From a span of a few days, she felt she went from an independent woman to a Praxton female. *I guess I don't mind being submissive to him, but this change I've gone through is bewildering. I hardly recognize who I've become.* She wandered outside to the patio, drinking a glass of juice and ice.

Shara was already sitting in a lounge chair, sun tanning topless. "Sorry about teasing you at the table."

"I don't think you are." Evelyn grinned at her, pointing a finger at her. "You like the thought of me having Max as my guardian and like to imply what he's going to do to me."

She laughed. "Yeah, I guess I do. But you're a perfect match. I just feel you should know what is expected of you when he's in charge. Stop pretending you're going to resist him."

"It's complicated. Where I grew up women just didn't follow a man's orders. My first thought when a man tells me to do something is to give him my opinion where he should go."

"Fair enough, but you're on Praxton now. And isn't there part of a woman in you that wants to obey him?"

"I suppose so. I'm torn between two emotions at times."

Evelyn took a drink and relaxed, envying how Shara could so easily adopt to obeying Philip without question. *Each command I receive from Master Philip, or now Max, I think of the consequences first if I don't obey. I'm still fighting this submissive female thing.*

She began to doze when her mobile rang. Startled, she looked at the caller, cleared her throat and sang out a hello.

"Hi, just calling to see how you're doing today. Any special assignments on tap?"

"No, Max. Just relaxing outside with Shara. That was a great dinner last night. I really enjoyed the evening."

"Me too. I wished the night could have lasted longer."

"That would have been nice. But I live under the rules of this household and cannot stay out all night."

Max asked, "Speaking of rules, did you or didn't you?"

Evelyn decided not to be coy and ask him what he meant. "I left them off, but I don't want you to think I accept you as my guardian. I'm still an independent woman." She glanced at Shara who was listening to her side of the conversation.

"Not meaning to imply you aren't independent. But it is nice to hear you followed my request."

"I thought it was more of a threat if I didn't." She kept her voice light, letting him know she didn't want to start an argument. "I decided it was the lesser of two evils."

He chuckled. "I may have come up with some other requests."

"Seriously? Are you on a control kick?"

"What are you wearing?"

"A skirt and a blue top."

"Take off the top."

"Max…"

"Take it off."

She heard the deep command in his voice and a sudden desire to obey him. "Yes sir." She put down her phone and took off her top, gathering looks from Shara. She sat bare-breasted except for nipple jewellery connected by a chain. "Alright I took it off."

"Good. I'll see you tomorrow when you get to go to your own place again."

"It will be nice to see you again." *And see what other orders you're going to give me.*

After they said goodbye, Shara grinned at her. "Did he just order you to take off your top?"

Evelyn blushed. "Yes. I didn't want to get into a fight with him so I did as he asked."

"Ordered."

"Whatever."

Shara laughed and chanted. "Evelyn has a guardian, Evelyn has a guardian."

Evelyn rolled her eyes and took a drink, feeling embarrassed.

* * * *

Evelyn prepared for leaving the Philip household the following morning, but agreed to go with Shara to shop first. "What are you looking for?" she asked.

"Nothing in particular. Maybe a new collar, or maybe a belt."

The mall was busy and Evelyn found that the new belt Shara was referring to was wide, stiff, black and lockable. It had a variety of rings attached to it, but the main feature of the belt was that it was wide enough to almost qualify as a bodice.

"It looks hard to breathe in that." Evelyn inspected Shara as she modeled it.

"It is. But I like the look and feel of it. It looks like I have this small waist and it's easy to cuff my wrists or elbows to it. It also has a place where you can attach this strip that goes between my legs." She held up a leather-like strap. "Master Philip likes crotch restraints and I think this combination will look sexy."

"I suppose it will." Evelyn wondered what something like that would feel like between her legs.

After the purchase, Evelyn strolled with Shara when she spotted a men's store.

"Let's go in there."

Shara shrugged. "Sure. Buying something for Max?"

"More like a few questions on what men wear."

Evelyn asked for the store manager and she was surprised to see it was a woman. Jenni smiled at her surprise. "My guardian owns the store and discovered men like to get a female's opinion on certain styles. So that's what I do."

Evelyn explained she was a reporter and wanted to get more information on what males wore on Praxton. "Like why do males wear such heavy boots and how do they manage to wear them all day long?"

"Tradition is why they wear them. At one point in Praxton's history males were true guardians in that they had to be prepared at all times to fight raiders that wanted to steal his land and females. So the heavy boots were good for fighting and the guardian had to be prepared at all times for an attack. Therefore, he usually never took them off while he was awake."

"Good grief."

"Actually the boot is usually worn with a heavy sock and the inside is padded and breathable. They aren't quite as uncomfortable as they appear. They also boost the height of the male, making him appear bigger."

"What about the shirts and pants?"

"Usually tapered with the shoulders exaggerated. Open chest and the shirt is usually fairly loose fitting. The pants normally are high waisted and loose fitting as well. There is also the famous open fly or more accurately a fly with a see-through weave to it."

"Most males wear a mesh underwear underneath, don't they?"

"Yes, I suppose the males want to show off what they have. The underwear is specially designed to lift their package and push it forward. Somewhat like a push-up bra on Alliance worlds."

"I can relate to that."

Jenni smiled. "There are different styles of underwear and some give a more enhanced lift than others."

Evelyn thought quickly. "Could you ship a pair of underwear to a friend of mine? Maybe a couple of pairs that provide lots of lift." She grinned. "It will be a nice surprise."

* * * *

Terri exchanged a glance at the other female candidate, who looked nervous and uncomfortable standing in the waiting room. The male candidates looked more relaxed, but none more than James McKinney. He was confident, smiling and shaking hands with anyone who came close. Terri decided not to approach him, or any of the candidates, preferring to watch how they handled themselves. She was also interested in how they spoke to the audience, and was agreeable to being the last one to speak. After a great deal of debate by the organizers, they decided instead of the normal alphabetical order for the candidates, they would follow Praxton tradition and have all the males speak first, then the females. The other female candidate's last name was Alfredson, placing Terri last.

A bell chimed and the all the candidates were ushered to the stage and seated in a row near the back. At the front and centre was the podium, where a young man gave a short introduction to the filled auditorium.

Terri watched as the first male contender crossed the polished black floor to the podium. What he said wasn't anything she didn't expect, having heard his views before in various media. She did pay attention to his style of presentation and how the audience reacted to him. The next two aspiring candidates were not as smooth as the first one, but their message was similar. All three preached they would fight to maintain Praxton values and customs and to resist what the Alliance worlds wanted them to do.

Then the incumbent, McKinney, spoke. He paused at the podium and began to speak in an authoritative voice.

"My friends, we have heard what these fine gentlemen have to say. I will not disagree with them that we need to keep Praxton as it is. This is our home. This is where we live. Some questionable laws made on Sol should not just be rubber stamped here." His voice suddenly grew louder. "In fact, I suggest the Alliance worlds copy some of our customs and laws."

The crowd applauded and cheered as he raised his hands.

His voice started quietly again, increasing in volume with each sentence. "But I ask you, who should represent us in this critical time? Someone new? Perhaps. However, I humbly submit to you that I have been in the forefront of defending Praxton laws and customs for almost two decades. I know our laws. I know the people who enforce them. I understand what the damn Charter of Conduct Office wants, and I know how to resist them." He pounded his fist on the podium.

Cheers erupted as McKinney spread out his hands.

He shouted, "Allow me to fight for what Praxton is and what is dear to your heart. I won't allow Praxton customs to go quietly into the night."

Terri watched McKinney retreat from the podium to cheering and the chanting of his name.

Tough act to follow. The next candidate, a male, made a quiet speech that received quiet applause. The female candidate stuttered her opening remarks before settling down.

"Praxton needs to have a female voice, a voice to protect female rights and to show the Charter of Conduct Office we are complying with their demands. Otherwise we face more sanctions, and we need to keep our economy strong."

Terri heard the soft applause and a couple of jeers as she spoke. She saw her wave at the crowd as her speech ended and hurry back to her chair.

Terri heard her name announced and walked calmly to the podium. "Thank you for coming out tonight to hear myself and the other candidates. I suppose I can't call you friends yet, as we haven't actually met. But I do hope I can gain your trust." She smiled as she looked out at the audience.

A ripple of applause followed her last comment.

"Some of the speeches here are interesting, but they have one theme in common. To resist change. To fight the Alliance and Charter of Conduct Laws. To hold on as long as possible to what Praxton had before the invasion. I'm not going to shout or pound my fist and tell you that if I'm elected, I can stop the integration of foreign laws. Because I'm going to tell you the truth."

She paused, watching the audience focus on her next sentence.

"We had a war, an invasion. At the end, we showed the Alliance worlds we were more than willing to defend our planet. The result was a compromise. We were able to keep aspects of our culture that are most important to us." She pointed at her collar. "We also had to adopt some new laws, such as myself running for office. I personally consider that a good thing." She grinned, receiving some laughter.

"I'm not going to ask for your support because I'm a female, but because I am the best choice for males and females. Maybe we can adjust and negotiate some of the Charter of Conduct Laws, but the reality is we have to adopt some of the new laws. The Alliance worlds have given us a timetable to integrate these laws. There's no point in trying to pretend they won't be enforced. If you will elect me, I will prepare Praxton to use those laws to our advantage. We are entering a new era, an era where Praxton can be the leading economic power in the galaxy." She raised her voice slightly. "Perhaps the day will come when Praxton culture will invade every Alliance world."

Applause and cheers filled the auditorium. Terri smiled, raising her hands and then boldly walked away.

As the moderator made a final speech, Terri saw McKinney eyeing her. When he noticed she had caught him looking at her, he gave her a short smile and nod of his head.

Terri spoke to various reporters in the conference room. She answered their questions, none of them too serious in nature. Most of the reporters already had their main story written and with a deadline approaching in a few minutes, only wanted some minor points clarified.

Evelyn approached her last, smiling as she waited for the last reporter to leave. "Very good speech, Terri."

"Thank you. I hope I gained some voters."

"You did." Evelyn looked at her tablet. "According to this you have jumped up in percentage of support. You moved from seven percent to fourteen points. That makes you virtually tied in second place with Allan Stevens. McKinney is still the leader at thirty-two, but you sure closed the gap."

"Well done, Terri."

Terri looked at McKinney as he approached her at the side. "Thank you, Master James."

He spoke quietly in her ear. "At least I now know who my main competitor is. I trust you'll understand why I won't wish you good luck." He touched her shoulder and walked away to a group of his supporters.

Evelyn spoke. "What did he say?"

"He gave me a compliment. Interesting male. I can see why he's been so successful as a politician."

"I think he's right when he said you were his main rival. I'll bet he was shocked how well you handled yourself and the direction of your speech."

Terri thanked her and headed to meet with her support team.

* * * *

Evelyn wasn't surprised to see the number of reporters covering the speeches. The first women candidates in Praxton history were generating a lot of interest. Alliance world reporters were also recording the event, and among those was Max Tremblay who made his way to Evelyn.

"Very good speech by Terri Baxter. She's giving the voters something to think about."

"Yeah. In the past hour since her speech, her rating has gone up even more. She's at eighteen points with McKinney at thirty."

"Good for her. Praxton needs someone with a new viewpoint."

They gradually walked out of the hall and stopped as a line of shuttles appeared to pick up passengers.

"By the way, that was an interesting gift you sent me."

She grinned. "Well if you can order me to go without panties, then I should be able to pick out underwear for you to wear. Did you try them on?"

"No, but they do look a little different."

She smiled. "I'll bet they look even more different on."

"I need to go home and change. How about I come to your place around seven and we go out for a drink?"

"Sure." She opened a door to a shuttle. "Wear that new underwear."

She waved goodbye, seeing a perplexed look on his face. *You don't like it so much when someone tells you what to wear.*

* * * *

Evelyn changed into a dress, one with a single zipper on the side. The shoulderless dress was a pale green in colour and the light fabric showed off her figure easily. She left her panties off, still under Max's two-day restriction on wearing them. She studied herself in the viewscreen. *Looks good. I've gotten used to these Praxton clothes.*

The door chime announced Max's arrival and she opened the door for him. She resisted the urge to check his pants until later when it wouldn't look so obvious.

"Drink? I opened some red wine."

"Sure." He stood in the middle of the living room watching her as she went to the kitchen area.

Evelyn poured the wine and looked over at Max. There was a definite, although subtle, bulge at his fly. The light in the living room gave her a good impression of his size. She swallowed and put a smile on her face as she carried the glasses of wine.

"Thanks." He took the offered glass.

"I like the new look on you." She grinned.

He frowned. "I'm not really an exhibitionist and this is pushing my comfort level."

"But it's okay for you to order me to remove some of my clothing. Do you think I like going around feeling exposed?"

"I don't know about that. But I do know there are gender differences on Praxton regarding acceptable exposure."

"True. But I wanted you to feel like I do. A little uncomfortable."

"You managed that."

She restrained a laugh and covered her mouth.

"I detect a bit of a brat in that laugh. I believe an attitude correction is in order." He put down his wine glass.

Evelyn took a step back, and then another. "Max, you mustn't."

"Why not?" He advanced on her.

She looked behind her, seeing only the couch, and retreated to its edge.

"I think you should put down that wine glass."

She looked at the glass, took a quick sip and placed it on the floor. "Max, we don't have to do this."

He stepped around her and sat on the couch. "We both understand we do have to do this."

Evelyn nodded almost imperceptibly. "I suppose you're right. I was trying to avoid doing some Praxton customs."

"But here we are. It's time."

Evelyn sighed, came around the couch and lowered herself over his lap. "I can't believe how many times I've been spanked on Praxton." She felt his hand rest on her ass, squeeze her cheek and slide his hand over the dress. She waited, deciding he wasn't going to hurry the first spanking he was going to give her and relaxed on the cushions of the couch. She slowly released her breath, licking her lips.

A small slap initiated the beginning of the spanking, and it was followed by several more taps, each aggressively harder. Then several well placed smacks caused her to gasp and murmur, "Ow." She shifted her hips, feeling his hardness against her hip. He paused to lift up her dress, exposing her to her waist. She gasped, feeling a rush of warmth spread across her skin. Heat suffused her cheeks, as she thought how he had a clear view of her ass.

Evelyn curled her hands into fists as the first strikes hit her bare skin. She remembered being told Praxton females resisted crying out, and decided to do the same, but it wasn't easy. The smacks were hard, and she recalled Max had big hands, covering most of one cheek with each hand. She cried out from another strike. "Ouch. Oh, Max, yes."

She rolled her hips against his hard member, getting a grunt from Max. Then another smack and she let out a long groan. She twisted her head back to watch and saw her ass was already red. A moan escaped from her as his hand came down for another strike. Her mouth remained open as she took in deep breaths of air, releasing the air in a series of whimpers.

After several more hits, Max stopped and slowly rubbed her cheeks. In a cool, composed voice, he asked, "How does that feel?"

"It's a bit sore right now. May I get up now?"

"Yes," he murmured.

She slowly rolled off the couch and pulled down her dress, avoiding his eyes.

"Look at me." She raised her eyes and met his. "I meant did you enjoy the spanking?"

She picked up her glass of wine and took a drink. Warmth seeped out from her groin. She wondered how honest she should be with him. "Yes I did. I know you enjoyed spanking me." She looked at his fly, seeing what had to be an uncomfortable swelling. "I assume it made you feel like a Praxton male."

"I suppose it did." He smiled. "I like that part of the Praxton tradition."

"I guess I do too." She rubbed her ass. "Just maybe not too often."

"I was thinking about spanking you for a long time now. Especially when you told me about being spanked in front of others."

"That was an experience. It's one thing to be spanked, another when others can watch you being spanked. A little bit humiliating."

"But that makes it a more exciting, right?"

She laughed. "It does at that."

"Then I'll have to find a way to spank you in public."

"Max, you mustn't do that." She licked her lips, suddenly feeling anxious.

"Now correct me if I'm wrong but it was okay for you be spanked in front of others by Shara?"

"That was different."

"Nonsense. Also, a male can spank a female when he feels it is justified?"

"True, but we're Alliance citizens."

"On Praxton. So you better get used to the idea I'm going to spank you in public one of these days. A little humiliation is what you may need."

Evelyn gave a pretence of sighing. "Whatever. I guess I can't stop you."

After finishing the wine, they left for drinks and snacks at a downtown lounge. The dark interior allowed them to sit together unobserved in a corner booth. Evelyn felt the burn on her ass, and shifted positions a few times as she sat. She liked how Max had exhibited his strength of character, telling her she needed to be spanked. It wasn't quite an order, but rather a statement, and she was aware he was now likely to push his dominance over her since she had given in to him.

They conversed about a range of subjects and his hand rested on her thigh and slowly slid upward. He didn't slide his hand under the dress, but rather pushed it up.

"Max…" She rested her hand on his and gave him a smile.

"I want you to sit bare assed."

She sighed and lifted up her hem. "You seem to have gotten into a habit of giving me orders."

"I guess I have. Do you object?"

"No." She gave a short smile, knowing any argument of him not controlling her was over.

"After this drink, why don't we go to my place?"

Evelyn agreed, wondering if he had something planned. *He's been behaving very forceful the past few days, and I'm not resisting him at all. Could be dangerous.*

Chapter Seventeen

Evelyn looked around at Max's apartment. It was, as he mentioned before, larger than her place. She noticed, otherwise, the apartment was very similar to her own, including the artwork and the wall hooks. Max quietly offered her a drink, but she asked for a coffee instead.

"I think I've had enough alcohol for one night." She watched him go to the kitchen, curious that he had become quiet as they entered the apartment building and said little after they entered the elevator. "Is everything alright?"

"Yeah, fine." He gave her a smile as he passed over the coffee cup. He pointed at the couch. "Please sit. I have something for you."

Evelyn was puzzled but did as he asked. He went to the bedroom and returned with a white plastic box.

"For you."

She took the box and slowly removed the lid. "A collar with cuffs." She picked up the bright blue metal collar and turned it in her hands. "It's beautiful." She looked at Max. "Is this a special occasion?"

"Perhaps."

She examined the collar again and saw a metal tab that could slide to the side. Pushing it, she saw his name imprinted underneath. "Oh." She looked back at him. "This is a guardian collar. You want to be my guardian." Suddenly the words he used before her spanking made sense. 'But here we are. It's time.' *He was telling me we live on Praxton and we should start following its customs.*

"Well, what do you say?"

"There are some things we should discuss first. Like what are the rules if you're my guardian? Are we supposed to live together?"

164

He pulled out his tablet. "I have the contract here if you wish to agree to it."

Evelyn looked at the contract. It was short and to the point.

This agreement is between Max Tremblay, the Guardian, and Evelyn Montgomery. Max Tremblay shall have the authority to exercise discipline and control as he sees fit. Evelyn has the right to refuse any discipline and control measures. She also has the right to control her own finances.

"So you wouldn't have any control over me unless I allow you."

"Correct. Same as if we live on an Alliance world."

She nodded. "Are we to live together?"

"Stay the night. If you decide to sign the agreement, then we can look at sharing a place."

"This seems a bit of a rush. We haven't known each other that long."

"I know what I want. I don't want to risk losing you by waiting too long."

Evelyn gave him a kiss. "Thanks. I'm pretty happy with you too." She looked in the box at the matching two pairs of cuffs with assorted chains to join them together. "Maybe I can sleep on it, wearing the collar." She removed her collar and put on his, hearing the click of the lock.

They kissed again and she felt him tug down the zipper of her dress. It fell off her, leaving her naked and he took full advantage of her. She responded to him quickly and they tumbled off the couch. She helped him tug off his clothes, laughing as his pants were pulled inside out. She tossed them across the room.

Max rolled her on her back, staying on top of her, pinning her two hands above her head with one of his. He used his other hand to roam over her breasts and finally between her legs. He kissed her as his fingers penetrated inside her.

Evelyn cried out. "Please don't stop."

He continued to work his fingers and placed his mouth on her nipple.

"If you're planning on screwing me you better get inside me quick." She arched her back as a rush of heat washed over her.

Later, they sat naked on the floor. Evelyn grinned at him. "Coffee is cold."

"I can make you another, as many as you want."

"What I want is to go to sleep."

He took her by her hand and pulled her to the bedroom.

She looked at the large bed. "A real bed. Wide and it looks so good."

"You can sleep here every night if you want."

She slid across the bed. "Very tempting."

He stood at the edge of the bed. "One question. Would you like me to cuff your ankle to the bed?"

"A rather unique Praxton custom."

"It is. Something I suspect a Praxton female would expect her guardian to do."

"I suppose that's true. I did get used to it during my stay at Master Philip's home."

"So the answer is?"

She lifted up her foot. "It's your apartment and I guess you can cuff me to the bed if you want." She watched as he latched the ankle cuff to the foot of the bed. She also watched his growing erection. "You have me secured now. I guess you can do what you want with me." She grinned as he climbed into bed.

"I know exactly what I want to do with you. That is if you're not too tired."

"Feeling much more awake now." She wrapped her fingers around his penis.

* * * *

James McKinney sneered. "You claim to be a Praxton female, but you originally came from Earth as a spy for the Charter of Conduct Office. How does that qualify you to run for office exactly?" He pointed a finger at Terri as they stood in a television studio for another debate, but this time only the top two candidates were invited to speak. Her campaign manager, Thomas McGrath, warned her McKinney was likely to go on the attack. The polls indicated a virtual tie between them and as McKinney slowly began to lose ground, he needed to take a more aggressive stance on his speeches. The studio was filled with interested spectators, as well as several major news reporters.

Terri looked at him. "As you know, Master McKinney, I am qualified to run for office because Praxton laws state I can." She turned to the audience. "You point out that I originally came from Earth, and that is true. That is also true of our ancestors. Everyone on Praxton can trace their roots back to Earth. I am merely one of the more recent citizens to decide to live here."

"But you came here as a spy."

"I did." Terri looked at him and then directed her response to the crowd. "I was sent here as a spy, and as the court records show, I soon renounced my connection with the Charter of Conduct Office shortly after arriving here. I was found not guilty of the charges of spying." She paused as she took a deep breath. "After the charges were dropped, I worked for the resistance." She gave a grin. "Perhaps you saw the video?"

A roar of laughter answered her question.

McKinney clenched his jaw and adjusted his jacket. "I'm glad to hear you decided to actually support Praxton for a brief period. However, unlike you, I've lived on Praxton for my entire life. My entire life, not just a couple years. I doubt you really understand the tradition and the culture of Praxton. We have a history here—a history I vow to protect. I will not let the changes the Charter of Conduct Office wants for Praxton to proceed without a fight." He pounded his fist on the podium. "Praxton shall not change if I have any say in it!" He stood straight, absorbing the ripple of applause.

Terri waited for the applause to die down. "Master McKinney, science has come a long way over the years, but we don't have access to a time machine yet." She waited for the chuckles to die down. "We put up a strong fight to the Alliance government and the Charter of Conduct Office and kept our independence, but with conditions. We agreed to those conditions, and one of them is a change in female rights. Master McKinney said he won't let change occur without a fight. But the fight has already happened, and here we are now." Terri stepped around the podium and looked around at the people in front of her.

"Praxton was different a hundred years ago. Fifty years ago. Ten years ago. It will be different in the future as well. We have a choice in that direction. I want to help Praxton move to that new, better world. I do not want to live in Master McKinney's world. That's in the past and has no place in our future. I ask you to let me be your voice for our future."

Applause erupted as people began to stand.

Terri took a step back, her jaw dropping. Men and women were beaming at her as they clapped. She looked at McKinney, who looked shaken, his face pale.

The moderator made a short speech and ended the debate. Terri made her way back stage, barely remembering her brief handshake with McKinney.

Allison gave her a hug she entered the backstage room crowded with her supporters. "Wow! You just kicked his ass!"

Terri smiled and nodded as she heard everyone laugh. "I think I did okay." She saw Evelyn standing near a wall with a camera mounted on a tripod beckoning her over.

Terri made her way to the reporter.

Evelyn held a microphone. "Would you say this was a surprise to you that so many people responded to your message of working toward the future?"

"I was a bit shocked." She smiled. "I didn't plan that speech. It just came out and I was pleased others shared that view."

"It seemed that you had taken the whole room to your side. Instapole has just released the new statistics for the debate. Would you be surprised to learn you have jumped twelve points and climbed alone to first place? You now have forty-one percent of the support compared to McKinney at thirty-two. Your speech has put you in the lead with just two weeks to go in the campaign."

Terri covered her mouth with her hand briefly. "That's very good news." She looked over at her supporters. "Excuse me. I need to thank them for their help tonight."

Terri went to talk to others in the room, receiving a hug and kiss from Romie. She listened to Evelyn talk to the camera.

"We have just witnessed a massive change in the support between the old guard and the new voice of Praxton ideals. Terri Baxter's huge jump in support came almost entirely at McKinney's expense, and that will make the rest of the election very interesting. Unless there is a drastic change in voters' opinions, Praxton will have at least one female Member of Parliament. There has been a fallout to the other ridings as well, with many other female candidates enjoying an increase in their popularity. Evelyn Montgomery, Pearson News reporting."

* * * *

Evelyn was watching Max Tremblay give a report on the recent election debates on Praxton. Besides her own interest in him, she also wanted to hear what the more serious network was reporting. Images of the speeches and crowds were shown as he spoke.

"The leadership race on Praxton is heating up as Ross Nichols made a surprising electoral promise that if elected, he would end the present relationship of the military and the government. The military currently has veto power over most government bills, even to the extent of deciding government employees on the executive level. Nichols claims the military is holding back progress on Praxton with its intrusion in government affairs.

"In a world where the military is highly revered for its fight against the Alliance world forces, it is surprising that polls are supporting Nichols' viewpoint. Indeed, he has now moved to the front of the four-man race. If Nichols holds on to that lead, it will lead to a drastic change in the how the Praxton government operates.

"Max Tremblay, Interworld News."

Evelyn used a control to find another report done by Max Tremblay.

"One of the bigger surprises of the election is the contest between the incumbent James McKinney and Terri Baxter. It was expected that some of the female candidates would squeak into one of the one hundred seat assembly, but what is happening in this electoral riding is shocking. Terri Baxter ran her campaign, not as someone who could give Praxton government a female voice, but rather as a leader for change that Praxton needs to go through. She has focused on the future of Praxton, and it seems the voters are quite willing to follow her there as the polls have put her a solid sixteen points in front of him."

Evelyn listened to him sign off. *I could listen to that voice some more but I need to talk to Shara. She should be arriving at work about now.* She left her suite and took the elevator to the main level, and found Shara at the front counter.

Shara looked up from her work. "Hi, how was your date last night?"

Evelyn smiled. "Very interesting." She waited as Shara stared at her, expecting her to continue.

"You have a new collar." She stepped around the counter, taking a closer look. "Hey, that's a guardian collar." Her mouth opened.

"Max asked me if he could be my guardian."

Shara grinned and gave Evelyn a hug. "I'm so happy for you."

"Well, it's a slightly different situation we have than the usual Praxton arrangement. We're not registering our agreement with the government and I can refuse his commands if I want."

"Still, you now have a guardian. I knew you'd give in to him."

"Thanks. Look, we're going to live together and he suggested that I look for a place we could share. Both our suites are a little too small for two people. I was wondering if you could help me find a place."

"Sure. Actually, we have a unit that recently became vacant. Want to see it?"

"I'd love to."

The penthouse suite was more than double in size of her own. The living room and the kitchen were not significantly larger, but the master bedroom was more spacious, with a larger but hidden shower. The second bedroom was closer to her current bedroom in size, but besides a shower that had a glass wall to the living room, it also had access to a sunken bath that was exposed to the master bedroom and the outside wall.

"I don't know about taking a bath where the outside world can see me."

"We're high up here. Someone would need awfully good eyes to see you. But it's really nice to take a bath at night and see the city lights. Very pretty and relaxing."

"Hmm. There is that."

"Come. This suite has a discipline room."

Evelyn looked around the discipline room. The rectangular shaped room featured a curved bench with one end attached to the wall and the bottom on the floor. "That is interesting."

"Picture yourself naked as you're stretched out restrained and with Master Max holding a whip."

She rolled her eyes upward. "Nice image." She looked around the room with the wall hooks and chains hanging from the ceiling. She saw an interesting item in the corner, a set of iron bars that formed a triangle with the two walls. "Is that a cage?" She walked toward it.

"Yeah, a small one as there isn't much space here." She swung open the door, pushed Evelyn inside and closed the door. "How does it feel?"

Evelyn looked around in the small space. "Confining."

"It's supposed to. Sometimes you'd also be in restraints."

"Hmm. Interesting." She pushed the door open. "I don't know if Max would do that to me."

"Is there anything you can think of that makes you believe he wouldn't? Besides, I can tell you like having him as a guardian and taking control of you."

"Maybe."

Shara grinned. "You do know you're going to have to buy some whips? If you leave it to him, he'll buy whips with stiff strands. Buy some that won't hurt you."

"That's only if we take this suite."

"Evelyn, as soon as your eyes saw the discipline room, I knew you wanted this suite. You can deny it, but I know you want to be taken to this room by Master Max." She smiled. "There's a similar suite to this but without a discipline room. A bit smaller, but is meant more for couples who don't see any need for a discipline room. Much more Alliance world in design with all the rooms. Do you want to look at it?"

Evelyn shook her head. "How much is this suite?"

* * * *

Evelyn followed Max into the large hall, a circular structure with a ring of raised seats around a platform. She wondered if the hall doubled as a concert hall, but today it was for the Affiliation ceremony between Terri Baxter and Romie Fevero.

Max held the end of her leash. An invitation sent to guests suggested all females be on a leash, with sufficient adornment of cuffs and chains. Evelyn complied, ensuring chains went between ankle and wrist cuffs, plus a chain from her nipple clips through her collar's centre ring. She felt comfortable in her restraints and Max leading her, something she would have been shocked at only a month ago. She still felt she was in control of her choices but Max had also made her feel secure and relaxed.

The proceedings began with the master of ceremonies standing between a row of females and a row of males. All men were dressed identical, except for Romie, who wore a more elaborate suit. The women, save for Terri, wore simple white frocks. Terri wore what Praxton considered a traditional Earth wedding dress; white with lace on the front of her torso and a bare back. The gown was long and loose, although a slit was made along its length at the sides. One unusual feature was that all the women were without collars and cuffs, and Evelyn had a sudden thought; that it made them look like they hadn't finished dressing.

Evelyn watched and listened carefully, noting the words of the master of ceremonies were very similar in their meaning to weddings she had attended on Earth. A similarity here was also the low level playing of music. Although she didn't recognize the piece, it sounded much like classical music.

The music tempo changed and the master of ceremonies stepped back as the men stepped toward the women. Terri moved toward Romie and they stood next to the master of ceremonies and watched as the men in unison reached up to the necklines of the women's gowns and in a quick motion, ripped away the thin fabric. The women stood nude facing the men and then turned around, crossing their wrists behind them. The men used a thick, white rope to bind their wrists together. A second rope went around their upper arms and torso, framing their breasts between layers of rope. A white collar was added to their necks and they were led behind a single wall of iron bars. The cage didn't have backs or sides to it but rather appeared to be symbolic of a cage.

Next, it was Terri's turn, and she simply stood as Romie removed her dress by undoing a series of buttons on the side. It was carefully folded and put to the side.

Romie performed a more elaborate rope tie on Terri, using the white rope. Her wrists were also tied behind her back, and the elbows were tied together separately. A rope around her arms and torso criss-crossed around her breasts, accenting them. Another rope was folded in half and wrapped around her waist and sent from her back to between her legs before being secured at the front.

Max whispered to her, his eyebrows raised, "That's a rather interesting tie."

"It is meant to secure her, but also to show he has control over her vagina," she whispered back. "For her sake I hope it isn't too tight."

"Maybe it's something we can try."

Evelyn looked at him, wondering if he was serious, and decided he was. "Maybe, but I don't want us to go overboard on Praxton customs. Just don't make it too tight. I do like how they used the rope around her chest."

"I need to buy some rope obviously."

She leaned against him. "Obviously." *Lots of rope.*

A white flogger was passed to Romie. He walked around Terri, lightly whipping different parts of her body. She stood, without flinching, as her skin turned a soft pink from the strikes. After three passes around her, he stopped. A jewelled, ornamental collar was presented to him on a velvet cushion by the master of ceremonies. The thick metal collar shone and sparkled as he lifted it up to her neck.

Evelyn saw her shake slightly and saw the wetness in her eyes as the collar was placed around her neck, locked and a matching leash attached to it.

Terri carefully dropped to her knees, leaned forward and placed her face at Romie's groin.

For a moment, Evelyn wondered if she was actually going to perform oral sex, but moments later Terri leaned back on her heels and looked up at Romie. She smiled as tears rolled down her cheeks.

Romie helped her up, and together they circled the platform before exiting through a flowered covered terrace to a set of double doors.

Evelyn, like the rest of the guests, stood up and applauded the end of the ceremony.

After the ceremony, Max led her to one of the waiting shuttles. "So maybe I should take a rope tying course."

"I suppose so. You're my guardian and I knew what could happen when I agreed to the contract." She paused. "Being tied up in rope sounds interesting."

He was silent for a moment as they entered a shuttle. "Good to hear. Perhaps tied up in the discipline room."

He doesn't know that I supplied the whips for that room and this is the first mention he's made of it since we moved in. "If you decide I need to be taken in there, I must accept it." She turned to look him in the eyes. "All the suites I looked at had a discipline room. I assumed when we took the suite that we would be making use of it at some point. I think it would be good for us to try it out."

"Evelyn, I wouldn't do anything I didn't believe you would want. I believe you like the thought that I could take you to the discipline room and use those whips. Now you may fear the pain a whip may cause but I would use them to stimulate you, not to cause you pain."

"Good. I do like the thought of you holding the whip. Just not the part of you using it." She laughed.

"I would use it but with light leather kisses." He grinned at her.

Rather than go home, Max and Evelyn went to a lounge for a drink. After a few drinks, he spoke of another Praxton custom. "When a guardian gets a new female they usually celebrate by throwing a party."

Evelyn held up her hand. "Nice try. I know of that welcoming party. The female gets stripped naked in front of everyone and often is spanked or disciplined. No thank you. You can have me naked and you can discipline me, but not in front of others."

"Okay. But you were spanked in front of others already."

"That was part of an assignment. It wasn't such a big deal as Shara and the others had already seen me naked."

"So what you're saying is that you don't mind being spanked in front of them."

Evelyn laughed. "Okay, you have made your point. Maybe sometime you can spank me in front of them. Time to go to the reception. I just hope you don't get any more bright ideas from there."

* * * *

They entered the large hall located in one of the more prominent hotels. Evelyn had been warned by Shara what to expect, but still was surprised by the amount of nude females on display.

Topless servers walked around with drinks, although the multiplicity of fine chains attached to the nipple clips made it look like they wore a small vest. There were four filles d'affichage that Shara had explained to her meant female on display. The blindfolded, nude women slowly tangled and untangled their limbs and body in coloured ribbons attached to a bed sized frame raised off the floor. In careful movements, the women slowly twisted and turned as the ribbons seemed to be barely enough to stop them from falling.

Max breathed out a "Wow" as they watched one performer.

"Shara told me it is very difficult to do. She tried it once and kept hitting the floor with her ass. These females are in very good shape to be able to do this. It's a very specialized art form on Praxton."

"I have to say it is eye catching."

The second group of nude women were on tables. Their wrists and ankles were secured to opposite ends of tables with food placed around and on them. Small cloths were placed on the body where the food rested on the skin. The skin was also decorated with sprinkles and drizzled with various sauces. One model had dip directly between her breasts where the occasional guest could use it for vegetables.

Evelyn took a few snack items to go with her glass of wine. "Praxton sure has a way of presenting food."

"No kidding. I have to say this is better than a centre piece."

She laughed. "I think we need to have naked men presented like this."

He shook his head. "No we don't. This is much more visually appealing. Any disagreement will earn you a paddling."

"All right, no argument." She looked around and commented, "A lot of people here. Must be an expensive venture to do this."

"Are you recording this? I can't recall seeing anything like this on any Alliance world video about Praxton."

"I am. I doubt any Alliance citizen has ever been to an Affiliation Ceremony before. It should make for an interesting report."

Evelyn pointed at the crowd by the head table, where Terri in her white dress was surrounded by her aids in black dresses. "Let's see what's going on."

They approached the small table that held a wedding cake. The multi-tiered circular affair looked exactly like what would be seen on Alliance worlds. However, comments and excitement around it indicated it was a rare sight.

She quietly mentioned to Max, "It looks like they haven't seen a wedding cake before."

"Likely because they don't have weddings here normally. I think Terri Baxter has brought some Earth customs here."

They moved away and saw Terri and Romie having a rare moment where they weren't surrounded by well-wishers. Evelyn tugged on Max's hand and approached them.

"Hi Terri. I wanted to introduce you to my guardian, Max Tremblay."

Terri smiled warmly. "A guardian? Evelyn, you certainly are adapting to Praxton customs."

"I am, some more than others." She laughed. "This looks so much like an Earth wedding, if you don't mind me saying so."

"We wanted to combine Praxton and Earth customs here. Master Romie was kind to allow me the discretion to do so."

Romie laughed. "I was willing to do anything to keep her happy. She can be very determined in getting what she wants."

Max noticed the crowd were going to various tables. "I think it's time we sat down at our table."

"I believe it's near the back. Us being near the end of the guest list puts us away from the head table."

Evelyn walked with Max to the table. She noticed most of the women like herself wore dresses short on coverage and high on glitter. A few women were also under leashes, but most of the women were free to socialize. Their table had Max and two other men, and four other women. They chatted with them as wine and salads were served, not revealing they were reporters. With Evelyn's short hair it was quickly surmised they were Alliance citizens but no one asked why they were on Praxton.

Like Alliance weddings, the new couple was introduced to the room and various speeches followed during the meal. Just after dessert was served, music began with the first piece a rehearsed dance with Terri and

Romie. Others joined in and Evelyn wasn't surprised that Max was a good dancer.

He held her close during a slow dance, whispering, "Nice party."

"Hmm, it is."

Evelyn's thoughts turned to how the reception seemed to be much like wedding receptions on other Alliance Worlds. The Affiliation ceremony was very different from a wedding, she recalled, but here she felt comfortable. Dancing, good music, drinks and friendly conversation. She briefly left Max's company to chat with two women in the wedding party, wanting to learn more on how they enjoyed the ceremony. She listened how they described their own excitement of being stripped and secured in front of the crowd. She heard chairs being moved and the giggles of women and laughter of men. She looked to her side and saw two women being led by men by a leash attached to their collars to a pair of chairs facing away from a nearby table. The two women were smiling, as they went past a small crowd to the chairs.

"What's going on there?" Max asked.

"They're going to be spanked. I suspect they won't be the last females to be placed over their guardian's lap tonight."

Evelyn moved to a new position to observe the women. One of them removed her gown by undoing a zipper, leaving her in a pair of panties. The other had her skirt lifted to her hips and rested over the knees of her guardian. He gave her a quick smack on her rear and then pulled off her underwear.

She watched with the rest of the small crowd as both women were spanked. The spanking wasn't hard, and seemed more playful than punishment. One woman was allowed to keep her clothes on during the spanking but the other was naked. Both remained over their guardian's laps without struggle until they were allowed to stand up. The one still wearing clothes was blushing as applause announced their ordeal was done.

Evelyn recalled the conversation she had with the women shortly before. *I suspect they won't be the last females to be placed over their guardian's laps tonight. Damn. So much for a normal reception.*

She returned to where Max was refreshing his drink.

"Hey, you returned in time for another dance, this one a slow one."

"Sounds good." She placed her hand behind his neck.

Max spun her in a circle. "Did you see the excitement at one of the tables?"

"I saw a bit of crowd around one table. I think some Praxton custom was happening."

"Two females were spanked."

"Oh?"

His hand drifted down and lightly squeezed one cheek for a moment. "I was thinking I'd like to give you a spanking."

"I know you would. Perhaps later tonight at our apartment you will find a reason to do so, Master Max."

"I was actually thinking of here."

She looked up. "Here? In front of everyone? I don't know about that."

"I am your guardian. Doesn't that give me the right to choose when and where discipline occurs?"

"Yes, but this is like a wedding. Maybe etiquette means we shouldn't be doing anything that might upstage the big event. Maybe that spanking is only for certain members of the wedding."

"We can ask, but the end result is going to be a spanking for you. In public."

Evelyn pressed her head to his chest. "Max, why in public?"

"Because I think it adds something to your spanking. Do you disagree?"

"No." She sighed. "You are really taking this guardian role seriously."

"I am. Shall we ask about the protocol of you being spanked here?"

"Don't bother. I know the answer will be in your favour. Can we at least wait until most of the people leave?"

"Sure. I'm warning you it will be more than just a token spanking."

"Damn, but I'm not surprised."

Chapter Eighteen

Gradually the hall emptied, leaving as many staff members as guests. To Evelyn's mild surprise, Terri and Romie remained well after many guests had left. Evelyn and Max approached the happy couple and offered well wishes.

Terri grinned, acting like Evelyn and Max were close friends. "I do hope you enjoyed our celebration."

"We did." Evelyn touched Terri's elbow and led her away from the men. She lowered her voice. "Master Max wants to spank me. Here."

"Then you have to let him, according to Praxton customs. He's allowed to spank you, and you shouldn't even protest. A Praxton male can spank his females whenever he feels it is necessary. It's entirely his decision, period."

Evelyn blew out air from her mouth. "I knew you were going to say that."

Terri smiled. "Don't tell me you don't want to be spanked by that big, strong male."

"I won't deny it. But in public?"

"Praxton custom is that public display of discipline is expected. Don't feel embarrassed. Enjoy the moment where your affection for each other is shown to others."

Evelyn nodded and returned to where Max and Romie were talking. She slipped a hand through his arm as the couples parted ways.

She remained quiet as he walked to the far corner of the room.

"Time for your spanking."

"I know. No objection," she said as she walked with him, stopping at a table.

He raised his eyebrows but said nothing.

She stood as he sat on a cushioned chair that he'd pushed away from the table. Evelyn licked her lips and slowly made her way to his side. She glanced behind her and saw several guests looking in their direction.

Her mind went into a dream state as she lowered herself over his lap. She felt his strong hands on her cheeks, the slow massage, the initial, soft hits on her ass, then the lifting of her dress, and the smacks on her bare skin, which grew harder and harder. She heard the shuffling of shoes as a crowd gathered around them. She moaned. *My heart is ready to jump out of my chest. Come on, Max, let's get this going. If I'm going to be spanked in front of others, make it a good one.*

Then she felt the tug at the waistband of her panties as they were pulled down her legs. Slowly, but deliberately, he tugged them down past her knees and she lifted her feet as he slipped them over her shoes.

Evelyn gasped as she swivelled her head around, seeing numerous legs of the crowd that had come to watch her spanking.

"Spread your legs, darling," he ordered.

She lowered her head and obeyed, slightly, gasping when he spanked her hard. "Ouch!"

"Further apart," he demanded.

She complied. *That's as far as I want to spread them here.*

As he assaulted her ass with several hard smacks, she kept her hands on the floor, deciding she wouldn't offer any objection to his discipline. She knew her cheeks had to be red by now, and she hoped he hadn't noticed how wet she had become. Evelyn groaned as his hard, big hand spanked her ass repeatedly. Her body shook and lifted with the impact of the strikes. She occasionally kicked a foot and cried out. He stopped, pushed her dress upward to expose her bare back. His fingers did slow traces on her skin.

She remained in position as he played with her body, touching and occasionally slapping her ass, causing her to jolt each time. Then he stopped, to her disappointment. *You could've stripped me completely and I would not have minded at all.*

Max helped her stand. Evelyn glanced at her panties on the floor and stood straight, crossing her wrists behind her back. She heard the chatter of the crowd behind her but focused her attention on him, staring at his eyes for a clue what he wanted.

"I believe it is time we went home."

She nodded. "Yes, Master Max. Whatever you say." She ignored her panties on the floor, focusing only on him.

Evelyn followed Max, giving a short smile to those who'd witnessed her spanking. The shuttle ride to their apartment was uneventful, although her lack of panties made her feel vulnerable. She had to shift position continuously, the spanking making it uncomfortable to sit properly.

She stopped moving, though, when Max ordered, "Sit still. I know it hurts. It's supposed to."

Her cheeks felt hot, both the ones on her face and her ass when she glanced around and saw the smiles from other passengers, but she obeyed his order.

When they reached the lobby of the apartment, he gave her another order. "Take off your dress and put your hands behind your back."

She slipped off her dress immediately and after handing it to him, turned around with her hands behind her back. He joined her wrist cuffs together and gently guided her by the elbow to the elevators.

Her heart was pounding with the anticipation of what he was going to do next to her as the elevator began its journey. She knew there were cameras in the lobby and the elevator and wondered if anyone was going see her naked journey to their suite.

Max took liberties with her, cupping and fondling her breasts. He lightly pinched her nipples and slid fingers between her legs, playing between her lips. She moaned and closed her eyes. "Not fair." *But don't stop.*

He gave her a devilish smile. "Don't come yet, we still have things to do."

The elevator doors opened and he again took her by the elbow to their suite. They entered and she paused to kick off her shoes before he took her directly to the discipline room. She breathed in through her mouth as he pushed her into the small cage in the corner. Evelyn watched as he closed the door and stared at his captive.

"I'm going to pour myself a drink. Would you like one too?"

She nodded.

"I'm planning on whipping you, using you. As per the agreement we signed, you are allowed to refuse this."

Evelyn gulped and nodded. "You can do what you want to."

She saw passion rise in his eyes at her comment, turned then walked away. She observed him through the discipline doorway as he removed his own clothing, tossing them on a chair. She was pleased he was wearing the underwear she had purchased for him, but the fabric was straining to hold his swollen cock. When he was nude, his erection stood stiffly away from his body. He disappeared and returned with two amber coloured drinks.

"Turn around."

She complied and felt his hand release her cuffs.

"Your drink."

Evelyn accepted the glass from between the bars. The whisky was strong, and she almost coughed on the first swallow, but soon found it calming her nerves.1

"I'm nervous about whipping you. You will tell me if I hurt you too much, won't you?"

"I'll be alright. I want you to do this." She took another drink. "Ever since we moved in here I was wondering what it would be like to have you punishing me." She finished her drink and took a deep breath.

He opened the cage door, surprising her by hooking a finger into her collar and pulling her to the centre of the room where two chains hung from the ceiling. He quickly attached a chain to each wrist cuff, went over to a wall where a switch activated a motor.

Evelyn was lifted off the floor. Moments later Max circled her, carrying a whip with a single thick strand. She remembered reading the package when she bought it, giving her a bit of a laugh. The whip had been approved by the Charter of Conduct Product Standard Board, and the heavy cloth whip was not supposed to cause undue pain or skin damage when used as directed in the instructions. *We'll see how well that theory works.*

She saw him take up a position in front of her at first. As she saw him raise his strong arm then flick she cringed and closed her eyes. The whip stung as it wrapped around her. Max took his time between each strike, trying to hit a different area of her body, moving completely around her each time. He stayed away from her neck, but concentrated on her back and breasts. When the whip hit her ass, she flinched as the sensitive skin reacted. The pain wasn't severe, but she wiggled on the chain, trying to give the impression he was hurting her. She remembered that Praxton females resist crying out and gave out moans instead.

He stopped using the single strand whip and replaced it with a flogger. Again, he walked around her, slapping the whip on her legs, back, breasts and stomach.

Her body tingled with a hundred hits, and a wave of warmth spread out from her groin. Suddenly he posed in front of her and his hand cupped and pressed against her vagina, probing inside with his fingers.

"Please, I need to come." She gasped.

"No. Not yet."

She noted the lustful glint in his eyes.

The chains lowered her to the floor and she lay there, too weak to stand. After a moment, he grabbed her hair and coerced her into crawling over to the curved bench. He secured her so her feet were on the high end of the board and her hands underneath. His hands rubbed over her skin, squeezing her breasts until she groaned. Then he lowered himself, sliding his member over her face. She stuck out her tongue as his cock went past her lips. Carefully she licked his testicles as he positioned himself over her. She opened her mouth wider and he pushed his erection inside. She gasped for air as he held it there and slowly pulled out, only to repeat the slow pumping action.

She could tell by his pace he was ready to come. He suddenly stood, spraying her breasts as he pumped his thick cock with his hand. He lowered his penis so she could lick it again. Finally, he stood over her again, like a warrior over a defeated opponent. Then he undid her restraints and helped her stand.

"We're not done yet."

Evelyn nodded, feeling the cool liquid dripping down from her chest. She dropped to her knees and took his limp cock into her mouth, working the member with her tongue. It began to swell faster than she expected, and soon it was stiff.

He gently took her by the shoulders and placed her on the curved board again, this time with her feet near the floor.

She spread her legs, sighing as he entered her. Evelyn wrapped her arms around his neck and lifted up her knees by his hips. "Fuck me, please." She jerked her hips in time to his plunges and her climax felt like an explosion.

Afterward she climbed into bed feeling exhausted, but took notice as he attached a chain to her ankle cuff.

"I like this custom of chaining you to the bed at night," he murmured.

"Hmm, I do too." She slid half on top of him, falling asleep on his chest.

* * * *

In the morning, Evelyn sat nude in the living room drinking tea and looked at Max as he read his tablet. He was dressed as usual and she spoke.

"So it's all right for you to be dressed, but I have to stay naked," she complained, a deep scowl on her face. "That's hardly fair."

He looked at her sternly. "Fair has nothing to do with it. My decision. I want you to be naked."

"And your other rules? I can't wear panties without asking first when I go out. I have to have a collar and cuffs on my ankles and wrists. This is pushing things a bit."

"You can always invoke the clause in our contract and refuse to obey."

"I could. But I also know that will lead to you spanking me or taking me to the discipline room, which you know I'm too weak to resist." She grinned at him.

Her phone buzzed and she looked at the message. "Shara is coming up to see me. Can I please put something on?" She stood, poised to go to the bedroom.

"No. She has seen you naked before. You will stay this way."

Evelyn let out an exasperated sigh.

He pointed to the couch. "Over my lap right now." He marched over to the couch and sat down. "Don't make me wait."

Evelyn pursed her lips and quickly rested her hips over his lap. She rested her fingertips on the floor and spread her legs slightly.

184

His hand came down hard and fast, striking each cheek a half dozen times.

"Ow, ow." She kicked one foot and squeezed her eyes shut.

"I don't want any attitude from you. Understood?"

"Yes, Master Max."

"Are you certain?"

"Yes, Master Max. I will do as you say without objection."

"Good." He helped her stand.

The door chime went off and she quickly inspected her ass. *Great, it's already red.*

She opened the door. Shara looked momentarily surprised at Evelyn but quickly gave her a hug.

"Sorry. Master Max has ordered me to stay naked, even with company coming over."

"That's okay." She touched Evelyn's arm. "Some interesting marks on your skin. Were you in trouble earlier?"

Evelyn shrugged. "I don't think it was anything I did, but Master Max took me to the discipline room last night and punished me."

"Lucky you." Shara went over to Max and bent down to kiss him on the cheek. "Nice to see you, Master Max."

"You too."

Evelyn and Shara sat in the kitchen, with Evelyn relaying the events of last night at the Affiliation ceremony. "It was like an Earth wedding in some respects, but with naked females." She laughed. "Max got on a real power trip and spanked me at the hall. It was so embarrassing. He took off my panties and with my dress lifted up I guess everyone got to see all of me."

Shara laughed. "I wish I'd been there."

"Then when we arrived at the apartment, he ordered me to take off my dress. I had to ride the elevator nude."

"Ohhh. Would it be okay if I checked the video records? I'd like to see that."

Evelyn nodded. "Sure. I'm getting used to being exposed now. In fact, I'm getting used to everything Praxton." She glanced over at Max who met her gaze with a twinkle in his eyes.

* * * *

After Shara left, Evelyn went to the bedroom. When she returned she was wearing a belt that had a strap that went between her legs.

Max looked at her with a mildly surprised look on his face. "What's this you're wearing?"

Evelyn passed him a remote control. "Something that gives you far too much power over me, but I'm very curious how it feels."

Max used the controller.

Immediately Evelyn gasped. "Oh my." She began to drop to her knees. "I think there is such a thing as too much power in one man's hands."

Max smiled as Evelyn rolled onto her back on the floor, her hands gliding over her body. "I do like this new toy."

Evelyn felt wave after wave of pulsating vibrations go through her. She touched herself, squeezing her breasts as she rolled on the floor. Max used the control to change the vibration rate, causing her to suddenly lift her hips off the floor. She called out for him to stop, to continue and finally just his name.

He kept his finger on the remote until she cried out in ecstasy.

He stood above her, grinning. "We have to make use of that toy more often."

She panted on the floor, her body limp from exertions. "I may get a heart attack from it."

* * * *

Evelyn sat across from Terri Baxter in Master Romie's living room.

"Thank you for agreeing to being interviewed. The Alliance world will love to hear from the first elected woman to hold office in Praxton history."

Terri smiled. "Thank you, but two other females were elected as well and they should be remembered as well."

"I'm sure they will be, but you were the only one to win by a sizable margin. It was also announced that you were given the position of Minister of Education and Employment. That is quite the responsibility and one has to wonder what your first actions will be."

"My first priority will be to look at where we are now in terms of education and skills and what we will need in the future."

"How do you propose to introduce more females in the workforce? I'm making an assumption that will be something Praxton needs to address."

"It certainly is an area we need to look at. Part of it is going to be to change the attitude of guardians and females about females working. Currently many people on Praxton feel the main purpose of a female is to serve her guardian. The guardian in turn takes care of all her needs. While it is true some females do work and contribute to the family's income, she usually doesn't see her earnings and receives just an allowance from her guardian. This lack of seeing the actual result of her work takes away from the incentive of being employed."

"How do you, or the government, propose to change that?"

"I spoke with our leader, Ross Nichols, about that very issue. He is very supportive of advancing more females into the workforce. One bill he will be introducing is the Freedom of Choice Bill. The bill has several parts to it, but to summarize, it will allow females to control their own finances by making it possible for them to own dwellings, businesses and bank accounts. In addition, any female working will be required to receive a statement of earnings, even if her pay goes directly into her guardian's account."

"Those are very strong measures. Do you expect much resistance to them being implemented?"

"There will be resistance, but part of these changes are mandated by the war ending agreement with the Charter of Conduct. Also, many females already have a contract with their guardians that stipulates what she is allowed or not allowed to do. Her income may already be directed to his account. So change will be slow in some respects, but as new guardian and female contracts are signed, there will be a possibility for the female to have more independence."

"Is this eventually going to end the guardian-female relationship we see now on Praxton?"

Terri thought for a moment. "Praxton has seen changes in the role of the guardian throughout its history, and this will be just one more phase it shall go through. I honestly cannot see a time when females on Praxton will not be wearing a collar that shows who their guardian is. As a female, I enjoy the thought of being able to do what I want, such as running for election. I also love the thought my guardian is here to protect me and advise me. I haven't a conflict with being independent in making business decisions and later submitting to my guardian."

"Will these changes eventually change the ratio of females to males on Praxton as you bring in more skilled workers?"

"Yes, we will see a change there. We will be adjusting our criteria for both genders to immigrate to Praxton. Both will be required to bring skills that Praxton needs. Also, everyone wanting to live on Praxton will be required to pass a course on our history and culture."

"What will that course entail?"

"For males, to understand the role of the guardian. They are to protect and be supportive of their females. They are allowed to control and perform disciplinary measures but cannot abuse them. For females, they must be accepting of our social norms. If they are not willing to wear a collar, then perhaps Praxton is not for them. They need to understand that when a guardian accepts them into the family, there will be a contract to abide by and must be comfortable there will be other females in the household."

"Interesting way to maintain the Praxton culture by requiring immigrants to take a course. Has your government received any backlash from the Charter of Conduct Office?"

"To be honest, they didn't like that provision. However, at the same time they said they wouldn't make an official protest against it."

"I can see there are many changes coming to Praxton in the coming years. Thank you for your time and agreeing to this interview."

Evelyn cut the recording and turned to Terri. "You certainly are forging ahead with change. Praxton for so long resisted any change at all and now this."

"Well, the Charter of Conduct Office was going to force changes on us anyway, so rather than resist every little item, we decided to hit them with a number of measures all at once. That includes our culture courses, which would have been difficult to pass alone. What I didn't specify in the interview is that we are using the courses to weed out those who are only here for the money. If a male figures he can have a few females at his beck and call, he won't pass the course and he has to leave Praxton. Same thing with a female. She must understand that when she has that collar on, and she has to wear one to live here, she must obey her guardian. If she has the attitude I'll wear the collar and do what I want, she won't pass the course."

"A very clever way of keeping Praxton the way it is in the home." She stood. "I have to admit that I never thought of myself as anything but an independent woman before. But with Max as my guardian I feel very comfortable wearing his collar and having him in control when we're together."

Terri walked her to the door. "That's good to hear. Not all females like the male in control, and that's fine. And not all males like the responsibility of taking care of females in his household. For those people, they are welcome to visit Praxton but must understand this is what we choose to have on Praxton and we will not allow it to become weak."

"I never thought of Praxton as being weak. Max and I have been offered a position on Mars to report on international affairs with Interworld News. If we decide to go there, I will not be removing my collar." She touched the metal edge. "It means a lot to me and I love how it symbolizes our relationship."

"Are there any wedding plans?"

Evelyn grinned. "Maybe an old fashioned Earth style wedding with a couple of naked Praxton females doing the filles d'affichage. That sure would raise a few eyebrows."

Terri laughed. "Check with me, I have a list of names that would be happy to perform for your wedding."

"Thanks. It has been great to have met you. I mean besides professionally as a reporter."

"I want you to know that you have restored my confidence in Alliance reporters. It is wonderful to know that unbiased news is coming out from Praxton. And it was wonderful to meet your acquaintance as well. I hope we can continue our friendship wherever we are."

"I'm sure we can." She touched her collar with her fingers. "I can't believe how this collar has changed how I view the world. I feel so much more content with Max in control. There are some restrictions I don't like, but I've learned not to argue with him."

Terri grinned. "Discipline measures?"

"Yes. Besides the discipline room, he will restrict what I can or cannot wear." Evelyn recalled having to stay at the apartment for two days because she wasn't allowed any clothes to wear. "It's all right. I like it when he takes charge, even when I don't feel I deserve to be punished."

"Are you going to continue the Praxton lifestyle if you leave for other Alliance worlds?"

"I think so. We'll need to be more discreet on how we do things. But if we move we'll still have a discipline room. I would like to have a cage as well, and I found that there are several Praxton companies that will ship cages that can be stored in a collapsed position."

"Sounds like you've worked things out." She gave Evelyn a hug. "Stay true to your heart."

Epilogue

The spaceport was busy with hundreds of travellers. They had little impact on Terri Baxter and the rest of the Praxton delegation as they were escorted by Alliance Forces security to the V.I.P. area. They received long looks from passers-by as they made their way down the concourse. Terri looked around the spaceport, remembering the last time she was there.

Several years ago, she had left from the same spaceport on her way to Praxton, as a spy for the Charter of Conduct Office. Her mission was to report the abuse of females and the irregularity of laws on Praxton to help justify an invasion of the planet by Alliance Forces. As she studied the Praxton society and became involved with Romie, gradually her allegiance and views changed. She became part of the resistance to save the Praxton culture, and eventually helped save part of the society from the Charter of Conduct Office ideals.

The Charter of Conduct Office wanted females to be free from their male guardians on Praxton, a position that Terri felt was overly simplistic and could not work on Praxton. *How ironic that all these years later I'm an elected representative of Praxton and I have pushed forward legislation that allows females to have much greater rights and not to be dependent on male guardians. It's certainly not what the Charter of Conduct Office had in mind, but in some ways was exactly what they wanted to accomplish. But at least it was done on Praxton's terms.*

They entered the V.I.P. room and were immediately offered refreshments. Terri took a fruit drink and watched a monitor giving the latest news. A pair of newscasters, a dark haired man and a blonde woman, took turns reading the latest developments. The man spoke on a topic that attracted Terri immediately.

"Preparations are being made for the first Praxton official delegation of government officials to Sol in the planet's history. After a long drawn out battle many years ago when Alliance Forces battled Praxton to free the female population…"

Invaded Praxton and the female population didn't need to be freed, thought Terri.

"…there finally appears to be a final resolution to the disagreements on Praxton's laws."

The woman continued with the report.

"Praxton continues to be an economic force, and Sol is anxious to establish strong trade relations with the sequestered planet. While the Charter of Conduct Office wants to push for greater reforms from the Praxton government, that is tempered by the realization that Praxton has the clout to make demands of its own."

The man took over reporting. "It should be noted that while the President of Alliance Worlds is very conservative in his beliefs that run against Praxton's view of underdressed women, he was also the leader of Haven when it was taken over for violating acts in the Charter of Conduct office laws. That may give a basis of understanding between the two governments."

The woman finished up the report. "There will be keen interest from other governments what agreements will come out of the meetings. If a major contract is signed, then Praxton may not only continue as an economic force, but perhaps also give credence to their culture. And as we know, that culture is the submissive attitude of women toward men."

The dark blue Alliance Forces ship took them directly from the spaceport to the top of a Mars building that poked its top above the bubble that protected the city population underneath.

The delegation was greeted warmly by dark suited Alliance government diplomats. Terri replied to careful words and soon they were led to their private suites.

The view she had from her window was impressive as she stared at the vast Martian desert. The sky varied from pink near the horizon to blue to almost black, as she looked higher up. The journey to Mars had taken its toll on her and she soon fell asleep on the bed.

Hours later, she awoke, unsure what time it was, not helped by trying to understand the clock that showed Martian standard time. She undressed, after determining it was after midnight and went back to sleep.

The morning brought breakfast in her room and she checked her messages, which included a private invitation for morning tea with the President's wife, Irene Thompson. Surprised by the request, she nevertheless quickly replied to the affirmative. *What should I wear?* was her first thought. *Praxton or Earth fashion?* She considered where she was and why she was on Sol. *Praxton.*

* * * *

Terri followed a two-guard escort to a shuttle that quickly deposited her to a bank of government buildings that contained a private dining room. A table sat in the middle with a formal setting as two servers brought in covered plates. The table, although it could seat six, seemed small in the richly decorated room.

A fair-haired woman of average height and wearing a blue dress smiled as she entered the room.

"Hello, you must be Terri Baxter. I'm Irene Thompson."

They shook hands and Irene gestured for her to sit at the table.

"Welcome to Mars and Sol, although I understand you were here a few years ago."

"Yes, but under much different circumstances. But it is interesting to return."

"I suppose you are curious why I invited you here. I read about your remarkable rise on Praxton after arriving there only six years ago, and I thought I would like to meet this woman who now is in a rather prestigious position on Praxton."

"Thank you. It's very nice to meet you as well. I understand you were the Premier of Haven at one time, so it seems you had your share of being in a powerful position."

Irene laughed. "So you did your research on Haven's history. Yes, I took over as Premier after my husband resigned being Premier to be

Haven's representative in the Alliance government. Then when Rod became President of the Alliance World government, I resigned. It was that or we would be living apart on two different worlds."

"I can imagine how hard that would be."

"Your husband, is that the correct term? Didn't come here to Mars with you."

"No, he felt I should show that I can be independent of my guardian on important meetings. I call him my guardian, although husband is close enough. He, and the rest of our family, will be joining me in a week's time when we will vacation on Earth."

"I saw a news video of your Affiliation ceremony with him. Very different from a wedding here."

Terri grinned. "Yes, on Praxton women are expected to be exposed a lot. One has to get used to the nudity if one lives there."

"For women. Men remained fully dressed." Irene raised her eyebrows.

"Yes, that and other Praxton traditions bother some people on the Alliance worlds." Terri returned her stare. "I understand Haven had its own culture challenged by the Charter of Conduct." Terri took a bite of a pastry.

"Good point. I can say Praxton certainly has an impact on fashions. Some of it I have to say is very interesting. I noticed hemlines have gone up and many women like to wear collars as a fashion statement."

"You don't approve?"

"Actually I have my share of short skirts. I like wearing new fashions and if I had my way, I'd be wearing bright colours and short skirts. But being the President's wife I have to be conservative in my dress. Heaven forbid if I ever went without a bra. However, I do have some of those fashion collars as well, although I have to be careful when I wear them. If I wear a collar, then some might interpret that as making a political statement of support for Praxton. So I pick my spots when wearing them."

"I have to ask. Do your collars lock?"

Irene laughed. "I see what you're driving at. Yes, they can be locked. I haven't worn them locked but would if Rod asked me to."

"He isn't the dominant type?"

"Wait until you meet him. He is the dominant type, but is careful how we are seen in public. In private, he can be most persuasive." She paused to take a drink of wine. "That includes giving me a spanking. Don't ever repeat that to anyone."

"I won't. I'll have to send you a Praxton collar that locks automatically. It will make you feel different wearing one."

"If you send me one, I'll wear it. Discretely, of course. Tell me, don't you find those chains between your cuffs and collar cumbersome?"

"No, I'm used to them. I can remove them for some activities, as they usually aren't locked. My guardian likes the look of chains and cuffs, so I usually have a full complement of chains attached to the cuffs when I'm at home. Otherwise, I usually leave them off."

"I understand Praxton women are subservient to men. Doesn't that make it difficult to run your department?"

Terri laughed. "It can be. I usually ask rather than order. There was some resistance at first to me from some men but that has disappeared."

"So has the fashions on Praxton changed with the contact of Alliance worlds?"

"Yes, but also due to more women entering the workforce. Short, tight skirts are not that practical at work. Generally speaking, Praxton fashions have become more conservative I suppose."

"And Alliance fashions have gone the opposite way."

"A blending of two cultures in a way."

* * * *

Terri felt her stomach tighten as she and the other Praxton delegation were introduced to Alliance government officials, including President Rod Duggan.

She had seen and read about Duggan before, but seeing him in person was different. Tall, broad shoulders with a handsome face made her stumble out her greeting. He didn't react to her slight miscue, but clasped her hand in his own large, masculine one and made her feel like she was the most important person in the room as he spoke.

"It is an honour to meet someone who will make such a profound effect on the future of Praxton and possibly all of the Alliance worlds.

195

You are indeed an inspiration to many who wonder what they can do to make a difference."

Terri mumbled out a reply. Blushing she made her way to the conference table. She sat nearly opposite Duggan at the round table, and kept being drawn to his eyes. When he spoke, his deep voice captivated her.

"We have made progress on several issues already, and I hope we may continue along this line. However, the representative from the Charter of Conduct Office, Natt Perkins, has an agenda item we should work through before proceeding on other issues."

A slim, medium height male with long blond hair coughed slightly and quickly scanned the room. "It has come to the attention of the Charter of Conduct Office that there are certain aspects of Praxton society that may require the intervention of our office. Specifically, there are reports women are being spanked and otherwise punished at the workplace by their male supervisors. It is of our opinion that Praxton laws need to be adjusted to prevent such abuse."

President Duggan looked at Ross Nichols, the president of Praxton.

Nichols looked at Perkins, frowning slightly. "What Mr. Perkins is suggesting is making it illegal to practice some of Praxton's unique customs. I fail to see how this is a benefit to Praxton or other Alliance worlds. To my knowledge no other world has a law banning social standards."

Perkins objected. "We are discussing spanking a woman in a work environment. Is this really a social standard we want to encourage or permit?"

Duggan replied, "Mr. Perkins, I allowed the Charter of Conduct Office this agenda item. However, the purpose of this meeting is to foster better relations between Praxton and the rest of Alliance worlds. This challenge of their social norms hardly will help in this regard."

Perkins blustered. "Don't you believe it is wrong?"

"There are many things I believe are wrong. But it would be equally wrong to legislate against everything we didn't like. I am going to end this discussion now and move to the next item on the agenda. Before we do so, I would like to remind the representative from the Charter of Conduct Office that the Charter Office does not have the power to enforce legislature on Alliance worlds. That power disappeared two years ago under Bill four fifty-seven, making the Charter of Conduct Office under the jurisdiction of the Alliance government."

Perkins shrank in his chair as Duggan looked at Nichols. "I understand you have a proposal to make."

The afternoon meeting with the Alliance and Praxton governments continued until a break was taken for dinner. When the meeting resumed among the ten dignitaries, the leader of Praxton delegation, Ross Nichols, spoke.

"So far I believe our meeting has been informative for both sides. I am pleased that President Rod Duggan has agreed to look into our request regarding the Charter of Conduct Office investigation of our laws.

"However, I would like to move the discussion to one of economics." He looked over at Terri. "Perhaps you would be so kind as to deliver our proposal."

Terri took a quick glance at her tablet before proceeding. "According to news reports, the Mars port used for repairing and building ships is in need of a serious upgrade or replacement. Several Alliance worlds have put forward proposals to build a new spaceport, providing they receive sufficient funding and help with bringing in skilled labour." Terri paused and directed her next statement at Duggan. "Praxton is in a special situation here. We have resources, both in material and financial to help build a new spaceport. We also have a population that can supply the skilled labour, providing we receive assistance here for training."

Duggan looked straight at her and at Nichols. "That is an intriguing proposal, and certainly requires closer scrutiny. But I see the merits in what you are saying and I move that our two governments explore a way of seeing this through. If we can find a way of increasing employment, especially among women on Praxton, it would go a long ways to satisfying gender equality."

The meeting finally adjourned, and Ross Nichols walked next to Terri. "Well done on your presentation. Short, concise and to the point. President Duggan commented to me later that he was impressed that someone so new to politics could handle herself so well."

"Thank you, President Nichols."

"I told him you were a remarkable individual and were just starting to make your mark." He touched her shoulder, stopping in the hallway. "You've certainly exceeded my expectations, and they were high, when you became part of our council. I don't see anything stopping you from continuing your journey. I just hope you don't plan on becoming Praxton's first woman president before I'm ready to retire."

Terri laughed. "I don't know what to say about that."

"Say nothing. But believe in yourself. You'll go where you need to be."

* * * *

Evelyn and Max were happy to meet with Romie, Terri and the rest of his household at one of the Mars restaurants.

After several minutes of exchanging hellos, Evelyn broke the news she was engaged. She held up her engagement ring to show the others.

"Max said it doesn't seem right that he has to supply both a collar and an engagement ring. I told him a girl can't have enough of pretty things."

Terri remarked how pretty it was as Dezine and Erica examined it with interest.

Dezine smiled. "Wow, it really sparkles. I can see this catching on on Praxton."

Romie laughed. "What? Do you know how much those rings cost? Remember I have three females. I could go broke."

Erica pouted. "Aren't we worth it?"

Romie shook his head, grinning. "How about I let you go shopping in Amsterdam instead? It'd likely be the same cost."

Evelyn spoke to Terri. "I hear Praxton has successfully won the right to have the new spaceport facility. That is a major coup."

"Yes, it'll help create those skilled jobs we are preparing for. Over half of the new spaceport workers will be female during construction and after it is completed. We also get to place fifty percent of the crew on the new Explorer class ship the spaceport will be building."

Max added, "So it will seem the Praxton influence on Alliance worlds will continue in the future."

Terri smiled. "I guess there are some members of the Charter of Conduct Office now wishing they had never ordered the invasion of Praxton."

Max laughed. "Many years ago they ordered the arrest of Rod Duggan when he was leader of Haven for violating Charter of Conduct Laws, despite the fact it wasn't part of the Alliance worlds. Then he became President of all Alliance worlds. Next, they ordered the invasion of Praxton. Now they have been given spaceships to spread their culture among the stars. I would have to say the Charter of Conduct Office is going to have to learn to stay out of other people's business."

THE END

Note To Readers

Praxton Four ends this series of the Praxton, Slaves of the Rogue World. That doesn't mean I won't be doing spin off books concerning this universe—indeed I already have one out—but the Praxton world won't be the main setting of new stories.

This is a science fiction series that came out from another novel I wrote called Haven. Haven is a non-erotica book, based mainly on a lost planet that came back into contact with Alliance Worlds. A brief mention was made of Praxton in it and I decided to give it a story of its own. Going back to the Praxton world itself, I made several statements about the future that dictated how Praxton came about.

1) In Haven I described there were many habited planets that had strong ties with Earth. Later, a previously unknown phenomena caused the destruction of many types of electronics, isolating the worlds. When things returned to normal, many worlds had decided to remain independent from Earth's influence. Thus, Praxton evolved to its own unique culture.

2) Drugs have a major impact on humans in the future. These drugs, besides providing health benefits, could also alter DNA and genes to make physical changes. A person could use pills to improve hair, body features and retain youth.

3) Human male birth rates declined compared to female. Roughly 55% of the population is female, which leads to some females deciding it is better to share a male with another female rather than live alone.

4) Praxton encouraged female immigration with inexpensive drugs. A ratio of three females to one male became the norm on the planet.

5) The women on Praxton were not slaves, but were dependent on

the male guardian. Women on Praxton did not have the same rights as men. However, once a guardian accepted a female into his household, he became responsible for their well being.

The reader may have their own thoughts on how a society may evolve with the above conditions. I tried to address the positives and shortcomings in the various books. I hope you enjoyed the series, and I welcome any comments you may have on the Praxton universe.

-Nick Howard

About the Author

Nick Howard lives near Grande Prairie, Alberta where winter is never far away. There he pursues a dream of writing and taming weeds on an acreage. So far the weeds are winning but perhaps the writing will allow him to feel a small measure of victory.

He shares the green jungle with his wife, and a dog that thinks itself as human. Rumors that the dog assists him in writing are greatly exaggerated, as the dog is horrible at grammar.

Nick invites readers to email him with their views at nshwrd@yahoo.ca He also has a website at www.nshwoward.com, which has other books and a few free stories. Please be warned the website is intended for adults, so please close one eye if you are sensitive to ladies in delicate situations.

One last thing, thank you for reading this story, and I do hope you enjoyed it.

Other works by the author with Melange Books, LLC

Praxton, Book 1: Slaves of the Rogue World
Praxton, Book 2: The Battle for Freedom
Praxton, Book 3: The Proposal

Haven

The Witch and the Hairbrush